Shot Bolt

Andreas Vassilakis, appointed to the World
Health Organization and summoned in mid-
honeymoon to Geneva on the sudden death of his
predecessor, was plunged into unfinished business of a very doubtful nature. New contacts had
sinister undertones, and apparently innocent
acquaintances lived under threat of violence
which gradually encroached on his own life and
that of his English bride Siân. The background of
greed, foreign intrigue and scandal merged into
nightmare with the discovery of a dismembered
body at the sluice gates to the Rhône. The related
disappearance of a dinghy and a murderous
crossbow left in their charge cast suspicion over a
wide area which included them both, members of
foreign delegations and a Genevese family locked
in bitter dispute over inheritance and recent
divorce.

Within this framework of suspense and murder
runs the story of a new marriage being painfully
forged in ironic parallel with the ruin of another.

CLARE CURZON

Shot Bolt

COLLINS, 8 GRAFTON STREET, LONDON W1

William Collins Sons & Co. Ltd
London · Glasgow · Sydney · Auckland
Toronto · Johannesburg

Shot Bolt is a work of fiction.
Although reference is made to actual places and
institutions, the characters and incidents of the story are
entirely imaginary.

This is for Elizabeth,
as poor thanks.

First published 1988
© Clare Curzon 1988

British Library Cataloguing in Publication Data
Curzon, Clare
Shot bolt.—(Crime Club)
I. Title
823'.914 [F]   PR6053.U7/
ISBN 0 00 232170 X

Photoset in Linotron Baskerville by
Rowland Phototypesetting Ltd
Bury St Edmunds, Suffolk
Printed in Great Britain by
William Collins Sons & Co. Ltd, Glasgow

Part One

CHAPTER 1

On Siân's map the lake had looked like a sickle, with the sharp ends pointing south. Coming in to land, as first one wing and then the other dipped to allow glimpses of mountain ranges, plain, and misted water, she saw it was less regular. The A300 had circled clockwise, crossed the Juras from eastern France, then the lake, and briefly re-entered French airspace before straightening for the run in. A soft landing after an uneventful flight so short that there was barely time to open the token magazine and deal adequately with the food tray thrust on one. Certainly no time to adjust to change: mentally Siân was still in England, living out her abruptly interrupted honeymoon.

She looked up at her husband who was solemnly involved in reclaiming their hand luggage from the overhead locker. For him it must be even worse, dropped helter-skelter into his new job weeks before he had been due to take up the appointment. All because Professor Theodorakis had pre-empted his own retirement plans by dropping dead on his way to work at WHO. And fate had offered Andreas no alternative. The imminent World Conference was important and he must attend it fully conversant with the Greek report. There would be plenty of supportive data from his nationals in the Secretariat, but final responsibility for presentation must rest with him. So, while she herself was merely off-balance at the suddenness of events, for Andreas the change was more crucial and demanding. In this new phase of their lives she admitted she could have little more than a background role at present.

As she emerged on to the metal stairway and was confronted by the austere face of the Cointrin airport she experienced a flutter of panic. What had she let herself in for? An alien land, a mixed marriage, no continuity with past friends or interests. Only Andreas would be the same, and he was of necessity already withdrawing, caught up in activity where she could have no place.

Issuing from Customs, both saw at the same instant his surname block-printed on a white card held high by a man in chauffeur's uniform. My name too, Siân reminded herself, and looked swiftly at Andreas for inclusion. He responded with the comic grimace he reserved for her, inflating his cheeks and collapsing them like a burst paper bag. And his eyes meanwhile watchful, apprehensive, apologetic: his admission of almost unbearable emotion. She reached for his arm and gently squeezed. 'It's all right. Everything's going to be fine,' briefly loving him with her eyes as he started to push the trolley with their luggage out among these milling, alien people.

Andreas had firmly declined the offer of hotel bookings near the Place des Nations, determined to prolong their privacy as far as possible when off-duty. He would need a bolt-hole where he could get his head down to studying his new role, and it was left to Siân to find one. So, as agreed between them, they said goodbye cursorily now. Andreas was swept off to the demands of his new office and Siân took the airport bus to the Cornavin station.

Her father had explained the convenient hotel booking system offered at any Swiss railway terminus, and she started dialling from one of the booths where hotel names, selected by pressing a button, came up as lights on a map of Geneva. A board alongside gave details of facilities and tariff. Nothing simpler, as her father had assured her; except that May was a month of conferences and not only were the nuclear nations holding a scientific Summit, but the anti-nukers were present in force for mass protests, holding on to the cheaper lodgings as well as squatting periodically across strategic roads. The Press presence to cover the dialogues had also trebled as possible blood-letting was scented on this second front.

All recommended hotels were politely regretting no

vacancies. With growing dismay Siân continued pressing buttons on the illuminated panel and dialling numbers. At the eleventh attempt she had an offer: double room with bath and shower, breakfast but no restaurant. It looked relatively inexpensive by Swiss standards and must do for the present. She noted down the address on the reverse side of a label on her suitcase, and trundled her trolley towards the exit marked 'Taxis'.

Outwardly unappealing, the entrance lobby of the Hôtel Stresa was dark and dingy. It didn't conform to her expectations of things Swiss any more than the depressing streets of neglected houses between airport and station had done. Nor did the dull and humid weather live up to the postcard propaganda of gentian sky and dazzling sunshine.

'*Je viens de vous téléphoner*,' Siân said hesitantly to the parchment-faced old man behind the Dickensian high desk. 'Madame Vassilakis.' It was the first time she had called herself this to a stranger. Would the man question the English accent and the Greek surname? Apparently not. He peered myopically at his daybook, running a finger along the lines.

'Double room with bath and shower,' he confirmed in English, reaching behind himself for a key. 'Breakfast is on the *entresol*.'

Siân handed up the passports. 'My husband arrives later.'

The man was writing particulars in his book. 'Ninety-three,' he told her, adding ominously, 'Ah!'

Ah? She examined the key with its massive rubber ball attachment. 93A. What was this room, then—a converted broom cupboard between 93 proper and 94? 'The lift is round that corner,' the old man told her. 'Your room is on floor six.' He left her to move her own luggage, one piece at a time, into the lift, and went back to squinting at his writing where he'd entered her name.

Even before examining the room she went to the telephone beside the bed and dialled the number Andreas had given her. Her call was expected and at her name the woman's voice changed to English. Siân gave only the hotel's phone number, insisting hopefully, 'It's just temporary, tell him. For one night.'

That done, she took stock of their new quarters. Old-fashioned, undistinguished, but quite clean. Double bed, firm mattress, no squeak. The bathroom was windowless and narrow, but adequate. Clear water ran out of the taps, and quite a lot of steam from the one marked 'C' for *Chaud*. Back into the bedroom and over to the single high window where she reached up to look out. Like Paris backstreets: rooftops, a vista of slates; tiles; upper windows; occasional small balconies crammed with flower troughs, wooden boxes, and lines of washing. Gauntly obtrusive, five or six giant cranes indicated where rebuilding was taking place in invisible canyons between existing blocks. In the distance, proving it to be a south-west aspect, rose the two mountain masses of the Grand and Petit Salèves.

And—wondrously—over to the left in the middle distance and issuing above dark rooftops, the incredible white plume of water which was the famous Jet d'Eau. Actually visible from their window! Now she could believe it. Their move to Geneva was real.

The lone young man lounging at the outermost table of the brasserie terrace, Place du Bourg-de-Four, leaned forward to watch the redhaired girl approaching up the street below. She passed almost under him and he swivelled to follow her with his eyes, curious to know where she was heading.

A good mover, he appreciated, but this wasn't her normal pace. She was hurried, perhaps conscious of being late. It gave a slight jerkiness to her gait, making her heels flick up behind and rolling her neat little buttocks under the straight, black skirt. Her cotton blouse was of clear buttercup yellow cut to emphasize the fine waist, and her dark red hair bounced on her shoulders with every step.

Her face had been—interesting. No classic beauty, and certainly not pretty—which in his estimation would have required a degree of silliness. Intent on getting somewhere, she looked even a little daunting, the brows quite straight and the chin upthrust. Not a tourist, he guessed, but if she was local he would have spotted her long before this. Not too certain where she was arriving, she stopped at the upper point of the triangle and began to riffle through her shoulder-bag, pulling out a folded plan which she turned about to match with the pattern of roads meeting there. Her back expressed doubt, hesitation, then a dogged sort of hope. She refolded the plan, keeping it in her left hand, and went on in the general direction of the Collège Calvin. Niall O'Diarmid returned to considering the grounds of his *café filtre* and pondering the blight which inopportune death had cast over his expectations. He was just deciding that it might prove no more than the latest challenge to his unquestionable ingenuity, when the waitress came by for his money. She lingered over picking it up and he teased her by seeming unaware; then, lurching suddenly to his feet, he picked up his clarinet case, rapped the girl smartly on the seat, throwing '*A bientôt, Thérèse,*' over his shoulder as he moved off. Without a backward glance he was striding the rest of the way uphill, on his way home.

There was a grey car parked outside at the kerb and from habit as he approached he noted the local registration, a two-year-old Fiat, licensed to a car-hire firm across on the Right Bank. As he went up the front steps three people were entering the lift across the hall. There was a momentary flick of black skirt topped by buttercup yellow before the door slid shut.

Old Antoine Régnier, ex-retainer of the Zuelig family and now the concierge of their town house, was still peering through the open window of his little office. As he passed, Niall sang out, '*C'est bien la Grecque, celle-là?*' confident that so much familiarity would guarantee a slapdown.

The old man stared back with his customary disapproval. Stiffly he informed the young bohemian that it was indeed Monsieur and Madame Vassilakis who had just arrived.

To view the dismally magnificent apartment of the late Prof Theo, Niall already knew, having been forewarned by Céline on the first floor. The old trout was a great source of gossip. Now that he'd seen the girl he was all in favour of new neighbours, two floors down from his own more modest garret. Not that Old Theo's bachelor rooms could have much attraction for a young couple. It would depend on what alternatives were available. If ever there was a saturated city, populationwise, it was Geneva.

He should have realized earlier that the new man would be offered his predecessor's lodging. It was an administrative shortcut. For himself too it could be much the same. Delete Theo, write in the new man; why not? In view of the time factor and with the man close at hand here, and the wife so worth his attention . . . Yes, he should certainly add what persuasiveness he could to the housing agent's silver-tongued inducements.

The agent in question was a UN rep from the Housing Bureau whom Niall knew distantly. And it wasn't difficult to slip on the penultimate step down as the couple finally came out with the man on to the landing. Niall sat nursing his left ankle in a welter of sheet music which escaped helpfully from under one elbow. While the others sympathized, collecting the papers skittering across the ceramic tiles, he warded off the husband's offer to examine the injury. 'No, no, it's a terrible coward I am. Can't bear to be touched at all,' he insisted, playing up the stage-Irish for all it was worth because, joy of joys, weren't they all speaking English!

The girl stood a little way off, clutching his music, her head tilted ever so slightly as if she wasn't entirely convinced by his performance. And how wrong he'd been earlier, because she *was* a beauty. He gave her the sad, slow smile proved capable of stirring butterflies in the least sexual of female breasts. 'You are going to take it, aren't you? The apartment, I mean.'

He thought he'd overdone the impudence. The husband gave him a hard stare. It wasn't easy to assess him in that dim light, but his stance gave a first impression of solidity —male, dark, athletic, contained. Not, Niall thought, unimpressed, like my own indolent, irresistible self.

The girl had turned to face her husband. 'Are we, Andreas?' she demanded abruptly. 'I don't think I can stand the Stresa much longer, with the laundry right overhead.'

The man looked doubtful. 'We shall have to consider it,'

he temporized. His English was good, but not perfect like the girl's. She must have spent a lot of her life in the Home Counties, or might even be English herself.

'If you do come, I hope you like music,' Niall offered, with just the right touch of boyish diffidence. 'I play the clarinet. Not that that should bother you, me being two floors up and out most of the day besides.'

They'll not wish to hurt my feelings, he assured himself, having in mind a clear picture of himself folded pathetically at their feet. 'I'll be a totally inoffensive neighbour, I promise.'

They both smiled, as he'd intended they should. 'You're Irish, of course,' the girl said.

'Ah, me accent . . .'

'The blarney.' Now she was laughing at him.

'And you as English as they come,' he marvelled. 'Yes, I'm Irish by birth, from County Cork; a bit of a wanderer, though. Genevese by adoption, at least for the present. I teach part-time at the Conservatoire here and play professionally with a small wind ensemble. You may even hear me sometimes on Radio Genève when they augment the Orchestre de la Suisse Romande. It's a witless, unambitious life as befits me nature, but I do little harm; so I tell meself.' He treated them to his feckless, disorganized smile, and all the while his blue Irish eyes mocked her from under near-black, overlong hair, saying, *I could eat you, five of you before breakfast, and still want more.*

'If I can't assist you . . .' Vassilakis reminded him of his presence.

'Ah, you were surely on your way out, and haven't I delayed you?' Niall raised himself weakly to his feet, drooped a little, brushing with long, white fingers at his trousers, long, dark lashes lowered over eyes still aware of the Greek's wife, her finely tapering legs, the neat figure, her femininity. He had always found redheads especially rewarding of his attentions, and wasn't the husband's present bristling evidence enough that he felt already the vibes passing between the two of them? But he mustn't put the man off. He could be so valuable. Niall turned to him now, all open and likable.

11

'It's a lovely part of town,' he assured him, 'perched between the old and the new, as it were. A good address means a lot in Geneva. And it's a pleasant apartment besides.'

'But it isn't yet available,' the bureau man stated dogmatically. 'The Professor's family still hold the lease until the estate is settled. But the layout is the same as the one directly above it, which might become free in the nearer future.'

'Madame's own flat? She's giving up her last part of the old family home?' Niall was astounded. True that no one had really lived there since the old mother died last autumn, but everyone supposed that Madame would eventually move back here herself, sell the huge villa along the lakeside now she was on her own. It was no place for a childless divorcee.

No one offered answers to his questions. Perhaps the agent had overstepped the mark in disclosing what he did.

'We shall hope to meet Madame Zuelig shortly,' the Greek said to fill in the awkward silence. 'We heard of the place because I am Professor Theodorakis's replacement at WHO.'

'Ah.' Niall nodded. 'OMS.' He couldn't resist correcting him. 'The English name's out. Not World Health Organization any more, but Organisation Mondiale de la Santé. The French have taken over. Another political victory, like Standard Time.'

'So I understand.' Vassilakis appeared to have lost interest in the topic and was ready to leave. Niall hobbled backwards and left their way clear to the lift's open gate. He'd been a fool to mock the man. There were times when his puckish temptations just took off on their own. But maybe no harm was done: the man wasn't English himself, didn't appear goaded. Maybe Greeks even preferred the French to the English. Small wonder if they did.

The girl turned back before she stepped into the lift. 'Anyway, we do like music,' she said, peacemaking. 'So if we should ever come here to live . . .' She almost offered her hand to be shaken, but ended with a vague gesture and a shrug.

Niall let his long-lashed, half-closed eyes linger on her

12

while his curved lips said everything for him. His smile had barely reached full strength when the lift gate sighed shut. He went on smiling as the light passed downwards behind the glass panel. He stood on, thinking. A lot might come from this encounter. Opportunities, means to ends.

He squared up the edges of his sheet music, tucked the bundle under one arm, turned and took the upper stairs two at a time on totally uninjured ankles.

CHAPTER 2

The girl who came to the villa every morning with croissants and milk stayed on until twelve on Tuesdays, Thursdays and Saturdays to perform such cleaning duties as were required. Living on her own there, dispirited and feeling far from robust, Klara Zuelig did little that might disarrange the showpiece order of what had formerly been a family home. She spent a great deal of her time now—and time was all she was conscious of having left to her; far too much time—sitting at the great windows that overlooked the lake, wondering what on earth she could do with the rest of her life, the deserted rooms, the prolonged silence pressing in on her.

When she could not bear to look further ahead she looked back, and marvelled that what she saw in retrospect was not what she had thought she saw at the time. 'How can I have been so blind?' she would demand aloud, rising impatiently and walking the length of the drawing-room which fronted the sloping gardens. 'Why did I let it happen to me? When did I become such a fool?'

When she was angry enough with herself about the past she would take another hard stare at the present, which meant walking through the paralysed rooms, the deteriorating garden, facing her own features in the rococo mirror in the hall.

She was far too thin, with the drabness of premature middle age. Her skin, always a little sallow so that she could never wear clear colours, had faded with her hair to an indeterminate shade. She even thought in certain lights that she caught the glint of silver at the temples. Her brows were still dark and thick. Stubborn brows, her father had once remarked to her as a child, and he had sounded approving. He wouldn't think much of the mouse she'd become. No; the mouse that she now knew she *had been*. Hadn't Papi seen it coming on? Didn't he know—such a shrewd man when it came to business—that over the years she had been flattened, eaten away, made negative; had even *chosen* to take those two steps backward which allowed Victor to develop such a monstrously inflated ego? Perhaps Papi had fondly seen only what he chose to see—the fair exterior, the seemly truce that was presented as Married Harmony: My Little Girl Grown up; Her Husband; the Family Trio. Papi having a blind spot when it came to people he loved.

Well, hadn't she been the same, deceiving herself as well as him with her trite picture of domestic felicity? All the while, surrounded by luxuries she'd never needed, she'd been neglected, just tolerated, never listened to and so eventually not herself expecting to communicate. Until suddenly—no; spread over a period of months—her eyes had come unstuck. After the first poisonous whispers she'd come to see what the truth actually was under appearances. She'd forced herself to acknowledge the dark side of the handsome, soul-of-the-party charmer who'd been her husband for over twenty-four years but whose life she had never shared. And just when they were expected to celebrate a special anniversary, she'd found the late courage to rebel, even then not knowing the full balance of the account and still believing there might be something left to salvage.

And now—she looked around—what was left? Only *things*. With herself in their centre. Beautiful, costly things which *he* had acquired over the years, as he'd acquired her at the beginning. The things were still beautiful; their value had increased. While she had faded. She was forty-six, and that felt really old. Old enough for anyone to be.

When she recognized her melancholia for what it was she always tried to think of an immediate remedy, such as moving back into the town, rejoining societies she'd been in as a girl, filling the old Geneva house with lively people, going on long holidays abroad with carefully chosen friends. But what friends, and what lively people? The ones she'd been young with were either disillusioned like herself or engrossed in their children's careers and the novelty of grandchildren. So much had to be started over again, because in the false life between she had lost the values of her youth as well as the friends.

What a waste of life, because of a false conception— thinking that being a wife was a matter of blindly following, of unquestioning support and submission. That must have been the very worst thing she could do, feeding Victor's monster vanity until he grew to believe in the myth of himself which he'd created, at last losing the ability to distinguish between pose and reality.

'My fault,' she said aloud. 'I should have seen. Why did nobody warn me?'

Others had guessed. She remembered her father-in-law, dying painfully, holding on to her hands and saying he was sorry, so sorry, tears running down his sunken cheeks. But that had been too late. By then she had known for herself and was already half resolved to strike back.

Klara leaned her forehead against the triple glazing that overlooked lawns and shrubberies terraced down to the surly waters of the lake choppy under a tricky wind. There were a few boats sailing far out, and close to land a single windsurfer on a shoreward tack. Idly she watched as he manœuvred to turn, fought the wind, was forced over and capsized. For a few moments he struggled to right the board, seeming competent enough for safety. The lake bed had a ledge near there. If he came just twenty feet towards land he'd be in his own depth. The struggling man drifted away behind her boathouse. Klara thought: I should go and pay Monique: it must be time she went home.

The girl was setting a tray in the kitchen: rye bread, unsalted butter, Camembert and a sliced tomato. 'It doesn't look enough,' she said sternly, adding the big bowl for hot chocolate.

'Oh, not that,' Klara protested. 'I'll make some tea later. There's a box of Earl Grey you can open.' She looked at the tray. Basic foods. Perhaps she ate too much dairy produce. Should she substitute an apple for the yogurt afterwards? But what was the point of a healthy diet? Wasn't it so that you would live that much longer?

Better perhaps if she regularly drank herself into a stupor, which she knew could become a very real risk if she let herself go. All those wonderful wines down in the cellar, and she'd always had a taste for wine, especially red Burgundy. In moderation, of course. For twenty-four years her whole life had been conscious moderation. It wasn't so any more. Mightn't she now wallow in drunkenness at least as profitably as she wallowed in misery?

'*Alors, à mardi, madame,*' Monique said, holding the door ajar and her head on one side. Klara wondered how long she had been waiting like that to make her escape.

'Your money. Did you find it?'

'I have taken it, madame. And left your change with the list.'

'Thank you. If I want anything for next time I will ring you.' She wouldn't. The freezer was full to bursting point and had been so, untouched, for a couple of months. '*Au revoir, Monique.*'

It was always doubly silent after the girl's quick footfalls had died away along the twisting stone path from the terrace. Klara looked sourly at the tray and turned her back on it, going through to switch on the radio.

Oh God, Stravinsky! True, only too true, what he had to say; but she couldn't take it and didn't have to. She snapped the music off. And heard the kitchen door re-open and somebody come in across the tiled floor.

It was Monique again. 'Oh madame, there is a man here, half-drowned. He asks to use the telephone.'

The windsurfer. Klara saw him beyond the girl, dripping at the outer door, shiny like a seal as he began to peel off the black wetsuit. Young, tall, beautifully built, revealing long, pale limbs and minimal swimming trunks. He shook back the straight, dark hair from his eyes. Laughing blue

16

eyes and near-black hair. Surely she had seen him somewhere before, but not like this.

'But isn't it Madame Zuelig?' he exclaimed in English.
'What luck. You won't remember me, though. I'm one of
your tenants at the town house. My name's Niall. I live at
the top.'

The Irish musician. Céline had spoken of him. They had
never been formally introduced because the agent dealt with
such matters, but she'd caught sight of him once when she
called there. 'Ah yes. It's Monsieur—?'

'O'Diarmid, madame. And devastated I am at needing
your help at all. I was doing quite well and then a squall
hit me so I went bottoms up. When I struggled to make the
shore I found I'd torn the sail on the boathouse steps. It's
a goner, I'm afraid, and I'll need a taxi home.' Woebegone,
waiflike. Teasing, of course.

'You haven't any clothes?' It had slipped out, unthink-
ingly. What a fool he'd think her, questioning the obvious,
but her mind, like her eyes, had been on his firm young
body. She felt herself flushing.

He crowed with laughter, flicking back his wet hair again.
'Windsurfers travel light!' There was dark hair too in the
depths of his armpit. He was almost indecently naked to be
in the kitchen so.

'There's a bathroom along the passage. Monique will find
you a towel and a robe.'

'But your floor, madame.'

'The tiles will dry off.' Now they seemed to have exchanged roles; she careless, he concerned. But he wasn't
really like that. He was the reckless kind, momentarily
trimming his exuberance to accommodate what he saw as
her domestic fussiness. He must recognize that she was
uptight and unwelcoming. The trouble was she'd forgotten
how to be casual, how to let the talk flow with a stranger.
She seemed even to have lost the right words.

Monique ushered him into the bathroom. He walked
beautifully, on bare feet. Pantherlike, the muscles flowed
under firm, shining flesh. There was more than a hint
of indolence, perhaps even insolence, in his assurance. It

wouldn't be so disturbing when he'd covered himself up.

'Shall I stay, madame?—' Monique, impatient to get back to cook her husband's lunch.

'No. It's all right. I'll see he gets his taxi home.'

'The lake's cold in May. I saw him shivering. I could heat up your chocolate for him.'

'Don't bother. I can give him whisky, or whatever's in the cabinet.' Monique nodded, said goodbye again and withdrew.

It was the first time Klara had unlocked the spirits since . . . since. Well, it had to happen sometime, and it didn't mean she would throw herself at the bottles. Just a polite glass now, so that the man hadn't to drink alone. There was nothing to be afraid of in that, was there?

As steadily as she was able she took down two tumblers and the half-filled decanter of scotch. There was nothing to go with it. No soda, not even dry ginger.

He came in quietly behind her but she could feel him there. She swung round, his glass in her outstretched hand, trying to be casual, feeling only reckless and already a little intoxicated before she'd touched the stuff.

It *wasn't* better now that he was covered. In the towelling robe and slippers, with his hair wildly unkempt, he looked as if he had come straight from bed. A husband figure. Any stranger arriving now would take him for that, or for an overnight lover. She had never had anyone in her bed but Victor.

'There's no soda,' she said wildly, pushing the tumbler at him. 'Would you like water?'

He made a rueful grimace. 'Haven't I had my fill of that already?' Then he laughed, showing white, feral teeth. Again a rapid change of humour and he was regarding her seriously, head tilted. 'This is uncommonly good of you, madame. How can I hope to repay your kindness? If ever you capsize outside my door on the fifth floor . . .'

'I shall choose it for my next shipwreck,' she heard herself respond and then she was laughing with him, as though none of this was at all strange but just an incident during a

18

crazy party such as people used to throw when she was a girl.

'To your health, madame. And the future.'

He held his glass up and she did the same. Then she was drinking down the fiery liquid. Drinking to the future: it was ironic.

They talked a while, first about his music. It was still difficult for her. She was short of things to say because so much of what she was thinking wasn't permissible, but the Irishman made up for her silences. Then gradually it was coming back to her, spasms of speech. She felt freed and rash and a little desperate turn and turn about. Her tongue was beginning to function independently. When he spoke again of phoning for a taxi the lie came out spontaneously. 'I was just going into Geneva myself. If you tell me where you left your clothes we can drive there first.'

'At the Petit Port, where I changed on a friend's boat. I become more in your debt every moment. Will you let me take you to lunch? Yes, I insist. Let me ring and book a table. Where shall it be?'

'I—no, I . . .'

'Yes, yes. You can't eat alone from that miserable tray in the kitchen. Especially after whisky. You need something more satisfying.'

It was disturbing the way he uttered that long-drawn-out final word. As though it meant more than the context allowed. But she could see it was just typical of the man. He was a terrible joker, hadn't a gramme of real seriousness in him, was perhaps a little of a rogue. Now she had left it too long to protest and he was lifting the phone, while she wasn't sure she ought to drive at all. Whisky, on an empty stomach, when she'd been alcohol-free for months. And, after she'd poured him a second drink, hadn't he lifted the decanter and done the same for her? She was almost sure of it. And her glass was empty again now.

'I must—change my dress,' she said suddenly, and left him to make the reservation.

It took only a couple of minutes, then he picked up the Geneva directory and ran his finger down the section H.

Luckily the Vassilakis girl had burst out with her dissatisfaction with the Hôtel Stresa. She was already keen to take the empty apartment, and between them they ought to be able to clinch it with Klara Zuelig. After that, if the girl knew her business—and what redhead didn't?—she had only to win over the Greek husband.

His call caught Siân as she was entering the hotel foyer and she was cautiously willing to fall in with his suggestion. Her husband was spending his Saturday working.

'You don't even have to book yourself a table,' he assured her. 'Just walk in and look around. I'll do the rest. You can charm the lady off her chair. Then, bingo, the flat is yours.'

She started to have doubts about the rents in that part of the town, and he put the receiver down in the middle of her reply because Madame Zuelig was coming back. He heard her cross the hall and come to a stop before the huge mirror. He moved to where he could watch. Klara Zuelig was frowning critically at her own reflection, leaning in to examine herself minutely from brow to chin, for all the world like a schoolgirl who imagines a beau is really interested in her face.

CHAPTER 3

Niall left them to their coffee together, pleading a suddenly invented lesson he'd to give at the Conservatoire. As he beckoned the waiter across to settle, Klara Zuelig waved her hand to dismiss the man. 'My father had an account here. It still exists.'

'But, madame . . .'

'My pleasure, Mr O'Diarmid.'

Well, okay, if she wanted it that way, his gesture said; and he grinned inside because his guess had been correct. Old Zuelig had had a share in this restaurant. He'd been into hotels and catering chains in a big way, even for a Swiss merchant banker. 'Then I'll thank you once again and take my leave. I hope we meet again soon. Really, I must fly. So sorry.'

With a generous wave of the hand and a display of even, white teeth he left them. At the door he looked back to where their heads leaned together over the table. Confidentially. Good! Queen's Bishop's Pawn to QB4, he thought impishly. A confident opening gambit, and much might come of it.

Striding down from the Old Town to the New, he considered the Zuelig woman's reactions. She was still knocked off-balance by the divorce and her need to seek it. It left her wobbling between relief and the desolation of finding herself alone. Cocooned from birth by wealth and her father's powerful connections, it must at first have been her choice to distance herself from others: you received that impression of conscious superiority. Now that the protective layers had been peeled away—her father dying some ten years back, her mother eight months ago, and the divorce as recent as Christmas—she was plunged in a new chill element. A strange woman, with a certain distinction; impulsive yet tongue-tied, perhaps capable of great passion while strictly schooled to conventional correctness. Very Swiss, owning so much but missing so much more. One might think what an opportunity for a skilled predator. But intuition warned him there was a layer of steely shrewdness under her apparent vulnerability, even a touch of the tiger freshly wakened.

At the villa she had been putty in his hands, moulding up nicely, and it had helped that she wasn't used to drinking. But sensible. When he'd paused by the driving door of her Mercedes she'd been quick to catch his raised eyebrow and flick him the car keys. But later—whether it was something discordant at the Petit Port, the cut of his clothes once he'd resumed them, or her re-emergence in public with a man alongside—the inhibitions had come back. She had kept to mineral water at lunch, held him firmly at arm's length and expected to be deferred to, as in the matter of who paid. Noncommittal, until the girl put in an appearance. Then the thaw began; Klara started to open out.

The girl had been just right—hesitant, slightly embarrassed by the introduction, deliciously young and frank. The older woman hadn't resented her intrusion, was unconcerned when he asked the girl to join them, and had herself called the waiter to have him set a third place.

Later, when he'd mentioned the Theodorakis apartment Klara had flatly stated that the lease was legally frozen for the present. She'd been taken aback that he knew her mother's old apartment was possibly to come on offer.

'I haven't finally decided,' she said defensively, and the distraught look had come back. 'I might want to use it myself, take up my old life in Geneva. It was my home, you know, as a child. We used the whole house then. Now it's too big, but I'm not sure I'm ready to cut all ties with it.'

'There are five floors,' Niall explained to Siân as though she hadn't seen it. 'It's one of the most elegant eighteenth-century additions to the mediæval city. There's a carriage block and stables at the back, with a cobbled courtyard and a beautiful fountain.'

'But it hasn't a real garden,' Klara said regretfully. 'We always grew geraniums and fuchsias and miniature roses all over the balconies and window ledges, but I longed for a garden. Mother too.'

'You certainly have your wish at the villa,' Niall said admiringly. 'And a glorious view; terraces right down to the lake; your own boathouse; every modern innovation one could want.'

And silent ghosts, Klara thought; but she struggled not to be engulfed by the lost past. 'In the winter,' she said, smiling determinedly, 'when Freddy was small, we used to ski down the orchard. It was a wonderful nursery slope. He learned to slalom between the apple trees.'

'That's one thing you couldn't do in the city.' Niall pushed the point home before she could slump again into gloom. Was she starting to think on the right lines, considering— as finally she must—which place to settle for as her base?

'Are you and your husband any nearer finding somewhere suitable?' he had asked Siân at that point, switching sympathy back to her situation.

'I scour the newspapers,' she said drolly, 'but by the time it reaches print every place is snapped up. The *Journal* and the *Tribune* had some lovely houses for sale, but they're too far out and they cost too much. It will have to be somewhere rented. And we don't want to join the international set on the Right Bank. Andreas would never be free of his work.'

'You make me feel guilty,' Klara Zuelig said, 'having a choice and unable to make up my mind.'

This was the point at which Niall had opted to quit the field, leaving the English girl with the Greek name to win or lose the day. He grinned, reviewing his strategy. Stage-setting was his line rather than full manipulation. He enjoyed 'agenting', a stage short of acting puppet-master.

Siân had just explained about the interrupted honeymoon. She produced a leather wallet from her shoulder-bag to show a photograph of the wedding. She was romantically in white, on the arm of a broad-shouldered man with a squarish, dark-skinned face. He looked solid and dependable with the hint of a quirky smile. 'Andreas is a doctor from Athens, but we met when he was working in Crete. He's a marvellous person,' she said.

'So was the man he follows,' Klara told her. 'I had great admiration for Professor Theodorakis. Such a convinced ecologist. Did you ever meet?'

Siân shook her head regretfully. 'It's strange that Andreas should succeed him, being a practising medical man and not political at all.'

'Oh, the Professor wasn't political either. A distinguished academic, of course, and very concerned about the earth's resources and the way they are mismanaged, but it took only a child's cough or an old person's gnarled knuckles to remind him he was a doctor too. I think he rather regretted that at World Health he was dealing with results more than causes. Perhaps your husband has been chosen to harness his ideas to the human scene. The Professor was almost obsessed with the problems of famine areas and natural disasters. Probably your husband will complement this by concentrating on the results and their cures.'

'Perhaps. His outlook isn't confined to his own country either. I was afraid at first that having a British wife might

23

spoil his chance of selection. I'm so glad it didn't. He was keen to come to Geneva as a delegate because he thought our marriage would start off more evenly here, with us both in a foreign land and finding it equally difficult. Mixed marriages have special problems. I said so once to my stepmother, and she said, "Don't be daft. All marriages are mixed: what can you expect with a man and a woman in harness together?"'

'I like that,' Klara said. 'What a practical woman.' She looked round the emptying restaurant, then signed the luncheon chit with a determined flourish. 'If you have nothing pressing to do now, why don't we take a look at the town house? I'll show you my mother's old apartment, stuffed with all the family relics I don't know what to do with. It's like a gloomy old museum.'

'I find it so dark,' Klara said, standing later in her dead mother's drawing-room. 'The whole house feels starved of light after the villa. I really don't think I could live here again.' Better to endure the ghosts and the silence, she thought. This house goes back too far in time. At least the other one is mostly relevant to the living.

Siân gazed around. It certainly was gloomy, due to heavy curtains, dark wood panelling and sombre wall-coverings. In this room the insets were of ruby damask with too many heavily framed paintings. There were also large ormolu clocks and several pieces of statuary in bronze. The long room had been formed out of two square ones with the dividing wall removed and its earlier position hinted at by open screens of black wrought iron, all arabesques and vine leaves. Madame Zuelig had switched on every light as she passed, as though the gloom had to be kept at bay, but the effect remained sombre.

'What can I do with all this *stuff*?' she demanded. She had moved on into the dining-room where immense glass-fronted cabinets were built into the walls to display crystal, silver, figurines and dinner services: monstrous evidence of accumulated wealth. This was like a tour of Hampton Court Palace, Siân thought; or one of those historic stately homes.

'And you grew up here?' she asked in disbelief.

Klara laughed. 'I told you, we used all the house then. These were our State Apartments. My big brother Klaus and I had the whole top floor with our English nanny and a maid. When we were brought down here, to meet guests, we were thoroughly scrubbed and then made to stand with our hands behind us for fear we touched anything. It was on the floor below this that my parents had their bedrooms and we all met as a family. My grandfather had already installed a lift, so visitors were brought straight up here without seeing the other floors. As an old man Grandfather had his rooms at ground level with a live-in manservant, and an office so that he needn't go to the bank once Father had taken over.

'So the ground floor was the first part of the house to have strangers live in. A lawyer whom my father employed moved his chambers there after Grandfather died. When my brother first left home and then I married, my parents found it all too large. Father let my husband's cousin Philippe have the first floor, and his divorced first wife is still there, Céline Durochat.

'My parents gave away a lot of the furniture and kept to the next two floors, converting the nursery floor for us to use when we visited. Then my father died and after Mother had a stroke she withdrew to this apartment and was persuaded to let the next floor down to the Professor. The Irishman at the top came only last autumn. Less and less has this house any connection with me. Perhaps I should move out entirely, just keep it on as an investment, jointly with my brother.'

She turned briskly. 'Well, now you have seen this mausoleum, let's take another look at the late Professor's rooms.'

Relatively they were less forbidding because here the plaster walls were washed over with buff emulsion. The furniture was all of Zuelig origin and massively impressive, but Siân recognized now that the monochrome enlarged photographs which hung framed in every room must be records of the Professor's ecological interests. They had no labels but Klara was able to identify them from conversations she had had with Theodorakis. 'Nepal,' she said, pointing out collapsing hillsides and ruined terraces. 'Colorado; the Yangtse Basin; Ethiopia; Siberia.'

They moved on, to be confronted by a large, framed oil painting.

'And this?'

Klara grimaced. 'That is a Zuelig leftover, a painting by Freddy which he once gave my mother. She couldn't stand it, but she wouldn't risk offending him by getting rid of it. When she died we moved it down here. The Professor didn't mind it. He said it made a valid statement. Which was kind of him.

'Freddy is an artist, so perhaps I should try to find his work less distasteful. Lately he has turned to abstracts and they disturb me less because I can't understand them. They even seem to sell quite well. If you will help me lift it down I will take it right away now.'

Siân could only agree with Klara's opinion. The picture was more than frightful; it had a sort of gloating vileness. The scene was the lamplit stall of a byre, naturalistically painted in dull shades of ochre. A chrome cow had just given birth and a small boy, exaggeratedly foreshortened, had turned away outwards, his full-face features distorted with horror. Gentle-eyed and maternal, the cow bent to lick her calf struggling groggily to its knees. Against the gory post-parturition mess the thing was clearly seen to have two heads.

They lifted the heavy frame down between them and Klara found a dust sheet to cover the canvas in its transport by car. 'Can you manage it at the other end?' the girl asked.

'Oh yes. There's always Monique, and anyway I shan't move it far. Can I drop you at your hotel?'

It would have been out of Klara's way, and Siân declined, preferring to walk. Both said goodbye hoping to meet again. 'I shall ring you,' Klara promised solemnly.

At least Siân had something of interest to tell Andreas that evening, not just fruitless trailing from unsuitable flat to just-missed Eden. Andreas himself was never very forthcoming about his day's work and she was determined not to question him, however apprehensive his silence made her. The changeover from hospital action to administrative responsibility must hit him hard.

When she had asked him what his workplace was like he had said vaguely, 'Pretty big.' Which hadn't encouraged her to show interest. But this evening, because he was trying out a second-hand Peugeot which a colleague wanted to sell, Andreas suggested for the first time that they should drive out that way and she would see the building.

The colleague, a Belgian, was seated with Andreas at the front and Siân sat forward on her rear seat peering between them, keen to miss nothing. She memorized the code letters of buses going in the same direction, determined to take some time off from flat-hunting to explore on her own.

'Just after the Palais des Nations entrance, up the hill and on the left,' the Belgian said of the WHO headquarters.

They swept round an enormous traffic island, where on a weekday a bus fleet would have collected late workers from the UN offices, and turned up a wide avenue. The whole area was open and leafy, tamed country with added mod. cons. And there, on the left in a pleasant garden, she looked through to a gracious old stone villa, grey and quite big. 'It's lovely,' she exclaimed. 'Which is your office?'

The Belgian sniggered and Andreas drove right past. 'Part of the Russian compound,' he said. 'The original house had to be preserved. The main part starts now.'

Then came a formidable high wall with electronic surveillance gear and massive automatically operated steel gates guarded by a reinforced lodge with smoked glass windows. Behind it an extensive block of pale stone or concrete went on and on apparently without windows, like some monster albino imitation of the wartime Citadel in Whitehall. 'It's gigantic,' she said. 'But I thought that all the Embassies were in Berne.'

'It's just the Soviet Permanent Mission to UN,' said the Belgian. 'The Russians always need ten times the staff of any other country. For reasons of their own which we can only guess at.'

The Peugeot's winker was indicating left, and just short of a tall, châteauesque building housing the Swiss Red Cross, Andreas turned along the side of the Mission wall. Behind it the Russian grounds extended a considerable way in this direction too until, among mature trees, a brutally modern structure of dark grey which was BIT (or in English the International Labour Organization). Round the farther bend, and opposite, was the enormity of World Health. As Andreas had said: pretty big.

'I'm glad you insisted we shouldn't live near your office,' Siân told him when they had returned that night, the Peugeot deal accomplished. He was cuddling her in the crook of his arm while he sorted strands of her dark red hair over the pillow.

He made the brown paper bag face. 'It's—crushing, isn't it? I am only just beginning to feel lifesize again. The whole prospect is awesome.'

'You'll make a great success of it, Andreas. They're lucky to get you.' She wriggled round to face him. 'Did you ever meet the man you replaced? Madame Zuelig had a very high opinion of him.'

'Yes, my family knew him quite well in Athens. In fact he was the one who sponsored my application. I should never have been considered otherwise. His word carried a lot of weight. A dear old man. I wish he could have lived to hand the job over. It was a great shock, his dying so suddenly. Nobody dreamed he had anything wrong with his heart.'

'So there had to be an inquest?'

'Ye-es.'

'Yes or no?'

'It was adjourned. To be resumed shortly.'

Siân considered this. 'Doesn't that imply some kind of doubt, a need for further investigation?'

Andreas sighed. 'The medical evidence seems quite clear, but somebody is quibbling over his activities before the fatal attack. They want to know the possible causes, stresses, things of that sort.'

'Surely that's going rather far into it, even for a famous

personality? So what had he been doing immediately before? Playing squash, something like that?'

Andreas hesitated, frowning. 'He had just arrived for work in the morning, very early. But his car was abandoned near the bottom of Avenue Appia. There was nothing wrong with it when they examined it afterwards, but for some reason he had got out and—' He hunched his shoulders and spread his hands, palms up. 'Somebody said he was stumbling when they saw him—uphill, in the direction of World Health. He was still quite a distance from the building when he collapsed and died.'

Siân tried to picture it: the car—what colour, what make? —turning left before the Swiss Red Cross, along the side of the Soviet Mission. Under the high wall with its camera and electronically guarded gates. 'Did he drive the same way we went this evening?'

'It would appear so.' Andreas was beginning to tire of the interrogation. His tone warned her off. It would have to rest there. Because he was uneasy himself and didn't want her suspicions augmenting his own?

But his answers hadn't satisfied her. She saw too vividly the route the dying man had taken: uphill, and the empty road curving ahead towards the as-yet invisible place of refuge. Too early for office traffic; Theodorakis the only pedestrian. Stumbling—to or from?—alongside the wall of the close-guarded citadel of the Soviet Mission.

Soviet. It had to be that, of course. This was the origin of any doubts at the inquest: why they started looking for a cause for sudden heart failure.

CHAPTER 4

They rose late next morning, to the mixed clangour of church bells. The sun had made three or four attempts to pierce the universal grey: excuse enough to make a gesture of faith in the reluctant spring. Andreas took Siân for a short mystery drive. Certain of pleasing her, he went back along the northern shore, parked the Peugeot by the Ecole des Interprètes and walked her down to the Jardin Botanique. 'I wanted to be with you when you discovered it,' he said.

A sort of mini-Kew, Siân found, wandering delighted from water gardens to rockeries, admiring the way small areas represented various parts of the world, the habitats of plants creatively differentiated with their native soils.

'So if ever you get to feel foreign,' Andreas said, squeezing her hand, 'come out here to your own kind. There are associated clubs you can join, and why not apply to take postgraduate Botany at Geneva University?'

'Andreas, how long have you had this up your sleeve?'

He grinned. 'Since I knew there was a chance of coming to World Health. I didn't mention it before because . . .'

'. . . that would have been offering bribes!'

'I thought that if you were happy to come just as my wife, then you'd be doubly happy here with an interest of your own as well.'

'I love you, Andreas Vassilakis. I wonder why.'

They drove west to Lausanne, lunched there and explored the town, then returned in the evening to Geneva, taking in cold roast chicken, salads and fruit for a picnic on the bed. Bed was becoming the focal point of their lives, for more than the obvious purposes. After they had eaten, it even served as a table for playing Scrabble, while Swiss Radio Three poured out a Vivaldi oboe concerto.

At eight-seventeen the phone rang and it was Madame Zuelig on an outside line apologizing for such short notice but she had a proposition to put to them. Could they come out to her villa for coffee? Say, in half an hour? Was that too much to ask? They should cross the Pont du Mont Blanc and follow the Rive Gauche towards Hermance . . . Her previous hesitancy had gone; Siân barely recognized the decisive voice as hers.

They said they would be delighted, all the way there regretfully agreeing that either of the Zuelig apartments was too vast and would certainly cost more than they could afford at present.

Too suddenly they came on the gates to the Villa Montarnaud on a rising bend. Andreas had to reverse a few yards to enter the driveway. It curved down to the lakeside where a small modern house overhung the water on a stone platform. As part of the ground floor a triple garage faced them with a wide space in front for turning or parking cars. The house was shuttered and in darkness, but on the right a chain of standard globes lit a pathway up a terraced garden to a much larger house on its crown. Light poured from windows that stretched some fifty feet along its frontage, and a lone figure silhouetted there waved down as they started to climb.

In the dusk they could make out shrubberies and rough lawns to either side of the flagged path which sometimes sloped up and sometimes rose in a group of seven steps. The final stretch rounded a high, stone-built promontory up which roses and wild vines straggled. There was a bare patch where the pearly grey limestone had been uncovered and seemed smudgily stained a faded orange over an oblong a metre high and some five metres wide. Andreas put up his hand to touch this in passing and sniffed at his fingers. They went on up the last seven steps and stood on an even lawn set with tubs of scarlet and yellow tulips. Electric lanterns illuminated Madame Zuelig at the door to welcome them.

Seated to either side of her in the drawing-room with its breathtaking view over the silver lake and the distant shore lights, they were offered a choice and settled for tea from an English teapot.

'I drink tea quite often myself,' Klara Zuelig told them. 'I learned the habit at school in Sussex.'

The conversation followed a desultory course while they waited for the Swiss woman to make her proposition. She seemed to be giving Andreas a chance to declare himself, and for some reason he was curiously quiet, watching and listening. She isn't sure about him, Siân thought, and he won't make it easy for her.

'Yesterday you were telling me about the Professor,' Siân ventured, 'and I mentioned to Andreas how much you admired him. He knew him too in Athens, and it was

31

Nikolaos Theodorakis who sponsored Andreas as his successor.'

'Then he must have thought a lot of you, Dr Vassilakis. His work meant almost everything to him.'

'He and my father were contemporaries at University. He's a doctor too, a neurologist.'

She nodded gravely. 'You will be established in Geneva for some period?'

'Three or four years to start with. There will be projects and visits abroad, but Siân will probably remain here while I'm away. Which is why we are looking for somewhere permanent to live.'

'With a kitchen of my own,' the girl said with assumed anguish. 'Suddenly I have this domestic urge. I want to feed the man.'

'I don't think,' Klara Zuelig said with abrupt trenchancy, 'that either kitchen that we've shown you would do justice in that case. They are both too—old-fangled. Can one say that? Anyway I have had this better idea. To me it seems better, and I hope you will think the same. I didn't want to say anything until you'd seen it, because "boathouse" sounds so awful.'

'Boathouse?'

'Down where you left the car. It's very modern, just eight years old, and no one has lived there since I got rid of the gardener and cook. There are two large bedrooms, a kitchen, dining-room, lounge, study, bathroom and shower. I use only one car now, which leaves room in the garage for two more. And under the garage there are two boats; a small powered launch and the dinghy in which Freddy learned to sail. We used to have a twenty-four-footer but I sold it and let the open mooring to neighbours. You can see her from here, *Cacahouette*.

'Oh, there is central heating of course. Double-glazing; triple on the lake side, which can be slid open. What else? Electricity for cooking and lighting. An open fire for burning logs in winter. The one drawback you might find is the distance from your work, Dr Vassilakis. By car it is perhaps thirty kilometres, but by boat a matter of minutes across to the Rive Droite. We once had an arrangement with some friends on the far side about mooring. Perhaps it could be renewed.'

Siân was staring at her wide-eyed, speechless at the offer.

'Have I overlooked something?' Klara demanded.

'The rental,' said Andreas drily.

'Ah well. Let us look at it first, shall we? Then we can decide.'

She changed her shoes to go down the terraces, and threw a dark coat over her shoulders, locked the door carefully behind her and held on to the key. They walked in silence and Siân couldn't tell from her husband's blank expression which way he was likely to decide.

The little house was sound and bright and half furnished; perfect for them, and leaving room to have their few precious items sent over from England. There were two small plumbing jobs needing to be done, also a new cooker fitted and the telephone reconnected. Then Klara would get the kitchen repainted, possibly a pale apricot shade. Siân could see no reason for turning the offer down, provided that . . .

'The rent,' Klara said calmly,' would not all be in money. Whoever comes here will be a caretaker in a way. For my house when I'm away over a period.' She paused, staring hard at Andreas as if to challenge him. 'And when I am here—for myself.'

'Because there is some special risk?' he asked quietly.

Again she hesitated. 'To the house, it seems. Perhaps even to me. But certainly not to yourselves. I shall have to explain. Please sit down; it's a long and rather sordid story.'

Since she had seriously set about obtaining a divorce there had been a series of incidents. In November she had been using the villa only at weekends and dismissed the servants, but the heating was left on because the severest weather was yet to come. When she brought the whitesmith to change the locks they found the house freezing. The oil feed had been cut off from outside, but recently enough not to have caused serious damage.

Then one Saturday she had returned to find one of the steel shutters forced apart and half a brick thrown through the glass inside. She had approached a private security firm to arrange periodic visits. They had reported a number of rooftiles removed and the inner cladding torn away to expose the main beams.

The most recent incident was the painting of her maiden name—which she had elected to return to—in letters a metre high round the promontory of the upper terrace. It had been sprayed on thickly in bright orange gloss and could easily be read from passing boats on the lake.

Because of the timing and her ex-husband's known reactions, she could only assume the vandalism was his doing, or done at his instigation. 'It annoyed him particularly,' she recalled, 'that I should no longer be known as Madame Durochat. I was offered the choice of surnames by the judge who heard our case. It seems as if Victor identifies the house with himself: his realm, because he was the master here. Losing it was monstrous for him, but you see, it has always been in my name, since Papi bought it.'

There was a lot left unexplained but in her way she had been astonishingly open. For such a discreet and private woman it could not have been easy.

'So you see,' she summarized, 'we are not good friends at all, my ex-husband and I. It is better that we keep a distance between us. Sometimes—sometimes his anger becomes too much for him to contain, and he has mischievous acquaintances who lead him on. I don't know if he comes here himself or if they do it for him, but these things have happened; clearly not accidents—and the police agree. But nobody has been *caught* interfering with the house. And there has been nothing really dangerous, or not yet. Just annoyances, to cause me expense in putting them right, and to disturb the way I hoped to live, in peace.'

'It is intended to frighten you, madame.'

'Yes. But I will not be intimidated. I have been harassed, persecuted—' She clenched her fist and beat on her knee, screwing her face to hold back the tears. 'But—I will not —be—driven out—of my own home!'

For Andreas and Siân the matter of the boathouse was not something that could be decided at once. There had to be consultations between the two of them and then perhaps another meeting to allow questions and discuss details. Andreas suggested that they should all dine together in Geneva the next evening, and then sombrely they walked far enough up to the house to keep in each other's sight until Klara was once again indoors.

'I don't like it.' Andreas scowled. 'We don't have to take on someone else's troubles, just to save a little money.'

'It depends,' Siân insisted, 'on what help she needs. It may be enough just to have us around, like a dog that only barks. As she said, she wants to be able to see lights go on and off nearby at night. It's like holding someone's hand when you're walking along a wall. You're not leaning on them; you just know they're there and so you keep your balance. And she did inform the police of the earlier damage. They'll keep an eye open.'

'One community policeman from the village.'

'And the villagers. They must know all about it. They can't be blind.'

'We'll see,' Andreas said. 'It's you I would worry about when I'm away at work. Let's sleep on the idea. Tomorrow it may strike us differently.'

Next morning they awoke to a bright dawn, and whatever the sun's effect on Andreas, Siân was sure it augured well. Nevertheless, armed with her street plan and a copy of the *Journal de Genève*, she set out on foot to prospect three further advertisements she'd marked in the *Immeubles* columns. Crossing the lake's end to the more native Rive Gauche, she summarily dismissed the Bel-Air address as too noisy and commercial. Grand-Lancy, for the other two, was rather distant; she would take a bus out there when she'd looked in on the University, the main block of which was set in the public park of the Promenade des Bastions. To reach it she must first manœuvre the traffic of the Place Neuve, self-consciously French with its Grand Théâtre mimicking the Paris Opéra, and there, on the right according to her map, was the Conservatoire, where Niall O'Diarmid gave clarinet lessons.

There could be no harm in looking in there first, and if

35

she caught sight of the Irishman she'd thank him for the introduction to Klara Zuelig which might, or might not, have solved her housing problem. Without actually prying, she might also learn more about the lady from that glib-tongued charmer, enough to set Andreas's doubts at rest.

She made her way through the traffic, passed a bed of early geraniums, went up shallow steps to the entrance foyer, and found the porter's lodge empty. She pushed open swing doors to stare in on an auditorium with no less than four harpsichords grouped on a stage. Again there was nobody in evidence, so she withdrew, turned left and walked down a high-walled corridor past solid-panelled doors from behind which floated a detached sequence of sounds; horn, violin, harp, a sad soprano. She must have strayed among rehearsal rooms and classes. She had really no right to be here but it was strangely exciting, the dreamlike combination of narrow space and loftiness, the escaping ghosts of music, and herself walking alone through them as if inside an orchestra that was tuning up.

Back at the porter's lodge she found a uniformed attendant and asked for Niall O'Diarmid by name. The man shook his head, regarding her over his half-spectacles. '*Jamais le lundi et le mercredi*. On Mondays and Wednesdays 'ee is 'ome.' And ''ome', she knew, was the Zuelig house up by the Bourg-de-Four. Perhaps after the University she would call there, say that as she was passing she felt she must thank him.

There she again encountered the severe-looking concierge and suddenly recognized who it was he had first elusively reminded her of. Not quite Don Quixote, but Calvin. Flesh-less, unbending, hawkish, with a long, pointed beard, Régnier was short of nothing but the divine's long robe, Geneva tabs and close-fitting cap. The man had little English, and when she asked for O'Diarmid he showed her into the lift, pushed the top button and gave a stiff little nod.

O'Diarmid was at home. Siân could hear the exquisite notes of his clarinet as the lift gate opened. The solo passage was familiar; from the Mozart Concerto. Abruptly it broke off and he took it up again from a few bars back, worked through it, repeated the reprise. He was giving himself a hard time. Maybe he'd not wish to be disturbed. Or was it going so badly that he would welcome an interruption? Tentatively she knocked. The music continued and she knocked again, more loudly. He must have heard her that time. The clarinet flowed on, and she turned away. Practice time was evidently sacrosanct.

The lift had already glided away, so she started down by the stairs, recalling at each floor the rooms she had been taken through. When she reached the first storey the apartment door was ajar. A little, plump woman in a polka-dot silk suit, white on lilac, was just removing her key from the lock. She looked back over her shoulder and smiled. '*Bonjour, mademoiselle. Vous cherchez quelqu'un?*'

Siân explained, the other nodding. 'Ah, 'e will not answer when 'e plays, *non*. Will you write a message, per'aps? Come in, please, with me.' Siân followed her in. The flat was immaculate and decorated mainly in gold and pale green. In the hall the waxed boards of the floor shone a clear honey colour, leading into a drawing-room velour-carpeted in champagne to harmonize with the furnishings. There were three display cabinets of fragile porcelain figures and several lavish flower arrangements.

'I am Madame Vassilakis,' Siân explained. 'I came here the other day—'

'To see Theo's apartment. Of course. Niall told me about it. I am so pleased to meet you.'

'And I came yesterday a second time, with Madame Zuelig, to see her mother's flat.'

'Really? That I 'ad not 'eard. We are sort of distant *belles-sœurs*, Klara and I. We married two cousins. You 'ave 'eard of the Durochats, of course. *Non?* Well, you will soon get to know the Maison Durochat on the Quai Général-Guisan. It 'as such lovely things—silver, jewellery, porcelain, pictures.'

'So you are Madame Durochat?'

'Céline, please. I 'ave kept my married name, you see. But Klara—' she shrugged—'Klara 'as gone back to call 'erself Zuelig. I think she does not like to remember 'er 'usband.' Céline Durochat raised a plump little manicured hand to remove a twist of white veiling and feathers from her lacquered ash-blonde hair. An enormous square-cut emerald sat smugly among the diamonds on her fingers. 'Excuse me,' and she pulled off one elegant lilac pump after the other, briefly scolding them in French as she pitched them into an armchair. 'There.' She wriggled her toes contentedly. A red line showed through the fine tights where the shoe's rim had cut into each cushiony instep. 'Why do I make myself suffer so? Is it elegant to 'obble, I ask myself?' She padded happily from the room and called back to Siân from the kitchen, 'Will you 'ave coffee, madame? Or I 'ave some nice Vermouth.'

'Please call me Siân. And really you mustn't bother.'

'I don't. See, I 'ave decided for you, the lazy way.' She came back carrying a tray with bottles and glasses. 'We 'ave a Campari and soda, or Punt e Mes with orange. *Mon cher mari divorcé*—' and she almost winked at the saucy term— ''e always says, "Celine, you never bother, but everything is perfect that you do."'

'What a compliment,' Siân managed, taken aback.

''E appreciates, *mon pauvre Philippe*.'

The tense she used was certainly the present. Correctly, or due to the limitations of Madame Durochat's English? 'Have you been long—on your own?' Siân ventured.

'Let me see.' The stylish little lady curled up in an armchair opposite, propping her chin on one jewelled hand. She had a pretty Renoir-model face, rounded and smooth. There was only the slightest sag under her jawline, and her wide, luminous eyes were set in blue shadows. She had a spirited, humorous way of talking, using her doll-like hands, pouting her lips, and cocking one or both of her eyebrows, so that even seated she seemed constantly in motion and somehow ageless.

'It must be almost seven years, I think,' she considered. 'Per'aps 'e broke a mirror and so 'e thinks it is long enough!' She gave a little gasping laugh. 'But I should not speak with such levity to someone 'oo is so recently married. You will think me *cynique*, a naughty lady, *non*? Not like poor Klara, who truly suffers, *n'est-ce pas*?'

'She does seem unhappy,' Siân conceded.

'She is so serious. Now is the time to say, "Good, I am free. I can go anywhere, do anything. I am my own woman."'

'Is that what you did?'

'Of course. And I would not change back for the 'ole world. There is *mon pauvre Philippe*, with 'is young wife always tied to the child, and at 'ome everything so untidy. 'E 'as no comfort, no inspiration. So 'e comes to me and I am sympathetic. We 'ave changed places, 'is Caroline and I. Now I am the mistress and 'e brings me the pretty things, and comes to say 'ow awful is 'is 'ome, and 'is wife does not understand 'im! Of course—' Céline Durochat darted a warm glance at Siân, saluting her with a half-tumbler of amber Punt e Mes—'it is a great joke, and all Geneva laughs at 'im, but 'e can laugh too. 'E thinks now 'e is a wicked devil. And 'e used to be such a dull dog.'

'Is his cousin like him?' Siân asked. 'The one Madame Zuelig was married to?'

'Victor? Oh, completely different. You would never think they are both Durochats. Victor is quite spoilt, an only child, and always so 'andsome. Klara was so enchanted by 'im that she turned into 'is shadow. 'Is mother made a monster of 'im, I think, but 'e 'as nice manners. You will assuredly think so. Especially when you go to the Maison Durochat, for 'im to sell you something!'

A bit of a con man, Siân accepted. 'And is he unhappy too about the divorce?'

There was a pause and she thought that this time she had gone too far with her prying. She glanced swiftly at Céline and caught the gleam of Puckish mischief in her eye. She was not offended; rather, a natural taste for scandal was struggling against discretion. 'E is mad, right out of 'is mind,' she rejoined at last, 'because 'e 'ad not believed she would go through with it. It was ''*is* idea first; to frighten 'er when she found out 'e was unfaithful. And when she showed 'erself so determined to get free—*mon Dieu!*—it was the end of 'is world!'

'Was he so fond of her?'

Céline was almost convulsed with laughter. 'Of *'er*? *Non!* 'Er *money!* 'E lost it all. The father 'ad tied it all up in the settlement. Klara is one of the richest women in the canton, and now Victor is in debt!'

CHAPTER 5

Siân was making moves to detach herself from Céline's racy confidences when there was a sudden thump from the ceiling. Both looked up and Céline made a *moue* at the lustres of her chandelier which were swinging gently. 'It will be worse when new people move in. Theo was so quiet. You would not think there was anyone there. Fortunately this is a solid 'ouse. Oh!' She spread her fingers artistically on her breast and pretended some confusion. 'But of course, next it could be you and your 'usband above me. I am sure *you* will not drag furniture about all night.'

'I'm not sure that we'll be coming.' Siân's plans were still too unformed to share with the gossipy little Genevese. To divert her curiosity now the girl rose and picked up her shoulder-bag, smiling. 'Who was moving furniture all night?'

'God knows. Theo's family, per'aps. They must be sorting out 'is things. It started after midnight, and now it seems they 'ave come back this morning.'

Siân thanked her for the hospitality, they said goodbye and Céline closed her door. As Siân moved towards the lift shaft the corresponding door closed softly on the floor above. She waited, curious to see who would come down, but the lift was not called and there was only a muffled scuffling of shoes on the steps. She went tentatively towards the staircase and listened. The sounds were receding. Then a cascade of liquid notes from Niall O'Diarmid's clarinet came suddenly louder and was instantly damped. Whoever had left the Theodorakis flat had gone up two floors on soft soles and let himself into the Irishman's rooms.

Siân shrugged, saw by her watch that it was time she

looked for somewhere to eat. Then, after an omelette and salad, she must go out to Grand-Lancy, look over the two apartments advertised for rent and duly report on them to Andreas when they met at four-thirty. She turned briskly into the Place des Casemates.

Niall O'Diarmid closed the apartment door softly behind him, padded straight through to the fridge, pulled out a can of beer and tore off the metal tab. As the cool draught went down, his eyes took in the stale, untidy kitchen. The remains of his late breakfast had congealed on its plate together with a crumpled cigarette packet and several half-smoked stubs. There was most of a dry croissant, the coffee things, last night's wine bottle and his heterogeneous collection of 'acquisitions'.

All symptomatic of minor panic, he told himself, surveying the débris. A stranger coming in might regard it as bohemian background natural to a young musician. The truth was that scruffiness offended him; he had a certain underlying need for order. Beneath the feckless Celtic image lurked the frustrated perfectionist who actually admired the Swiss ethos which he constantly mocked. And warring with both parts was the incorrigible romantic who saw himself as the first-person hero of a long-running epic.

'Now isn't that just the same squalid mess as yerself is in, me boy?' he demanded. Deliberately he chucked the crushed beer can to join the other rubbish on the formica-topped table. Then meticulously he began to sweep away the evidence of frustration. Not until the washed crockery was back in its cupboard and the little room straightened did he pick up his four acquisitions and carry them through to the living-room: *eeny, meeny, miny* and *mo*.

He stood a moment, head tilted, critical of the clarinet-playing on his practice cassette, waiting for the end of a phrase to allow him to switch off and extract the continuous tape. He slipped it tidily into the drawer that held his other practice recordings.

Then he returned to the four objects ranged on the coffee table, sat and examined each carefully, weighing it in his hand, pressing experimentally from every angle, alert for that barely discernible click which would confirm his suspicions. But nothing came open. All remained solidly what they appeared to be: a silver-backed hairbrush, a chalet musical-box, a flat tin of talcum and an aerosol can of shoe polish.

Only when he had dismantled the first two did he begin to feel any excitement at all. Not that he really *expected* success, but there just might be something inside one of the last two. A flat tin of talcum—such a hoary old hiding-place that even an innocent like Theodorakis could have known of the possibility. And the spray can was significant, because surely it was something a conservationist shouldn't have owned—propellants being accused of polluting the upper atmosphere or whatever. Moreover, it seemed palpably impossible to break into undetected, because any puncturing of a pressurized container involved some risk. A trick can could have a second chamber built in. It was anybody's guess what substance the boffins would put in as well as the token solution. Ammonia, or something more lethal? One had to remember that the old Greek had had his wits about him, for all his innocence, and this container might have been official issue on loan to him for the occasion. New gadgets were being developed all the time, the less likely-seeming the better. So he would save the spray shoe polish can to the last.

He picked up the talcum tin, inserted the end of his screwdriver in the seam under the shoulders and levered. The soft metal buckled in coming apart and a cloud of white powder puffed out, cool on his fingers and tickling his nostrils. 'Fern' was the perfume advertised on the label. Something grotty, certainly. It teased the sensitive membrane at the back of his nose and he sneezed until his eyes filled with water. When they cleared, disappointment again: a simple tin with a single substance spilling from it. No wooden block inside the shoulders cunningly drilled with twin holes to take reels of microfilm. Well, perhaps that device was too *vieux jeu* by now. There remained the aerosol can.

42

He carried it into the bathroom and took what precautions he could: opening the transom window fully; kneeling on towels and setting others to hand; first-aid kit open; cold tap running. God, his heart was putting out the finale of the *1812 Overture*, fire-crackers, cannon and all. He went back to the kitchen for rubber gloves, pulled on his oilskin sailing jacket, drew the hood close, fiddled about fitting a wet facecloth in as mask. Take every precaution, he told himself, because didn't curiosity kill the cat? One day it could well do the same to him.

Then there was no putting it off further. Get in, man. Think of the thing as a can of pilchards.

It exploded all over the bath and walls, shot out of his slippery hands and struck the tiles opposite, a miniature moon-rocket gone berserk on lift-off.

And he was still breathing, actually able to smell the white glop spattered around. It was acrid, almost antiseptic, familiar, not unpleasant. It was shoe polish.

Bulky in his protective clothing, Niall O'Diarmid lay back in the cramped space between bath and towel rail and laughed till the sweat ran down his cheeks.

He closed the door on the disaster in the bathroom. Result zilch, nix, nil, nothing! But had he really expected anything more of those four objects? Hadn't it been simply the romantic in him longing for the dramatic? The four objects had been the only fruits of his wildly optimistic search overnight. He'd brought them back as a dim last hope, and left dealing with them until daylight, by which time he'd been pretty certain that the Greek couldn't have transferred the data to microfilm anyway. It would have taken apparatus that wasn't in the apartment. The rooms were in fact singularly empty of personal belongings, considering how long the Professor had lived there. It was as though his ecological creed required him to travel light, leaving no tracks behind. A pollution-free habitat. Or had it been professionally sanitized since his death?

Frustrated, Niall had awoken late, breakfasted in haste and gone down a second time, determined on this occasion to look for what was *not* there. Nikolaos Theodorakis had been a simple man living without many of the crutches an ageing bachelor supports himself on, but some possessions, in Niall's opinion, he'd had more than enough of. Such as volumes of yellowed cuttings from newspapers and periodicals in half a dozen languages; and boxes of photographic enlargements, mainly of medical or geographical interest. Some of the famine and disaster scenes made the Irishman's flesh creep, but he worked sedulously through them.

The walls as well were hung with photographs, poster-sized and lightly framed, the paper seals old and undisturbed. They were all on the same themes, as though the Greek had to keep reminding himself of his function in the world. There was no denying his camera skill, but the subjects contrasted grimly with the opulent Zuelig furnishings.

Sunlight had been slanting across the buff-washed walls then, and Niall became aware of a space between two sets of photographs. It seemed that at its centre there showed a slightly lighter oblong.

Stepping aside to get a different angle on it he had collided with a waist-high jardinière, and before he could field the thing it went over, jangling its fine brass chains against the heavy carving, and crashing to the polished floorboards. The empty bowl it held rolled safely away across the thick rug. Niall set the jardinière upright and restored the plant pot, listened for repercussions from elsewhere in the house, then cautiously expelled his pent breath. He stared again at the suspect patch on the wall, which had not shown up by artificial light on his first visit. There was no place in the apartment, he knew by then, where a framed picture of that size could be hidden. Already he'd had the panels off the bath, been behind the wardrobe, sounded for false partitions. So someone had taken a picture away, together with whatever was hidden inside it. Who and where remained the puzzle.

He had had to admit himself stymied. The only faint hope that lingered was that something small might be concealed in one of his four acquisitions.

Now, with the four suspects finally proved innocent, he could no longer discount the obvious. Whatever secret document Theo had held was no longer in the flat. Living right on top of it, Niall hadn't known it even existed. Just as now he didn't know exactly what form it was in, nor what it contained. Worse, he had no idea who else was interested. The only way he would find a clue to that last blank was if he caught someone with the discarded frame. And a picture of God-knows what.

Theo and he had been too scrupulous, keeping rigidly to the rules, not visiting each other but meeting only on the stairs or in one of the parks, or on a lake boat, as if by chance; stupidly correct in observing the don't-need-to-know code. Because of this each had incomplete knowledge of the chain they were links in. Someone should have foreseen a balls-up like this. But then the original script hadn't had sudden death in it.

Over at World Health the ignorant authorities had accepted 'natural causes', and they might even be right. But in view of what the old Greek was secretly engaged in, and then the disappearing picture, there had to be doubt. Yet no one had pressed to have the apartment sealed as was customary in suspicious circumstances. Did that mean that everyone concerned knew it was a case of bolting the stable door too late?

Niall would have to report in, admit he was snookered. Failure, when everything had looked set fair for a good break in this new venture. Unless, of course, it was his lot who had stepped in ahead and seized the papers the moment Theo died. In which case they would surely supply him with a new contact for the second half of the operation, which was bound to be the more dodgy part.

Maybe that was already taken care of. The Greek's replacement at WHO had been almost instantaneous, a young doctor at least bilingual Greek–English, and probably adequate in French, with a very attractive Brit wife. Who better? He had taken over Theo's office, had access to anything there that needed clearing away. Vassilakis had also been to the house and could well be the one who'd somehow spirited the missing picture away. In that case all Niall had to do was continue as instructed, with Vassilakis cast in place of the old man.

So, on to the next move. Following precedent, Niall had already deposited the concert tickets at the Conservatoire porter's lodge, and the other two had been picked up. But had old Theo reported in on that arrangement before he died? If not, Vassilakis wouldn't know to pick his up. Perhaps it should be sent on to him. That would at least demonstrate that Niall recognized who to collaborate with.

Today the Greek would be out at WHO, which was forbidden territory to Niall. The safest bet was to contact the wife, and she was already indebted to him over the introduction to La Zuelig. Yes, the girl Siân was the one to follow up, and hadn't that some pleasant personal advantages too?

Niall O'Diarmid accordingly dialled the Hôtel Stresa and asked for Madame Vassilakis. After a short wait he was told that there was no answer from her room. He dialled her at hourly intervals all afternoon with the same result. At six-seventeen he made his last attempt from Radio Genève before going on the air, and still drew a blank.

Siân and Andreas had appointed a trysting tree in the Jardin Botanique, a mature *Liriodendron tulipfera*. The delicate creamy-gold flowers were just opening their cups, and Andreas had been fascinated by the lopsided leaves, like a plane leaf with a bite taken out of the end. From under its branches they had a panoramic view of rockeries and the distant lily-pool. Andreas was already there stretched flat on the grass, hands clasped under his head, enjoying the novelty of warm sunshine when Siân dropped beside him and bent to kiss his rough cheek. Without opening his eyes he murmured, 'I give you just three weeks to stop that.'

She snuggled close. 'Andreas, the boathouse. What about it?'

'Nice place. But isn't it really a question of the lady— whether she has been quite honest with us, and isn't a head case?'

46

'Yes, and I found out a little more about her today. She does appear to be the innocent party in the divorce, if there is such a thing. I happened on a woman who knows both sides well. Are you interested?'

'Tell me, then.'

She gave him the outline of her encounter with Céline, ending, '. . . and I'm sure she's the sort who would make the most of malicious gossip just for the fun of it. She didn't appear to know the details of damage to the property, so Klara Zuelig has been very discreet over that.'

Andreas grunted. 'Does that help you decide?' Siân demanded.

'Perhaps. That and what I found out myself.'

'You've been delving too—where?'

'In the commune police post.' He grinned at her astonishment. 'Well, it was obvious, surely. Your Madame Zuelig claimed she'd reported certain incidents to the local police. I went along, explained my interest and asked for confirmation. They were cagey—as a zooful of agoraphobic monkeys. So I itemized the details Madame mentioned, and invited them to say if I was in error. Which they couldn't do.

'There are two policemen in the village. The younger one winked at me behind his colleague's back. The senior one showed me out, and said that my living locally could be only to the advantage of everyone: it was always good to have a spare doctor within reach. I think you might call that the green light.'

Siân grimaced. 'They expect to call you in for children's grazed knees and the seasonal wasp sting at weekends. But does that mean that tonight we accept Madame Zuelig's offer?'

He rolled lazily over and gazed at her through half-closed eyes. 'When you had already made up *our* mind, would I dare oppose it?' He sat up suddenly. 'Let's celebrate. We'll drive over to the Rive Gauche pier and take the hour trip in a *bateau mouette*. Then you can view your new home from the water.'

The little boat was only half full but the tour guide did a thorough job, trilingually, with the PA system at full volume.

In the bow, Siân's red hair streaming in the wind, they watched the cleanly sliced green water creaming back along the hull. Ahead the lake surface barely seemed to ripple and the dozen or so isolated sails were making little headway.

Dutifully they admired the points of interest as the loudspeaker listed them; including all the elegant estates of the wealthy and famous.

'Not overlooking,' Andreas whispered, 'the Château Vassilakis, home of an imminently impoverished Greek doctor and his adorable wife.'

They had watched the lakeshore glide past with the neat, modern boathouse poised over the water's edge, seemingly on stilts. In the shadows beneath, they made out the dark shape of two boats behind metal mesh gates. Beyond the tiled roof with its empty white flagpost rose the terraced garden and winding pathways leading to Klara Zuelig's splendid villa, ivory and honey-coloured against dense beech woods on the summit.

'There's a lot of unused ground there,' Siân said enviously. 'Do you think she would let me have a small patch to turn into an Alpine garden?'

'We can ask.' He turned to her seriously. 'Siân, you have considered there may still be attempts to damage the property? The person responsible for the vandalism must be unbalanced, and there's no way of knowing how he may view our being there.'

'I'm prepared for a little hassle, yes.'

'Well, I thought perhaps a dog . . .'

'*Could we?* But if we go back to England there's quarantine. I'd never put an animal through that.'

'We would leave it here with friends over holidays, and when we finally quit, it could be good company for my mother. Greece has no entry restrictions for dogs.'

They continued to plan while the little boat frothed into a wide sweep, heading now for the farther side of the lake. 'This is the right way to see Geneva for the first time,' Siân enthused, as they made their return to a sunlit shoreline of cream and gold, so unlike the earlier overall grey. Distance and the glacier-green water between added a cool beauty to the well-spaced buildings and orderly tree-lined avenues over which rose the hump of the Old Town and the solid towers of St Pierre brooding with Calvinist severity over the materialist society it had spawned.

The guide was explaining now about the River Rhône which, rising in the high canton of Valais, flowed the length of the lake and out here, to pass via France to the Mediterranean. Eleven years, the loudspeaker claimed, was the time it took to make the journey.

'How can they tell?' Siân doubted.

'Scientifically. Random drops removed at source are marked with the date and then examined on arrival,' Andreas explained blithely. 'Simple, like ringing the legs of pigeons.' He evaded the gentle karate chop she aimed at his arm. 'But seriously there is a bridge here where they control the lake level, and you can see water drop over a metre down into the river. We could go there now on foot. The lake boats can't go further because the Mont Blanc Bridge is too low.'

They went ashore and, crossing to the Quai des Bergues, stood watching the foaming water thrash and tumble at great sluice gates guarded by chained bundles of long rods which also served to hold back any flotsam borne down by the rapid current. Above, on the Pont de la Machine hung lifebelts, grappling hooks and sinister-looking gibbets which presumably were used in salvaging large items. The roar of the water cut off the sounds of traffic; and the bridge, for all its solidity, trembled slightly under them with the force of the flow.

Andreas pointed downstream. In that direction, he said, the Rhône was joined by the Arve which drained the snows of Haute Savoie. One day they would take the river boat down into France. He'd heard it was lovely country, full of wild birds like herons and teal. But today, if they were to be punctual for Madame Zuelig, there wouldn't be time. They had to return to the Hôtel Stresa and change for their dinner appointment.

The phone extension in Room 93A had just stopped ringing as they came out of the lift. Niall O'Diarmid gave up trying for that day and went to take his place with the rest of the Orchestre de la Suisse Romande for their warm-up before the broadcast.

<h2>CHAPTER 6</h2>

Madame had recommended a small restaurant high in the Old Town where the atmosphere was sombrely rich, the smells mouth-watering and the tables discreetly spaced. High living at high cost, Siân decided, and even then was appalled at the tariff.

At first their conversation was general as they avoided personal topics, but Klara seemed tense, and when the waiter had refilled their glasses, Andreas said quietly, 'We should like to accept your offer, madame, if it remains open.'

She sat for a few seconds with her head bowed, her hands clenched, then she said in a low voice, 'Thank you. I . . . You cannot know how pleased I am.' She picked up her fork again and made vague movements with it among the food on her plate. 'There are times,' she said with apparent difficulty, 'when it is necessary to hold on to what is familiar. And at the same time to make a new beginning. Do you understand?'

'I think so, and we admire your courage. It is a little the same for us, making fresh decisions and being among strangers.'

The Swiss woman looked at him directly and nodded. 'Yes. It is not easy setting out in either direction. Really we are the two sides of marriage, like two sides of a coin.'

'I hope we can become friends as well as tenants,' Siân ventured.

'Tenant-caretakers,' Andreas reminded her. 'Even gardeners, perhaps. Siân, tell Madame what you were thinking of.'

Klara listened with growing interest. 'Of course. There is too much garden, and I know very little about the subject. Choose wherever you think the conditions are right. As a

50

good Swiss, I can only say that it is sure to add to the value of the property!'

She was comparatively relaxed by now, although Andreas appreciated that she wasn't the sort to find intimacy easy. It surprised him that so private a person had managed to admit to strangers what her situation was.

She told them she had already ordered the work to start on the boathouse kitchen, and it should be completed within two days. They were free to move in at any time after that. As to the idea of a dog, she had once considered getting one herself, but was a little too nervous. However, at one remove a guard dog did seem more acceptable. Then she could get used to it by degrees.

'We need a friendly animal,' Siân stipulated on their way back to the hotel, 'but one that looks tough and barks at strangers. Not a puppy either. So how do we get one?'

'I put a request on a notice board in a certain corridor, mentioning perhaps that I have an English wife. That is all that is required. There are thousands of British in the canton and some must be due to return home, faced with disposing of the family pet. All we need to do is wait and then start interviewing candidates. It could be a second Cruft's.'

There began a period of almost feverish activity for Siân. Taking advantage of the hour's difference, she phoned her stepmother in London after leaving Klara, and arranged for the dispatch of their crated wedding presents, linen and crockery. But even with these there would be gaps in the boathouse's furnishing. She drew up a shopping list and, with more curiosity than genuine intention to buy, included the Maison Durochat.

The manner of display—single items under a spotlight, rich drapery swathed as a background—was warning enough of price range. She found the opulence almost mesmeric, standing bemused before an exquisitely painted vase. It was Chinese, reputedly eighteenth-century, and to complement it the local display area was delicate *chinoiserie* lit by a flood of softest peach.

Well, that was not how she and Andreas intended to set up house. It was beautiful but irrelevant. The vase would

51

look well in the Zuelig villa, and was the sort of thing Céline filled her apartment with. They were both Durochat ex-wives after all, but while one seemed almost to despise possessions, the other thrived on them.

Siân moved on and was confronted by an androgynous person in a dark suit with a white stock at the throat. The voice was a woman's, the hands could have been a man's.

'Madame désire quelque chose?'

Madame desired a bookcase and a coffee table. Even in such an élitist showplace, there was a utilitarian area where such things were to be found. Siân was passed on to a nervous young man with haunted eyes, and entered a mock-up library. Marvellous, for a stately home. For a boathouse, out of the question. A coffee table then?

There was every sleek kind of wood; there was smoked glass and chromium, onyx on ormolu, marble with brass, table tops that were great sawn sections of unknown rocks ringed like the trunks of trees. And there was one unassuming, quite perfect circle of gleaming walnut set on matching little legs which seemed to prance. The price was alarming, but spread over all the years that Andreas and she would share and treasure it—nothing!

The Maison Durochat would deliver next day. To the Hôtel Stresa, of course. If the boathouse address passed through their books it might trigger off a new phase of the Zuelig husband's campaign of hate. If indeed he had been the culprit. Siân looked around for him. She saw a tubby little middle-aged man, moustached, with sparse hair economically stretched over a whitening dome. He was showing some crystal bowls to a thin woman in black and pearls.

'Philippe!' came a commanding voice from behind her, and the man started. So this was Philippe—Céline's cher mari divorcé, the 'dull dog' who thought himself such a devil.

The newcomer was tall, impeccably tailored, erect, with the proud chest of a male Bolshoi star about to launch himself on his pas seul. His stylish dark hair showed white wings. His face in profile was little short of aquiline, with an impressive nose, but the mouth was disappointing, too small and tight; petulant perhaps. If this was Klara Zuelig's ex-husband it was understandable that she had learned to take second place. Life could be more peaceful that way.

He smiled, and then he was total, assured charm, going forward to take the thin woman's hand. '*Princesse.*' He sounded overwhelmed.

Siân moved away. She had once heard an American address a bobby-soxer with that title, but this was the real thing. This was Geneva, where such ranks existed, on vacation or in exile. The Maison Durochat, evidently, was their select habitat. But not hers. Andreas would laugh when she told him. Or would he? Wouldn't he ask why on earth she went there in the first place? If she admitted it was out of curiosity, it would have to be a throwaway remark after he'd seen and admired the table—'Actually it came from the Durochat place. I think I may even have caught a glimpse of the infamous Victor.'

Really she'd been pretty silly. It was more than rash to spend all that money on one small item. She had been hypnotized into buying something they couldn't yet afford. The Greeks would probably have a word for that. She would keep a grip on herself from now on.

That evening Andreas was back late. He brought two boxes stuffed with papers, which he deposited in the hotel safe while they went out to dinner, warning Siân that he must catch up on his work that night. Over their meal she mentioned her purchases and he nodded as if they were simply ticked off a list. She threw in where she had been and who was there, but his mind was on other matters. 'Andreas,' she said when they had returned and he sat down to work with a cognac beside his papers, 'something's worrying you. Can I help?'

His mouth went into a stubborn, straight line, then he caught her eyes on him and relented. 'It's nothing, really. But I arrived this morning to find my office in disorder. Not badly, but things had been moved. By somebody other than the cleaners, I mean.'

'Andreas, your things or—?'

'Theo's mainly. So I brought some papers back to look

53

through. Whatever they were after must still be here. There hadn't been time to clear up afterwards.'

'I see. What are you looking for?'

'Anything odd, foreign to his main interest. I need to go through the whole lot, to see if there's one thing Theo held which could be specially valuable or else to someone's disadvantage. The trouble is that it's all been mixed up so. Needs sorting.'

'Can I help in any way?'

'Maybe if you took all the typescript and printed matter to sort into subjects. Say, correspondence, reports under their various languages, press cuttings. That would do for a beginning. I'll work on the handwritten stuff. It's mostly case notes in Greek from colleagues in the field.'

They started in on it, Siân silently observing that everything an ecologist worked on must be to someone's disadvantage. Exploitation of the earth's resources was a quick way to wealth. The ones who had to fear him, the enemies of mankind as he'd have seen them, were the profiteers. 'Was the Professor Left Wing?' she demanded suddenly.

Andreas replied without looking up. 'He was a socialist, of course. He believed capitalism was necessary but had to be controlled. State capitalism was the ideal—or would be if you could guarantee ideal men in charge of it. Which has never been achieved yet.' The dryness of his tone wasn't lost on her.

'So Theodorakis was the present Greek government's natural choice for a delegate. But you aren't. You are non-political, slightly right of centre if anything.'

'I was Theo's personal recommendation. I thought you knew that. There *are* Greeks who occasionally make decisions independent of party politics.'

She stared at the top of his head, then went back to sorting the papers, feeling she had been on the brink of some useful idea and then lost it.

After an hour or more of reading and stacking separate piles of documents on the floor along one wall, Andreas gave a sudden grunt.

'Found something?'

He shook his head but continued reading with a new intentness. Glancing across, she tried to make out the Cyrillic script, but the words didn't make sense. It struck her then that even Andreas was making heavy weather of it. 'That—isn't Greek.'

He looked up sharply. 'No. Looks near enough to it to fool a non-Greek at a quick glance.'

'So it's Russian?'

'Yes. And I'm not getting it all. But it's not encoded, and I think it could be important.'

'There's some Russian in this lot too.'

'There would be, naturally. Especially since Chernobyl. Printed reports, official handouts. But *handwritten* is different.'

She considered this. Different because not Tass- or KGB-approved. It implied someone making personal contact with the Professor. Giving him restricted information?

Eventually Andreas gave up, moving his spectacles up into his cropped, dark hair while he gently rubbed his eyelids. Then he held out his hand to Siân. 'Let's put these back in the safe and go out. We'll find some night spot that still serves coffee. I can't do any more now.'

'Do you think the Professor's family would help? Where are they staying in Geneva?'

'He had only the one younger sister, a teacher in Athens. She arrives tomorrow, and I'd like you with me when I meet her at the airport.'

'But who was seeing to his stuff at the flat, then?'

He looked at her inquiringly.

'The other day,' she said, 'when I was with Madame Durochat—' and she told him about the previous midnight's thumps, and again something knocked over in the Greek's flat even while she'd been there.

'It would be the concierge, or some workman he let in. The apartment was locked against anyone else.'

What she had told him seemed to prey on his mind all the while they sat over their coffee and walked back through the brightly lit streets. Between cleaning her teeth and running a bath Siân heard him use the bedside telephone.

Coming back, she raised an eyebrow at him as he lay ready for sleep. He said simply, 'It wasn't the concierge in Theo's flat. He was quite shocked that someone had been there. So I reported it to Security, both incidents. They will look into things, have the apartment officially sealed.'

'It may be too late.'

'I don't think so. You said the second occasion at the house was Monday morning. My office was searched during the hours of darkness since. An unfinished search, I think. So unless there are two separate parties at it, it seems to have been fruitless.'

He kissed her gently and turned his back, switching himself off as decisively as the light. Siân lay awake, staring at the dark ceiling. He'd mentioned Security. Whose Security had he reported to—the Swiss, UN's, or some other? It was a strange new world and she felt herself more than a little at sea.

Next morning Siân had planned to tackle the housekeeping angle, not perhaps buying in supplies but at least pricing main items in various shops and listing local specialities. She went out early, just after Andreas had left, and at the corner of the bridge met Niall O'Diarmid ambling towards her, his splendid white teeth bared in amiable greeting. 'Just the person I was looking for,' he claimed, 'or very nearly so. It's your husband I'd my sights on. Would the good man be up yet?'

'Up and away,' Siân said drily, almost certain that Niall had been watching out for just that to happen.

'No matter,' Niall grinned, 'because if I give you the ticket you'll see he gets it, I'm sure. For the concert. I always put one aside for old Theo, and this is it. So I'm passing it on to the next man. I'm only sorry there's just the one. Next time I'll put in for the pair of you.'

Siân looked at the envelope he'd pressed into her hand. 'What concert is this?'

'Tomorrow's. I'm sorry it's such short notice. I've been trying to ring you for days, but you're never in.' He cocked his head and smiled at her under his lashes. 'You haven't the least idea what I'm blethering on about, have you? It's one of *our* special talent shows, for isn't the Conservatoire one big sausage-machine for prodigies? As staff, we get these complimentaries showered upon us like bridal confetti, just to make sure the best seats get filled. But actually you'll find some of the music's quite rewarding, and the Genevese intelligentsia will even pay to get in.'

'Well, it's very kind. Thank you. I'm not sure Andreas will manage to make it tomorrow. He has a lot of work on at present. If he doesn't use the ticket, it won't go to waste. I'll use it myself. Thank you again.'

'It's a pleasure. I hope whoever turns up enjoys the programme. Franck's *Symphonic Variations* and some Benjy Britten as well as the stiffer stuff.'

'Will you be playing?'

'In the scrum, yes. You're in Row D, three in from the aisle, and I'll be looking for you to blow me a kiss of encouragement.'

'Well, if it's not me, I'll warn Andreas what is expected of him.'

'Be sure you do that. Have you found somewhere to live yet?'

'Yes. We've been very lucky—and I have to thank you again over that, for the introduction. We've accepted Madame Zuelig's offer—'

'Great! So we'll be seeing a lot of each other. Look, sorry to be rude, but I've a lesson to give in twenty minutes. Must dash.' He flashed his big white teeth again, made a rotary movement with one palm in her direction and went loping off towards the lake.

The girl stared thoughtfully after him, slipped the envelope into her shoulder-bag and remembered now what she hadn't told Andreas: that whoever had been clandestinely in the Professor's apartment had gone up two floors afterwards and let himself—or herself?—into Niall O'Diarmid's flat.

When she met up with Andreas at noon to welcome Kyría Elena Skoufas there was no time to talk to him, the plane

57

being twenty minutes early and Customs clearance a mere walk-through.

Elena Skoufas had distinction rather than beauty. In her middle fifties, she gave an impression of balance and good sense. She brushed away their expressions of sympathy. 'Nikos enjoyed a fulfilling life. Everything he did produced its own small reward, and he had no intention of staying on forever. As a boy he wanted to be a priest, but when the time came for training he said, "Perhaps that is aiming too high. I think I am better at keeping the second great commandment. Soon enough to concentrate on the first when I am dead."'

'Then he did as he intended,' Andreas agreed. 'Mankind had no better friend than your brother.'

'Not only mankind,' she said, smiling. 'He was no conventional Christian. I sometimes thought he also worshipped earth and water.'

'He loved life, and so everything that supported it.'

Elena Skoufas looked gravely at Andreas. 'I see you truly understood him. He told me, only a few months back, that you would complement his ministry, restore the balance by laying the emphasis squarely on the human aspects. He also said you were a healer. So what are you doing in administration?'

And there, Siân thought, she had put her finger right on it, asking directly a question which she herself had hedged over. She looked at Andreas now, to see if he would admit he'd compromised to suit his new, foreign wife.

'I have several reasons,' he said. 'One was that if Theo found it enough, it would be more than right for me. People imagine bureaucrats achieve nothing, compared with setting bones and cutting out tumours. But the work is just as much a challenge and a battle. In the end we may shift a whole people's ignorance, support life over wide areas of devastation, actually help to eliminate specific diseases. I want to add my weight to this work, and my gifts such as they are.'

'And what are they?' She was mocking him slightly, daring him to take refuge in phoney modesty.

'Medical knowledge; discipline; experience of others' suffering; a desire to be useful; two languages beyond my own; energy; patience.'

'And compassion.'

'To an uncomfortable degree at times.'

'Good, good. We should all weep over something; but not because Nikolaos Theodorakis has worn himself out in a good cause.'

Surprisingly Elena Skoufas had no wish to see her brother's apartment. 'I have so little time,' she explained. 'Will you have all his things sold off? I will give you the address of the fund the money should be paid into. No, there is nothing of his that I want. I have come merely to take his body home. I understand everything is now in order and we are to leave by the evening flight.'

'If you must go so soon.'

'I must. The summer term is specially important for my pupils. I don't want to be away any more than is necessary. In Athens, of course, there will be a memorial service and that means another half-day off school. I shall attend certainly, but I do not need reminding what a wonderful man Nikos was. And a memorial will be no benefit to him. Funerals are for the living, to make them come to terms with death in time.'

They took Elena for lunch to the Perle du Lac, and she seemed quietly to enjoy the waterside scene of sailing boats, windsurfers, and the frequent passage of the Léman *bateaux mouettes*. Afterwards all three of them strolled in the little park and fed the red squirrels with bread rolls which Andreas had slipped into his pockets. Then there were formalities which he had to help the Greek woman with before the body was surrendered to the airline, and Siân went back alone to the hotel.

In 93A the coffee table had been delivered. She removed the wrappings and set out their supper things on it—ham, cheese, biscuits, boxed salads, almond slices and wine. When Andreas returned Siân's mind was still on the woman they had met, so the disagreeable subject of searches and security was easily overlooked.

She learned that Elena had a husband with multiple sclerosis and two sons, of fifteen and twelve. Siân had imagined that so philosophical a woman would have lived alone—if not at actual Olympian heights—with something of the reputation of an oracle.

Lying together in bed after making love, pleasantly muzzy from finishing the wine, they discussed the next day. Andreas grunted. 'I'm afraid I have to go to Berne tomorrow, and it means staying over.'

'But that will be Saturday, and we're meant to be moving then. Can't you explain? I don't want to start at the boathouse on my own.'

'We can keep on this room for another day, or until Monday. It isn't so long.'

But she had been counting on it, planning ahead. Having so much time on her hands now that flat-hunting was suddenly over, she felt stranded like a beached whale. It annoyed her that Andreas had given her such last-minute notice. Berne—and presumably that meant the Embassy—could surely have left him free until he was settled in on the Rive Gauche.

'Will you be driving there?'

'Yes, it's more convenient.'

So she wouldn't have the car either. If that was a selfish thought, Andreas was no better. What had happened to the 'thinking for two' they'd once talked so much about? The hard truth was that only one of them was the breadwinner. Despite the vaunted liberation of women, she might as well be a nineteenth-century miner's wife (without the nightly fun of scrubbing her man's back in a hip-bath by the fire!) No such intimacies with Andreas: he washed the job off each evening before leaving for home, and in his bath he was clinically estranged. Their lovemaking was confined to when he had the time, the energy and the inclination. Perhaps she should start making some demands. It would be fatal to drift, become background, do a Klara Zuelig.

She knew, all the time that she was whipping up her resentment, that it was unreasonably exaggerated. But it was enjoyable too, like scratching at a sting. She turned away from him now, making herself rigidly untouchable, but had no way of knowing whether her husband had recognized it as withdrawal.

In the morning her mood, softened by the time they said goodbye after an early breakfast, hardened again as she put away the suit he had worn the previous day. In hanging up the trousers she noticed the bulge of a used handkerchief in one pocket, pulled it out and with it a folded scrap of paper. She smoothed it out.

$$\text{`}4 \times Z_{10} \quad 6 \times K_5 \quad 3 \times L_1 \quad 4 \times V_4 \quad 5 \times S_1 \quad 4 \times M_3$$
$$2 \times A_1 \quad 2 \times X_8 \quad 2 \times F_4 \quad 2 \times P_3 \quad 2 \times O_1\text{'}$$

What on earth was that about? Roman capitals, not Cyrillic, and she wasn't even certain that Andreas had written it himself. It was not a formula, so what did it refer to? A list of coded items and quantities? A stock order?

During the day she went back several times to stare at the paper. Each letter occurred only once. What in Einstein's name was V—some measure of volume? Or velocity? If M was mass, and X the proverbial unknown quantity, what did Z stand for?

Whatever the individual answers were, the whole thing represented another secret she was to be excluded from. She stuffed the folded paper in her shoulder-bag next to the Agatha Christie in Greek which she was working through. And discovered the envelope which Niall O'Diarmid had given her for Andreas. It was too late to deliver it now, and he wouldn't be here to use it. But *she* most certainly would.

The seat number was D10, another letter and figure combination, but grouped differently this time. The list from Andreas's pocket couldn't refer to numbered seats because of the varying quantities required before the letters. You couldn't have four Z 10s. No, obviously, there was no connection, except in her unsatisfied mind, casting around for random significance.

She would make use of the ticket. In her present rebellious state of mind she might even take literally Niall O'Diarmid's invitation to blow him a kiss of encouragement. Encouragement to play well. For anything else she felt rather off men at present.

Despite that proviso, she shook out her emerald silk dress, washed her red hair and swept it up with a pair of silver combs. It made her look older, certainly more sophisticated. She put on fresh mascara, picked up her white jacket and set out to be entertained.

The programme was broadly selected to display the students' proficiency, some quite small children struggling with a new medium, others at sub-prodigy level. The more stumbling violin pieces were mercifully short, the brass ensembles acceptable. They led on to more skilled performers—four voices with flute and piano, then the major work by Franck.

The platform was rearranged and the orchestra came on, Niall leading the woodwind section, strikingly handsome in dinner jacket and black tie.

Siân had been vaguely aware of people in the seats about her. Now she felt the man on her right lean in and turn to stare at her. '*Kali spera*,' he said softly.

Why Greek? It wasn't his own language; he spoke it too carefully. She followed the direction of his glance and saw the open shoulder-bag on her lap, the spine of the paperback thriller sticking out. He had read the title, recognized the language it was in.

'*Kali spera sas*,' she said politely back. This was Geneva after all, the home of internationalism. Perhaps it was the done thing to greet people in their supposed native tongue when you could.

They both had to stand then to allow a latecomer into the row; someone familiar enough with these talent concerts to avoid the earlier apprentice musicianship. In settling again, Siân let slip the bag and it spilled over the feet of the man who had spoken to her. He bent to retrieve ballpen, purse, paperback, handkerchief; and there was a brief exchange of social niceties between them while clapping announced the conductor's arrival.

Siân was amused by her neighbour's embarrassed eagerness, a little white rabbit of a man with rimless glasses and a twitchy mouth. Genus *UN bureaucraticus*, she noted.

By contrast, his companion, in the aisle seat, was large, expansive, extroverted, and engaged at present in waggling his thick, black eyebrows at her, blatantly making mating signals over the head of the little man in between. He was so unsubtle that she found herself laughing back at him. When she caught Niall O'Diarmid's stare fixed on her from the stage, missing nothing of the encounter, it struck her as developing into farce.

She closed one eye to acknowledge she'd seen him, and was repaid with glazed indifference. Best stage manners, she observed. He was, after all, a professional on show among amateurs, with the irresponsible part of him buttoned away under the tailored dinner jacket.

The girl soloist nodded at the conductor over her piano. He raised his hands, bâton poised. The *Symphonic Variations* got rompingly under way.

CHAPTER 7

After the concert O'Diarmid briefly deserted the clearing-up squad to look out at the departing audience. The manic train-catchers had already stampeded. As ever, there were little knots of friends who threatened to stay on chatting indefinitely and patting each other's offspring who had performed on stage, but the main crowd claiming his attention was a protoplasmic flow beyond the entrance doors, making plans to extend their evening out. He caught a glimpse of white and emerald where the redhaired English girl, freshly off the marital leash, moved away between the two Russians, the larger one waving his arms expansively as he told some anecdote punctuated by hearty guffaws.

Subarsky, however, was looking as if he'd shit himself, but he needn't worry: the girl was going over well, with just the right degree of amused disbelief in her expression. Young and attractive enough to hold the Security man's attention, with enough experience to act casually detached. There was more in that lady than Niall had at first supposed. Well, the play was all in her court now.

He grinned, winked suggestively across at a dowager with a well-known penchant for schoolboy pianists, waved a general goodbye and returned backstage, his curiosity satisfied. Fat Bear would undoubtedly suggest one of their few permitted public places for a little late supper. While she kidded him along, Siân would find an opportunity to communicate with Subarsky and pass him his final briefing. All the little twit had to do then was relax, listen and follow instructions. As for the girl, he just hoped she had a good head for vodka. Taken all round, it could be that losing Theodorakis had proved no great drawback. Except, of course, for the old fellow himself.

When Niall went back to lock up his cupboard, Susi Honegger was sitting side-saddle on the table, drawing hungrily on a reefer. Her violin case lay demurely alongside. She gave him a little snort of disapproval. He remembered then the date they'd made for the rest of the weekend. 'Patience, my sweet. I can't play duets all the time. Comes the moment for the *tutti*.'

'As if,' she replied tartly, 'it is ever a duet with you. Always your solo, my accompaniment.'

He leered cheerfully back at her. 'Then you must be more forceful. Become the prodigy yourself, the Paganini of the bedsprings' (running his long fingers up her shoulders, palpating the nape of her neck.) 'It takes only practice. In the words of the *maestro*, my place or yours?'

But there was one thing he must do before they relaxed for their weekend. He steered Susi to a corner table of *A La Barbare*, settling her behind a large Campari-soda while he installed himself in the telephone booth. His call was answered on the third ring by a breathless female voice. She spoke in a whisper, repeating the number in English.

'It's Niall O'Diarmid, Penny. Is David in? I'd like a word.'

'Yes, he's—Oh *God!*' The last anguished word, uttered at normal volume, failed to cover the siren wail of a wakened baby.

'Sorry, David,' Niall opened, when a male voice replaced the woman's. 'I forgot about the wean.'

'I wish I could sometimes. I'll ring you back in five minutes.'

Niall gave him the bar's number and waited. It was discretion, not the fretful but robustly vocal baby, that drove David out to a random public phone. 'What's new?' he demanded as soon as they were reconnected.

'It's done. They made contact. She's gone off drinking with him now, with a minder alongside. Kilo-Golf-Bravo written all over him in red felt-tip. He seems quite taken with the girl; eyes for nothing else.'

'Ah!' David took time to ponder this. 'Same method of linking them?'

'Consecutive tickets, yes. I thought it would be the lady's husband who used it, though.'

'Er, yes. Whereas?'

'Siân herself. She said that Vassilakis was busy elsewhere. Didn't turn a hair. Real cool: played it straight, even with me.'

'Ah,' said David again. Then, 'Nice to know. Okay. Be seeing you.'

'Ungrateful bastard,' Niall grumbled. Not so much as a thank-you for Niall's having taken the initiative. Bloody civil servant.

By now Susi was into the tight-lipped routine. He could recognize it right across the bistro. Niall collected an armagnac for himself and a second Campari-soda. Then he went across to join her, sliding a small packet across the table in her direction. 'Prezzy for a sweet girl.'

She leaned forward to read the label. 'Champagne Bubble Bath? I don't believe it!'

'Something I thought we might share. Asses' milk being so awkward in bulk.'

At last she was smiling, showing the small, very white teeth like a kitten's. He hoped that the smell of shoe polish spray would have completely disappeared from the bathroom.

*

65

From his window in the concierge's lodge Antoine Régnier watched the two couples who had just entered cross the hall and get into the lift: first Madame Durochat and her husband—(by suppressing the 'ex-' Régnier was just able not to disapprove of the first-floor tenant. If *she* had undergone the monstrous treachery of divorce, and *he* had since made an unsuitable liaison of merely legalistic worth, at least they still respected their original God-sanctioned union). Régnier wished he could be as sure of propriety in the case of the second couple, the young Irishman and his present partner. Peering through the glass panel to the corridor, he couldn't even determine if it was the same girl as last weekend. They all looked so similar now in their sloppy sweaters and jeans. Certainly she wore the same protective helmet which O'Diarmid supplied to all his pillion passengers. Perhaps that was intentional, providing anonymity, so that he could be promiscuous without the fact being widely recognized. His was a Hell-road if ever anyone's was. Lascivious, was Régnier's judgment on his ways; he considered the young man corrupted, corrupting and totally immoral.

There had been a time when such a person would have been forbidden the house. Now he was sheltered under its very roof. Was there no limit to the lowering of standards, even within the Zuelig circle? Truly the world was become the realm of the Devil!

'Ye walk every one after the imagination of his evil heart . . . therefore, behold, *the days come*, saith the Lord . . . For mine eyes are upon all their ways: they are not hid from my face, neither is their uniquity hid from my countenance. They have defiled my land, they have filled mine inheritance with the carcases of their detestable abominations!'

Shaking with divine passion, Régnier turned his back on the sight of human frailty and flung himself on his knees. 'Hear me, O God of Israel. Pour upon me the fires of thy wrath that I may go forth and condemn that which is defiled! Give me but the power to show these wilful sheep how they flock to the ravening wolf and call him shepherd!'

Niall O'Diarmid, having waved Susi towards the freedom of his bed, bath and kitchen, returned by the stairs to wheel his Yamaha round to the stables at the rear. In the ground-floor corridor he cocked his head at the sound of the reedy voice calling down divine retribution from the other side of the partition wall. Old Régnier was ranting again, poor devil; working up to a crisis like two years ago. They would have to watch him. Some day he could become dangerous, run amok as the Lord's Avenging Angel. And the result could be a right Jeremiah-load of universal mayhem.

Afterwards Subarsky never knew how he had got through that evening. Voronov was painful enough on his own, always talking, always taunting. He was the sort who built himself up on others' failings, never let them forget his power; at one moment gave free rein to his own follies and then would think nothing of removing whoever had witnessed them. So he was doubly treacherous. And now, in his impulsive lusting after the Greek girl, he was blatantly breaking all the rules. Even such a sympathetic venue as this Czech-run bar admitted members of the alien public. If Voronov went too far—half as far as he wanted—then, KGB rank or not, there would be a disaster. He, Subarsky, through having been present, would be tarred with the same brush, found unreliable and sent back in disgrace. And even if Voronov didn't crash, he would make certain that no possible witness to his indiscretions was ever left credible. Willingly Subarsky would have lost the sight of his eyes rather than be forced to defend himself against a trumped-up charge of treason.

The girl had declined to try vodka, claiming that Greek women seldom drank strong spirits. She ordered her own Vermouth, in French that was better than theirs, and then made one glass last while they tossed off almost a bottle. While Voronov went to relieve himself she quietly ordered something else. On his return she thanked them sweetly for their company and escaped to the waiting taxi. Subarsky suspected that their waiter was secretly laughing at their discomfiture, but the man turned his back and busied himself setting out glasses.

Then Subarsky was left to cope with Voronov's filthy

temper. He wasn't to be diverted until Subarsky invented some salacious gossip about Comrade Second-Secretary Malik's younger daughter in Berne, at present visiting the Delegation. Then the Security gorilla was suddenly quite eager to get back to the compound. Now the girl would need to take to her heels whenever the fat old lecher came anywhere near, thought Subarsky; but it would serve her right for scaring the shit half out of him with that half-starved mastiff of hers.

But despite the perils of the evening, he seemed to have emerged unscathed. And he had the coded note which the Greek girl had dropped for him at the concert. It wasn't until he was alone in his own room at the Soviet Mission that he dared to open it and read his instructions.

It was in a code which he didn't know. It made no kind of sense, was just a series of letters with numbers, a sort of mathematical list. The girl must have thought that Theodorakis had already supplied him with the key. But he hadn't. The wretched man had died the very morning before they were to have met. Subarsky sweated afresh, recalling the panic he'd been in when no one came to rendezvous with him. And later, when the newspapers gave an account of the Greek's death, with mention of his car abandoned under the very wall of the Mission, he'd been sure it was no natural demise. He'd waited for the axe to fall, could even now barely dare believe that the plan was still on and his intentions undiscovered.

And now this fresh setback. There was nothing for it but to get in touch with the girl and get the note decoded. It was vital to do it at once, because the instructions might demand immediate action. He didn't know what the arrangements were, he'd miss out, and then there might never be a chance again. Recall to Moscow, when it came, would give him no margin of warning. Once they knew he was booked for return, Voronov's lot would never let him out of their sight.

He sat on the edge of his bed and sweated and shivered as though he had a high fever. He had been so near, so very near, to escape, and now the beautiful future had burst like a soap bubble in his face. Unless he could trace the girl.

Vassilakis, she had called herself. Good that he'd been alert enough to latch on to that. (But too much to hope that Voronov had missed it. He was practised at registering details for dossiers.)

There was no privacy here in the Mission for him to make inquiries in safety, even if he knew where to begin. To demand a copy of the Geneva telephone directory would arouse suspicion, and anyway she had said she was new to Switzerland, so there would be no printed record yet. A request rung through to directory inquiries would be monitored inside the building. In any case he had to get outside.

The best chance would be to leave a message for her at the Conservatoire porter's lodge. Whoever had left the tickets there would surely go back sometime. When the children from the Mission went down for their *Solfège* Class he must go himself to help escort them. There seemed to be no alternative. More delays, more risks; would it never end? None of these complications would have occurred if Professor Theodorakis hadn't suddenly dropped dead.

If only—Siân told herself—Nikolaos Theodorakis had managed to carry on until his retirement date, leaving Andreas and herself just that little longer together. The way they'd had it planned seemed reasonable by all standards: ten days' honeymoon in England, a short break at home to collect things and turn round, then a full free fortnight in Switzerland for acclimatization, mental as well as physical. In that way they would have built up a base from which to withstand new challenges. As it was, they'd lost touch with each other; Andreas off doing his WHO balancing act elsewhere, while she performed as a sort of Aunt Sally on her own. Some circus.

It had hit her suddenly, by delayed intuition, while she was sitting drinking with those two clowns, that this wasn't an entirely accidental encounter. She'd been manipulated into being with them. True, it had been her own quirky decision to go on with them to this rather old-fashioned, over-ornate little restaurant, but the run-up hadn't been chance.

The thin, clerical one was so unnaturally tense. She couldn't tell if it was on account of his companion's extravagant behaviour, or from anxiety over how she might react to it. The contrast in the pair had struck her from the outset as amusing, when she was already looking for entertainment. So she had gone along with them, in more ways than one. And then, suddenly, they weren't Laurel and Hardy at all, but something quite sinister, with herself caught up in the middle, almost their prey.

Sergei and Ivan; they had said they were from Prague. Certainly the restaurant was Czech, but they hadn't received quite the welcome you would expect from your own nationals abroad. And all the way through, the language they had used was French. If that was to be expected while at the Conservatoire, yet on home ground wouldn't they have returned to their own tongue—at least in ordering from the waiter?

So, not Czechs. Possibly Russians, and she had done nothing to correct their assumption that she was as Greek as her name. They had called each other 'Sergei' and 'Ivan', but the waiter addressed the smaller one as Monsieur Subarsky.

What was it now made her feel so uneasy? Niall had given her Professor Theodorakis's ticket for the concert. Correction; he had meant it for Andreas. So this was one of her husband's situations which she had inadvertently dropped into, yet the fat Czech-Russian had shown no disappointment, was actually delighted to be making advances to her in his heavy-handed way. Could she assume then that he had merely come along for the culture or a free evening out? In which case it was the thin, nervy Subarsky who was meant to contact Andreas. And, yes, he'd taken the inside seat, leaving the aisle one to Sergei.

At first he had watched her from the corner of his eye, then glimpsed the Greek paperback and muttered a greeting while they stood up to allow latecomers in. It was only about then that the far one had seemed to notice her and began making unmistakable signs of male interest.

As she was there in lieu of Andreas (or Theodorakis), it was presumably a WHO situation, international politico-medical business. Could she go so far as to assume that? No, the way it had been set up was underhand.

Did that mean that WHO had secret functions the general public didn't get to hear of, or was this some other affair solely between the Greeks and Russians? She didn't think so, because Andreas neither represented his own side politically nor had any party affiliations. So a *private* arrangement of some kind?

She had to consider all those involved as individuals. Perhaps that would make better sense of it. Fat Sergei was quite delighted to meet her, but hadn't seemed to be looking out for anyone. On the other hand Ivan was decidedly tense. Even if put off his stroke by her substitution for Andreas, he wasn't letting on about anything to Sergei. Sergei, she felt sure, for all his jolly, heavy-breathing chumminess, was someone Ivan feared—too much to encourage her to talk freely in front of him. Afraid of Sergei's suspecting he had links with a Greek? Specifically with a representative of the late Professor Theo?

With a leap of logic she had two loose ends tied in together. Ivan-the-Terrified was the source of the handwriting which Andreas had discovered among the Professor's disordered papers. He had been providing Theo with restricted information. The job Andreas had taken on, as Theo's recommended candidate, involved the role of a spy!

Because Siân had never found the opportunity to tell her husband about Niall's offer of the ticket he had missed this rendezvous and gone off to Berne without hesitation on some other matter. They had had little enough conversation before he dropped that on her, and she'd no number to ring him at now. The only other person who might set her right about this whole business was Niall O'Diarmid, ticket-provider and assignation-maker. He must be involved. He would know where Andreas should have been sitting. It wasn't stretching the imagination too far to suppose he had taken a block of numbered tickets and so determined who should sit in the next seat. And it was Niall who had some connection with the searcher in the flat above Céline Durochat's, the late Professor's rented rooms.

She decided to ring O'Diarmid as soon as she reached her hotel, to thank him for a splendid concert, and then to see where the subject led.

She found his name in the directory, but when she rang through there was only the engaged tone for answer. She tried twice more, twenty and then thirty minutes later, with the same result. Perhaps, tired after helping with the concert arrangements, he had taken the receiver off, to ensure he would not be disturbed.

CHAPTER 8

Andreas returned in time for a late dinner on Sunday. Siân felt that he was not so much physically tired as preoccupied. Over their meal, in the nearby Brasserie Monopole, she tried to interest him in the concert of the previous evening. He smiled and asked polite questions, but his mind wasn't engaged. Whatever the business at the Embassy, it demanded all his interest.

Siân thought better of introducing her suspicion that Niall had set up some kind of contact with supposed Russians in the seats next her own. By the light of day the idea seemed fanciful, and her own behaviour questionable. She didn't wish to explain the rush of rebelliousness that had seized her and caused her to act so out of character, as she saw it now. There was no call to worry Andreas further. Instead she encouraged him to talk about what was already on his mind.

There had been serious discussions in Berne over the weekend quite apart from the specific subject he had gone to deal with, the focal point of them being a Californian researcher's new observations on AIDS-control.

The seminar had done nothing to stimulate Andreas. 'I am sorry to be so dejected,' he apologized, 'but the cynicism

72

of the political arguments baffles me. I find I get as exhausted facing polemic as digging out the aftermath of earth-
quakes, or after long hours in the operating theatre. And
with much less achieved. It is simple tiredness, I think. And
I have used up my courage for the moment.'

She reached over the table to him. 'Let's skip the dessert
and go back to bed.'

Tomorrow they were to move into the boathouse. No
great affair: everything here would go into the Peugeot, with
the shrouded coffee table aloft, on the ski rack which Siân
was to buy first thing. Andreas would accept a lift to work
with a colleague who rang him on their return from the
brasserie.

'Thank you, David. That will suit me very well. Good
night,' he was saying as Siân came out of the bathroom.

'David?' she queried. 'English or American?'

Andreas shook his head. 'Mid-Atlantic by the accent. He
could even be Canadian. He rang to offer any help we
needed. He's at BIT, or ILO to you.'

He stretched out on the bed and made room for her beside
him.

She awoke just before dawn, too excited by the prospect of
the new house to waste time in bed. Perversely she felt sorry
to be leaving the Stresa and the shabby shelter of 93A.
Mostly she would miss the rooftop view. She slid out of bed
and felt her way to the window. Beyond the first few streets,
left and right banks of the Léman merged in misty slate-blue,
the water between invisible, the ranks of buildings flat as
stage scenery. Behind, a dark silhouette of dense woodland,
then the two Salèves rose chalky pale against a mottled sky.
To their east and paler still, the Savoy Alps floated like thin
white cloud above the horizon.

In the middle distance three separate columns of smoke
were suddenly emitted from among the jumble of roofs,
chimneypots, aerials, masts and cold frames, as industry
made ready for the working day. She counted five gawky
cranes, their massive gantries at the horizontal, towering
over the canyons of streets. Closer in, there were blocks

of reconstruction where scaffolding was securely wrapped about with green netting. Irrelevantly cutting across them in the foreground, window-boxes were banked with early geraniums.

Gradually the sky lightened, colour entering the monochrome. The last neon advertisements were switched off on the rooftops. There was a brief period of anonymity before the invisible sun started to pick out the taller, east-facing blocks of concrete and stone, adding distance and depth. And still the great jet of water had not come spurting up like a broken-tipped feather.

An aircraft ran a golden vapour trail across a sky like silk. Siân latched the window fully open, and traffic sounds became more than a murmur, an active threat.

'It's Monday,' said Andreas, coming awake and open-eyed at once. 'It's unnatural to be so keen on a new working week. Come back to bed.'

She crept back and warmed her feet and arms which had grown chilled. But all the time he made love she seemed to see, behind her eyelids, the city panorama still unfolding to the growing light.

Andreas left at half past eight, having settled the hotel account. The suitcases and purchases stood ready in the foyer. Siân lingered over breakfast, then drove over to the Left Bank to buy a ski rack. Back at the Stresa a hotel porter helped her rope the coffee table on. Now she was ready for her grand entrance to the Villa Montarnaud.

She had barely parked and started up the zigzag path when she saw a girl hurrying down towards her with a carton under one arm and waving something in the other hand. '*La clef*,' she called as she came nearer, '*et quelques provisions*.' There was bread, milk, cheese, coffee, tea and a box of dairy goods. They were from Madame Zuelig, she explained, who would visit during the morning. She herself was Monique who helped to look after the villa and she had already left a basket of fresh vegetables at the lakeside door, samples of what her husband sold from his market garden.

She was plump and brown-eyed, perhaps three or four years older than Siân, and she wore her hair strained so

74

tightly into a topknot that it gave her a surprised look. She explained about the village shops, helped Siân in with the luggage and then hurried off.

Klara came down just before eleven. Siân switched the percolator on when she saw her start at the top. 'So,' Klara said in a rather German way, smiling round at the changes and waving away Siân's thanks. 'When does your furniture arrive?'

Siân explained that when it arrived it would be held at Air Freight until she was notified and requested delivery. 'Use my telephone, please,' Klara said. 'They haven't come to reconnect yours yet.'

They took their coffee and two folding chairs out on to the balcony over the lake. The water made little cluckings under them. 'I must show you the boats,' Klara said suddenly. 'And I have a little gadget for your car, which makes the garage open and the lights come on at night.' They went down by a stone staircase behind a door in the kitchen to a cold cellar, and through it to the inner jetty with a small motor cruiser and a dinghy tied up side by side.

'You both sail? Of course, your husband is Greek. I do not need to ask.'

'I'm learning to crew,' Siân admitted. 'Sailing comes naturally to Andreas. But are you sure you want us to use your boats?'

'They will only rot just lying there. We used to leave the dinghy permanently outside when Freddy was home. He would be in and out of it all day—just raise the sails and be away.' She spoke almost wistfully. This was her third mention of the boy. Siân wondered what had become of him. 'Freddy is the artist?'

'He paints, yes.' Perhaps aware that it sounded abrupt, Klara made an effort to cover up. 'He is living in France, near Annecy.'

'Not too far,' Siân smiled. 'So he can easily get home to see you.'

There was a moment of strained silence. 'I go there myself, usually. He—has not been in very good health.'

Taboo subject, Siân warned herself. With Klara there

seemed to be a number of areas to skirt around.

'I'll show you where the mooring rings are,' Klara offered. 'That large yacht out there is *Cacahouette*. We sold her to neighbours, and they still use our mooring. Otherwise you could have tied up the launch there.'

Siân promised to tell Andreas, but she thought they'd do little motoring on the lake. Even in poor weather he would probably prefer to cross to work by sail. The lake didn't look more than three miles wide at this point.

'Oilskins,' Klara said. 'They are hanging up below. Three sets, and life-jackets.' She drifted about the little house, seeming almost on the point of saying something more but finding it finally beyond her. At the door she turned back. 'After lunch, if you are free, we could go round the garden. Then you can start to plan your rockery.' She hardly waited for the girl's answer, turning abruptly away, strangely awkward.

Klara was more relaxed when Siân went up later to phone. She would be notified when the crate arrived at the airport, so that it could be delivered at her convenience. 'Then you can borrow Monique to help unpack,' Klara said happily. 'There is seldom enough for her to do here.'

She had carried a tray of tea-things on to the villa terrace and they sat looking over the glassy lake towards the north shore and the distant Juras. 'I have made some important decisions,' Klara said quietly. 'My new beginnings. First to wash my hands completely of past mistakes, and secondly to go away for a while.'

'That's wonderful,' Sian told her. 'Where will you go?'

'To France, I think. I should like to tour the Loire Valley, perhaps the Dordogne. No timetable, no set route, but just as the mood takes me. And then—' she sounded actually vivacious—'and then I shall go to New York, by sea. By freighter, if possible, not a millionaire's cruise ship.'

'How exciting. When will you be off?'

'As soon as my business arrangements are in hand. My solicitor has been busy. Your contract for the boathouse should arrive tomorrow, and papers for me to appoint a proxy, then I shall be gone. I will leave you my brother's

76

visiting card and a key to the main door to the house. Perhaps you would look in occasionally? Monique will come in once a week, when convenient to her.'

'How long do you think you will be away?'

Klara shrugged happily. 'I shall come back when I feel the need to. When I again feel this is my home where I can settle down free of all the sad past. By then all my connections with the name of Durochat will be broken. I have given instructions that everything else is to be sold.'

Siân looked uncertain.

'It was my grandfather's doing in the first place,' Klara explained. 'He came here as a young man from Zürich to represent his family finance house, and he married a beautiful Genevese. My father was their only child, a lonely little boy, but he had a schoolfriend in Montreux, Charles Durochat, from a family of hoteliers. They lost touch as they grew up, but in 1913 the Durochats had joined a combine to build two enormous luxury hotels, and Grandfather lent them money. Then the First World War came, so there were no rich foreign visitors, and afterwards the world had changed. No one had any money and the Durochats were almost bankrupt. They sold their interest in the big empty buildings at a loss, but Grandfather held on to his shares and gradually took over the combine. Then, much later, Father put Charles in to run the chain, and his son Victor trained to follow him. Charles had a brother who became an optician, and so did his son Philippe. They had a shop in Geneva and another in Lyons, which is where Philippe met and married Céline, a French physiotherapist.'

There was a silence while Klara frowned over how to tell the next part of her story. 'Our fathers kept up the financial relationship they'd inherited, still in touch but less close once money had linked them. I first met Victor at a party Papi gave one New Year. At the time I was very unhappy. There had been a man I was fond of but he would not ask me to marry him because he—he could not give me children. He went away and it seemed like the end of the world. My parents decided that Victor would make a suitable replacement!' There was bitterness in her voice now.

'He was charming, very handsome, very attentive. Why not, when there was so much to gain by it? He had learned his role well, and I, poor fool, believed that I was what he was after. He—he had such appealing eyes. And that is what he did—appealed and appealed and appealed. I gave in. I went away with him to the mountains for a skiing weekend. We made love, and I discovered my own passion. It was—overwhelming. I had to go on with this ecstatic life for ever. Which, with my kind of family, meant marriage, of course.

'It suited everyone admirably. I didn't know the cost in money of my becoming Madame Victor Durochat until after my father died, but it was considerable. Charles, already in ill-health, was able to retire and to afford an expensive nursing home for his alcoholic wife. Victor moved to Geneva and Papi set up the Maison Durochat in one of the most fashionable streets. Victor always had an eye for beautiful objects and he took on a partner who had been trained at Sotheby's in London. Cousin Philippe, by then an expert in lenses, jewels, and crystals, came back from Lyons to join them. This was the new Durochat empire, but really my father owned it. He also let Philippe and Céline take one floor of the town house where he lived himself with Mami, and he told Victor and me to choose a villa on the lake for our wedding present. It was Victor who found Montarnaud, and when I first set eyes on it—it was Paradise. I had everything then, and I was so grateful. To Victor.'

Now the bitterness was fully in the open. Klara sat there staring fixedly ahead, with her hands clenched on her knees. 'I saw only the surface, what I wanted to see. And I allowed myself to be moulded into a nothing, a shadow. And everyone danced attendance on the great Victor, the handsome, charming, successful Victor, who was so wealthy and generous. And I was happy to do the same. He *was* all those things, because the Maison Durochat was *ours*; I never once thought of it as mine. Nor did he.

'When Papi died I still thought of it as ours, but Victor couldn't bear to have it spelled out otherwise. He seemed even to have expected to be my father's heir, in place of my brother Klaus. He started to drink heavily and sometimes he wouldn't come home until very late. Then he would be very objectionable. There were complaints from some of my friends who were customers that he had been very rude and overbearing. And there were things he said to me from time to time which I didn't understand.

'I began to wonder. Then someone who worked at the shop—someone he'd dismissed after years of good service —came to me with tales. About Victor and his partner Kitty. I didn't believe him, except that at next audit what he said about the accounts was proved true. And then, one night when Victor hadn't come back for a special dinner, I left our guests, went there, and I caught them—Victor and that *man-woman*! She told me she had been his mistress for fifteen years! And she laughed at me.'

Klara sat hunched, shaking her head. 'I didn't know what to do or even who I was. I couldn't tell my brother about it: he has a string of girlfriends and is so casual over such things. But I'm not like that.

'Just a few days later—we'd barely spoken, Victor and I —it was my birthday. We always used to go out somewhere extra nice for dinner, to celebrate. This time he hadn't said anything, so I waited until afternoon, then rang my mother and we went out to dinner together, two women left on their own.

'When I reached home Victor was there with a large envelope for me. Do you know what was in it? A typed agreement for a separation, two copies, and I was to put my signature to both, under Victor's.

'I read it through, and suddenly I felt very strong inside, as if something could burst out of me like bursting out of chains. And I thought: Yes, this can be the end of it. And I signed, signed that I wished for my freedom, and to forgo all liabilities between my husband and me.

'It hadn't been drawn up by a lawyer. Philippe and Victor had put it together at the Maison Durochat that day, copying a similar agreement drawn up three years before when Philippe bought his wife off because his mistress was pregnant. Kitty typed it out herself in the office. Of course, it was meant to frighten me and bring me to heel, so that I'd make no trouble, such a little mouse, and nothing at all without my wonderful husband.

'But I signed it, and he waved it at me as if he had won some significant battle, had me cornered. Next day I took my own copy of the paper to my mother's solicitor and started divorce proceedings.

'The two cases were quite different, of course, because Céline had no property of her own and the dissolution was designed to protect Philippe's capital. But in our case it had the effect of wiping out any claim Victor might try to bring against my father's precautions.'

'And how did Monsieur Durochat take that?'

'He could not believe it, that I could even contemplate any move on my own. And then, when he began to see that I was adamant, he became quite ill. With anger, I think. He took an apartment in Geneva. He used to ring me up in the middle of the night and scream at me. I went away for a while, and he moved back into the house. I had him removed and the locks changed. Even then he once broke in, and there were those incidents I told you about. He will never forgive me. We are open enemies now, you see. And I find this a much more honest way to be. All the same, I remember, and it hurts.'

She linked her fingers over one crossed knee and turned to look at Siân. 'It has helped me, speaking of this to you, a stranger. By talking I have distanced myself in some way. I am outside it, and safer. Do you see why I am going away now?—to try and become intact, myself, as I was before I met Victor. And why I am getting rid of everything connected with the word Durochat.

'Except my home, because here there are some memories that I want to keep forever, once the pain is dulled. Over the past few weeks I have been discovering something important: that I am not so alone now that I have my anger for company. Anger can be a good thing. We need to make positive use of it. Constructively, I mean.'

Siân smiled, a little out of her depth.

Well, she was young, Klara considered, recognizing this;

but in time the girl would learn all about techniques of survival, once she was through surfing in on undiluted bliss.

CHAPTER 9

Next day's post brought a copy of the rental agreement for the boathouse. It looked satisfactory, but Andreas took it to work to get it checked. He went by car, having tied up the dinghy to the outer jetty, ready to try out on his return. A second item of mail was a prospectus from the University Department of Sciences with a list of summer outings of the Alpine Botanical Club. The next would be in two days, from Thursday to the end of the weekend.

'You should apply,' Andreas insisted. 'Get in at the beginning, make a complete record of the year's flora.'

Siân felt a need to put down roots herself. 'I'll see.'

'You must hurry if they have to book.'

'They'll be camping. It gives a list of what to bring. And we've got the Holiday Travel Cards Father gave us at the last minute before leaving. You could come too, take two days off to make up for working the last weekend.'

'I don't think I—'

'Think again, then. Think hard, Andreas, because I really don't want to go on my own.'

'We'll see.' He kissed her, looked at her with his head at an angle, smiled and said *au revoir*. Siân watched the car climb towards the road, then went up the path to the oil bunker where the villa's gardening tools were kept. Today she would take some soil samples from two places she'd in mind for the rockery, then get Klara to approve the site before she went off on her travels.

In the Rue Général-Guisan the postman delivered later, bringing a whole packet of brochures, orders, payments and invoices tied up with a yellow cord. He handed it to the nervous young man who left it in the office for Madame Kitty. She, having supervised the uncrating of some Meissen

81

porcelain delivered the previous afternoon, left its display to Monsieur Philippe and retired to the office for her coffee. It was a morning when Victor would not be in, having gone across to the Hôtel des Anglais with samples of Italian ceramic tiles.

Kitty undid the yellow string and poked the envelopes apart with a square-tipped index finger while she waited for the filter to perform. From their outsides she could guess what most of the contents would be, but one had her curious. It bore the imprint of a local firm of solicitors, not their own. She was quite sure that since a settlement for damages concerning chairs in transit the Maison Durochat had had no dealings with them. As she handled most of Victor's business affairs, she had no hesitation in slitting the envelope open and satisfying her curiosity.

She wished she had not. The letter itself was civil enough: a courteous inquiry whether the directors of the Maison Durochat would be interested in making a priority bid for the freehold of their premises when they came on the market. Instructions had been received from the present owner requiring a public notice of intended sale to be issued within ten days.

What could it mean? The owner, singular. If this had referred to the Zuelig merchant bank the wording would have been different. Perhaps it was a careless slip, or a typist's error, because surely the Board of Zuelig's owned the property jointly with Victor? She thought she knew, from years of familiarity with their insurance arrangements, who the landlord must be. The rental debits were entered for anyone to inspect, but the actual cheque was made out to Victor, by long-standing tacit agreement.

So, with Victor as owner, why should he want the Maison Durochat to move from this status address to somewhere down-market? That would be like cutting his own throat, however much he needed to free his capital. And it had to mean removal, because Victor wouldn't countenance paying rent to a landlord for what was once his own.

Could this sale mean that he was also intending to dissolve the partnership? After all the expertise she had brought in, building up Durochat's to an international reputation, was she in danger of being cast off? Victor couldn't afford to treat her like that. She knew too much. She was an integral part, the most vital part, of the firm. Customers knew that if Madame Kitty recommended it, then they were purchasing something of real value. Why, for years it had been supposed that she was a Durochat herself. That was why she had allowed her surname to drop out of general use. Who else could Madame be, having such authority— the spirit of the company, behind the mere façade of Victor? Why else would she have gone on with this farce of taking him to her bed, except that it had once solidified her position? Her heterosexual needs, never equal to his, had dwindled more years ago than she cared to number. It was the business that gave her satisfaction: the money and the influence. The Maison Durochat could not survive without her. Victor and Philippe were no more than window-dressing.

The phone had been ringing for some time and she'd not heard it. Now the boy came bursting in to answer it, leaving the door wide open, blundering into her where she stood exposed, arms wrapped tensely about herself, white and shaking with rage.

'Get out!' she shouted. 'Imbecile, get out of my sight. You're fired. Do you hear me? Fired!'

He backed hastily against the edge of the door and struck his head in jerking it back to avoid her venom. He fell awkwardly, his long limbs sticking out like a scarecrow's. She had to lean over the Florentine desk, gripping hard at its edges, to stop herself throwing things as he sprawled there in full view of heads turned curiously from the groundfloor showroom.

The phone ceased ringing. Monsieur Philippe came fussing in, distressed and useless as ever, hissed at the boy, 'Get up. Get—up! Really, I don't know what—'

'No, you don't. You know nothing,' said Madame Kitty scathingly. 'But you will when Victor gets back. We shall all know a lot more then about what he has been keeping in the dark. Go and see to the customers now.' She turned her back, running her big, square hands through her short-cropped hair. She would not go to lunch today, but stay and wait for Victor to return. Then she would have her explanation.

Her original of their partnership agreement was in her bank deposit box, but there was a carbon copy in the safe here. She unlocked it now and although she knew it by heart started reading through every legalistic phrase again to make sure there was no way she could be deprived of her rights.

Victor came in with a jaunty step. He had stayed on into the afternoon, celebrating with a liquid lunch the new order, which was considerable. He strode through to his own office and found the two partners there waiting. He saw the open Chinese cabinet, the brandy bottle and glasses, and then saw their faces, Philippe's stricken, Kitty's with a hectic flush like nettlerash staining one cheek and all down that side of her neck. He faltered. 'What is it? What's happened?'

'You tell us.' She handed him the solicitor's letter.

'I don't . . . What?' It was genuine bewilderment.

'Do you mean that this is news to you too?'

'Oh my God! That *bitch*!'

'Bitch?' Kitty had a face of stone. She knew at once who he meant: his ex-wife. But how could she have done this?

Victor was speechless, his hands jumping about with the lawyer's letter in them. Philippe moved anxiously forward. 'Sit down, Victor. Look, I tried to tell her . . .'

'Tell who?' the woman demanded contemptuously.

'Tell you, of course, but you wouldn't listen. You never do. So I thought I'd better wait until Victor—'

'Victor.' She stood over him where he leaned back, his face hidden in his hands. 'Do you mean *she*—Klara Zuelig —is the owner of this building? The sole owner? Since when? Was this written into your divorce settlement? Why didn't you warn me? Couldn't you see what she would do out of spite? God, what a fool you are!'

'She—no, it wasn't in the settlement. You know that that paper we both signed wiped out any rights to compensation

84

for her. We copied the words from the agreement Philippe tried, unsuccessfully, to get Céline to accept when they divorced. But our circumstances were different, Philippe's and mine, and it meant that I lost any rights to a matrimonial share of *Klara*'s property. And even without that written in, her father had tied up everything in the original marriage settlement.'

Kitty waited, contempt blazing in her eyes, but he seemed unable to continue. 'Then you can only mean that this place was always hers. And all along the rental payment should have gone to her.'

'It didn't make any difference. Her or me, it was all the same: expenses at the villa, they absorbed it.'

'Did you know this?' Kitty turned in fury on his cousin.

'Well, yes, eventually. But not when we helped Victor with the document. You're as much to blame as either of us. You were there, you typed the blessed thing. Didn't you read it?'

'Not seriously enough, it seems. Because she wasn't meant really to sign it. It was just to hold over her as a threat. Victor was so sure she'd capitulate entirely. And now we find that that was all part of his great fantasy of power, worth as much as his fantasy of possessions! He just didn't choose to face the fact that if she did divorce him we would be liable to pay her—'

'*He* would be liable to pay her. Instead of which he went on drawing the rent himself.' Philippe's voice rose to a near-hysterical squeak.

Kitty nodded ominously. 'Now at last she's got tired of being swindled, and so she's going to off-load him by selling the building over our heads. Despite the fact that she won't get a good price with us here as sitting tenants. Have I understood that rightly? Well, she's got more guts than I credited her with. Victor, you've driven her into ruining our business!'

'It's *my* business!' Victor screamed, suddenly erect. 'She took the villa, the boats, the car, everything! But this is mine! I made it! She can't—'

'*Who* made it?' The voice was full of deadly menace. 'How

far would you have got on your own? All you knew about was hotel front-desk, and there you lost money. Why, even poor Philippe here has more useful experience than you.'

'But what are we going to *do*?' Philippe stuttered. 'Can we make a priority bid like the letter says? If we asked for a bank loan—'

Kitty turned on him. 'They will want to look at the books, and all profits are kept trimmed to the minimum for tax purposes. We never needed to make big paper profits like a public company. And if you make war on the Zueligs you'll get no help from the other banks. They all stick together like bad surgeons. If anyone does offer to help, it will be to suck the life-blood out of us.'

'Be quiet, both of you. Do you want to send me out of my mind?' Victor glared at them, the whites showing round his starting eyes. A spasm showed in the corded muscles of his neck and he tore at his collar.

It could happen, Kitty recognized. Victor Durochat could go right out of his mind. Just as his mother had done some years back, according to rumour. And with Victor mentally deranged, it would be a worse tangle to get sorted out than things as they were at present. So, *doucement, hein?* She must try a new line.

'Victor, dear man, you have had a shock. We have all had a shock. It is not the best of times to make future plans or to consider past mistakes with sympathy. That moment will come. But for the present the *galeries* must continue as normal. Philippe and I will stay on this afternoon in case the staff cannot manage on their own, but Victor, you should go home and lie down. Ring me when you reach there so I know you are all right. I am going to call a taxi for you now. Do you understand?'

He went off like a sick man. He *was* sick. She would have to handle him carefully, win him back gently. Because if they had to tackle Klara Zuelig, it was even possible that Victor must be squeezed into kid gloves. If he wanted the business to prosper, free of outside interference, and still at this excellent address, he might even have to go back to being a husband. The Maison Durochat was surely worth occasional token sex? God knew, she'd paid enough in that coin herself over the years!

It was a full afternoon. Customers tended to arrive in little groups and drift from department to department, unsure of what they wanted. 'Something for a rich old aunt who has absolutely everything.' 'A wedding present for two young moderns.' 'Almost anything about this size—' (wildly waved hands)—'but it has to be blue, lightish blue, or perhaps marbled. We've had the drawing-room done and there's this awful space, you see.'

Philippe was fiercely glad to have his mind occupied. In the background he was aware of his brain's nervous fretting and a hollow apprehension behind the points of his tightly buttoned waistcoat, but at least he wasn't yet faced by the need to think about this new threat. By closing time he knew only that he must take precautions long overdue. If disaster struck now it would find him vulnerable. He'd spent far too much on the new car for Caroline; there had been her medical expenses; insurance premiums had increased; she had had the whole apartment redecorated; and the house-keeping these days was a bottomless pit. She was no manager at all. And then he always liked to take along something pretty for Céline when he called. And he had called quite often recently because they had so much in common to talk about, and she had a way of making a man feel wanted. With Caroline it was always complaints—about the apartment, or her back, or the child, or the neighbours, or why couldn't he get a better salary out of Victor, they were partners after all, weren't they?

When Norbert came in to operate the shutter mechanism for the display windows, he closed the order book on the desk with a sigh. 'Your head, how is it now?'

'There is a lump like a golf ball,' the boy said sulkily. 'And my eyes are muzzy.'

Yes, he should have been sent home, but then there would have been an irate parent on the doorstep and a doctor's account to settle. As it was, Philippe had inspected the injury himself, applied antiseptic ointment, and persuaded

Norbert that Madame Kitty had not meant what she said about firing him. She had been under pressure at the moment—a sad family bereavement—and one should show special patience with women at that age. It was unfortunate that he had been so precipitate in bursting in like that. Certainly it must have appeared rude, even if his intention was to be helpful. It would all blow over in time.

Philippe had made an entry in the industrial injuries register and made Norbert sign it. They were covered then for insurance purposes, and the boy couldn't later make a major scandal out of the incident.

Philippe phoned his home: a new delivery had arrived which he must stay on to check. There was no need to keep a meal for him; he would have something sent in. Caroline grumbled, but he knew she would be glad to have less to do. She and the child could make do with pâté and salad now, eaten on trays while they stared, mesmerized, at the TV.

Next he rang Céline. 'Ah,' she said archly, recognizing his voice, '*mon cher mari divorcé*!' He always pretended to share the joke with her, but really it made him uncomfortable. Somehow it lacked dignity, was unsuitable.

'My dear, I wondered if you were free this evening. If I dropped in, say in half an hour?'

'Delightful. Of course I shall be pleased to see you. Maybe we could go out together somewhere for dinner?'

'I think perhaps—if you don't mind—I would prefer just to sit and talk.'

'As you wish. *Tête-à-tête* and an omelette then?'

'Perfect, my dear. You always know exactly what is required. *Au revoir*.'

What should he take her this time? He must really cut down on the presents. Flowers maybe, or a plant: it was the thought that counted. But he was a little short of change, and he would need to take two taxis tonight. So, something from stock.

He picked out one of the Meissen bird groups newly in, and signed the internal purchase book. One of the sales assistants was still there, frowning over her cash computer.

He asked her to gift-wrap the porcelain while he went for a wash.

Céline was like a little bird herself; bright, quick of movement, chirping, curious. She listened to the tale he had to tell, head cocked, and made sharp, pecking queries over detail. 'What a very foolish fellow Victor is,' she said at its end. 'Did he imagine he could go on forever not paying her the rent legally due? Even if she could ignore the money her accountants wouldn't. He knew what cards she held. There is absolutely no excuse for putting you all in jeopardy so. Is there real danger, do you think, to the Maison Durochat?'

'Who can tell at this point? Whoever buys the property will get it cheaper because it isn't vacant possession. And their first move will be to have it revalued and raise the quarterly payment. It could easily be doubled, and if we are not prepared to pay that amount there are many rival firms who would jump at the chance of such a fashionable address. It might well be that one of them could even raise the necessary capital to make an outright purchase.'

'Which is exactly what Victor should be doing, of course. He should have thought of this months ago and instructed his lawyer to secure the business.'

Philippe sighed. 'You know Victor. You cannot approach him on some matters. Anything that threatens his superiority . . . I think he still lets himself believe he owns all the old Durochat interests Zuelig took over. Only a day or two back he was talking about the Montreux hotels, as if they were his. And Reynaud, from the boatyard, rang up all confused because he'd had a message from Victor to scrape and repaint *Cacahouette*. Well, we all know it was sold to the Petitjean family back in November. I tell you, my cousin has fantasies. He is no longer reliable, and this makes it dangerous to be in partnership with him.'

'What about the Kitty person? Doesn't she keep a tight rein on him?'

Philippe sighed again, sinking farther down in the armchair. 'I have never seen her so furious as today when the notice of proposed sale arrived. Usually she is so cool, like a rattlesnake. She had had no idea that Klara was sole owner. I knew, but I didn't know that Victor was still holding back the rent. That is what he has always done, keeping it for himself, and it never occurred to him that after the divorce Klara would insist on being given her dues.'

'She has enough money without that, certainly. But it's obvious that eventually her accountants would discover what was happening and go chasing after the accumulated debt. Really, Philippe, you and Kitty will need to squeeze Victor into a corner and take up the reins more yourselves.'

Twin charioteers, he thought; ridiculous! He tried to picture himself braced shoulder to shoulder with that formidable Amazon, both of them whipping the horses on, while Victor huddled hog-tied on the bouncing boards behind. Impossible. He shuddered. 'I am not so sure that Kitty is still in a position to exert influence on Victor. Today she went too far. There are things you cannot say to Victor's face: that he deceives himself, is a dupe of his own desires. Perhaps because he knows it is so near madness when it reaches certain lengths. There was his mother, you remember. First the drinking, then when she was in that home— quite, quite crazy. They had to restrain her. Well, Victor must think about that sometimes. It must get to him, you know. So you just don't—*say* anything.'

'M'm.' Céline didn't sound impressed. 'I think,' she said, as if her mind was far away, 'that you should go and see this firm of lawyers Klara uses, and find out just what she has in mind. Perhaps it is a personal thing against Victor, and she has not considered the repercussions elsewhere. It could be an empty threat to bring him to his senses and ensure the partners put right the irregularities. Zueligs have owned that property for over fifty years. They are hardly likely to let it go now when every year it appreciates above the best rates of interest.'

'But you see,' Philippe said desperately, 'although it appreciates, we have never had our rent raised. Even in old Zuelig's time he let it slide, because we were—as he said— family.'

'So maybe it is the son, Klara's brother, behind this move,

bringing values up to date, sounding out the market to see what it is worth.'

'No, no. You are mistaken, Céline. It is *this* house, the old Zuelig home, which Klaus has a half share in. He wouldn't concern himself with the business property, which is Klara's absolutely.'

'Nevertheless, I would go and see that lawyer, if I were you. What harm could it do to learn all there is to know?'

'That would be like going behind Victor's back. I don't think I could do that.'

'When your livelihood may depend on the outcome?' She was beginning to sound exasperated. 'I tell you what, Philippe. I will go myself. I have every right, being myself a Durochat. Do not distress yourself. I will make it my business to get every detail out of the wretched man.'

Like a small, bright bird, yes. Persistently tapping and tapping the snail's shell against a stone until it was all off the succulent morsel she intended to swallow whole.

CHAPTER 10

On Wednesdays he had no classes at the Conservatoire, and due to half-term he was free now for six days. With a spring in his step, Niall O'Diarmid crossed from the Place Neuve and entered the Promenade des Bastions. There was the customary flow of midday strollers between the three rows of chestnuts, and students on park benches, diving into lunch-boxes, sunning themselves while keeping a sexy eye open for fate's offerings with a book open alongside for sporadic study. One hardy girl, encouraged by fitful sun, sat in a half-lotus position exposing her delectable white flesh in a bikini, full under the baleful glare of Knox, Calvin, Cromwell and Co. massively present in stone along the battlements.

Niall gave an encouraging wave as he passed and wished old Régnier would take a lunch-time walk this way. It would bring him with a thud into the late twentieth century. Poor old sod, it was unfortunate, his obsession with Calvin. A case of over-identifying with his look-alike. And, brainwashed by the scale of the sculpture here, he saw himself as twelve feet tall, the ultimate earthly authority.

Swinging his rucksack of groceries, Niàll loped up the steps at the park exit and made his way towards the Bourg-de-Four and his favourite table. But Ginette was off duty, replaced by a dour, middle-aged metallic blonde. Niall trimmed his requirements to a packet of Gauloises and beat a retreat. Coffee and wine he had plenty of at home.

He might have accosted the bikini girl in the park, except that three squash racqueteers were already closing a strategic encirclement with each bash at the wanton shuttlecock. He suddenly remembered the redhead he'd first sighted on this very hill. It shouldn't be long before she was established in the Zuelig house, conveniently near. Something to look forward to.

Niall saw Antoine Régnier look up briefly as he passed on the way in. Madame Fouchet the cleaner was washing the floor of the lift so he stepped over her feet and the bucket, to make his way up by the staircase. Towards the top of the first flight he heard Céline Durochat's raised voice, and then the receiver slammed down on her smart brass telephone. '*Cochon!*' she shouted. '*Chameau!*' and the apartment door was wrenched open. She came out on a verbal high, saw Niall, drew breath, waved her hands above her head and filled the air with voluble complaint.

'*Plus lentement,*' he begged.

She switched to English. 'Niall, you will never believe. *Non, jamais!* That—*unspeakable* woman, what she 'as done now. *Sold—this—*'ouse! At least, she 'as sold 'er 'alf to 'er brother, and 'e puts it on the market.'

'Are you sure?'

'Sure? Of course I am sure. I 'ave been to see 'er lawyer about the—about another matter, and 'e told me. We are to be offered an inducement, 'e says, to make us leave, and then the 'ouse will be sold.'

'But it's her home, the Zuelig family house.'

'No, 'er 'ome is the Villa Montarnaud—'as been for

nearly twenty-six years. Now she does not want to keep on a place in town. And the brother, 'e could not care less. To 'im it is a moneymaker, nothing more.'

'So he wants us out?'

'Well, there are two apartments empty already, and the new Greeks are not coming after all. 'Alfway to vacant possession. So you and me, we are to be *pfuite!*—swep' out.'

'Then I suggest we stubbornly stay put and make him raise the inducement.'

'Not 'im. 'E will raise the *rent*, too 'igh for us to pay. I 'ave rung Philippe to tell 'im, and 'e thinks—'

She stopped, short of breath, her face suffused with colour. 'Oh, I 'ave to sit down. Niall, 'elp me.'

Such a little creature, but she was heavier than he had supposed. He had to lift her in both arms and carry her over the threshold like a bride—this *chère femme divorcée*. He deposited her on the champagne velvet chaise-longue. 'Brandy?'

'In the cabinet. Oh, my poor, poor 'ead!'

Which could only feel worse when she'd knocked back a couple. Poor old doll, and her sawdust spilling out. For himself it didn't matter so much: he travelled light, welcomed change, was indifferent to what district he lived in —what bed for that matter—provided his privacy was inviolate.

'E will not pay any increase for me,' Céline said shortly. '*Ce Philippe!* Not a centime more. In fact 'e says I would 'ave to find a cheaper place in any case, because 'e 'as to make economies. A Durochat economize, imagine!'

'So what is going to happen to old Antoine Régnier?' Niall demanded. 'He's too old for anyone else to take on as a concierge.'

''Ow do I know? 'E must 'ave money saved. 'E can retire.'

'He'll go bananas,' said Niall with certainty. 'Simple, Bible-thumping bananas. He's the captain here. He'll insist on going down with his ship.'

Klara stood in the drawing-room with its wide view over the lake, and surveyed the single suitcase she had brought

93

up from the cellar. It pleased her that she could contemplate travel with so little luggage. She would wear trousers and jacket; pack a suit, fresh blouses, a pullover, two dresses, underwear and shoes. Anything else she could buy on the way. Wonderful, at last to be so free of *things*!

She should have done that in the villa too, got rid of all the bad associations—that alabaster bowl his pipe used to lie in, souring the air; the piano he strummed on so abominably, making Chopin sound like Liszt, loud pedal sustained for bars at a time. How pleasant to come back and find it gone; just a space, an invitation to plan what she really wanted instead.

She walked round the piano, a full-size black Bechstein grand. As furniture it was all right, but she didn't herself play and she'd no intention of learning. It could stay locked, just as Victor always jealously required: the key was still in it.

She could send it to a depository and advertise it later for sale, on her return. That young Irish musician would know the best store for the hot months of summer. She would ring him and then get Antoine Régnier to arrange its removal.

She found Niall's number in a list of phones for the town house, but there was no answer when she rang. So she got through to Régnier and told him what she required. 'I'd like it removed tomorrow,' she stipulated, 'whatever the cost.'

She continued packing, fetched dust covers from the laundry room and left them in a pile for Monique to shroud the furniture. A depository rang confirming the piano order. Then she went out to see how Siân was getting on with the garden.

She found the girl seated on a stone step of the pathway, looking worried. Asked whether it was not working out, she seemed embarrassed. 'Oh, the soil is splendid. I shall need to get some fine grit before I start planting, but the site is everything I'd hoped for.'

'Then what is wrong?'

Siân hesitated, then, 'That,' she said, pointing to a cherry tree that hung over the angle of the path.

'I hope you don't want it removed,' Klara said quickly. 'It's a favourite of mine, with that droopy shape and the lovely blossom.'

Siân had gone to stand by the tree and Klara joined her there. The girl knelt and was running her hand down the bark, behind a little rounded shrub. 'Feel it,' she invited. Klara's fingers explored, felt a ridge. Or was it a groove? She traced it down obliquely, reaching two-thirds of the depth of the trunk. 'What—?'

'It's been sawn almost through, diagonally. The bush hides the cut, but I noticed sawdust. It's fresh, you see, and the bark is sticky. To save the tree we shall need to put some sealer on and dress it. Even then it may be dangerous. If it fell—'

'It could crush someone on the path below.'

'Do you know of a tree doctor?'

'No, but there is sure to be someone in the village—' She halted. 'Siân, do you mean that somebody came up here, deliberately, carrying a saw, perhaps at night when we were asleep, and did this thing? To kill a tree? The tree – or me, do you think?' The last question came out bluntly, her face expressionless with shock.

'Something like that, except that it could have been your own saw. The padlock on the bunker door has been forced.'

'Victor. He knew where the tools were. And he knew I loved that tree. When I am in a hurry I swing on it going round that bend. Imagine if I—'

It was horrible. Siân put out a hand towards her, then withdrew it. If Victor Durochat hadn't been responsible— and it was hard to picture that immaculate man at work with a heavy saw—then someone else was determined that he should get the blame. Was Klara herself capable of such deviousness, to gain sympathy? How far would that companionable anger go, of which she'd spoken yesterday? Did it stop short of active spite?

'I'll find someone to take care of it,' Siân promised. 'When are you leaving?'

'Tomorrow morning, early. I shall try to be quiet. I have

decided to pick up a small car instead of the Mercedes. I want to remain unobtrusive.'

'If Andreas and I were away for four days while you're gone, would that be all right?'

'Of course. Just let Monique know, so that she will look in every day.' She sat on a rock and kicked at the soil with her heel. 'Siân, you have been immunized against tetanus, haven't you? Oh, of course, your husband is a doctor. He will have covered everything. I don't want any harm coming to you in the garden.'

'Don't worry. We've thought about that. Forget everything and just enjoy your trip.'

'I really believe I shall. Oh, I meant to tell you about the piano,' and she explained. 'Would you see to that for me tomorrow? Régnier has arranged for it to be collected. The men are due between nine and ten in the morning. Monique will come up later to clear up.'

She stood up, smiling. 'Eventually, when I feel that I am winning, I shall send you a postcard. Well, I mustn't be late for the hairdresser, so I'll say goodbye. That is, *au revoir*. You will still be here, of course, when I return from my travels.'

Siân watched her go down and operate the garage door. The blue Mercedes backed out and swung up the drive towards the road. Meanwhile, she recalled, the tree bled. She would get her key and phone Monique from the villa.

Monique clicked her tongue. Her husband would come that evening, she promised. He had done a forestry course during his *service militaire*. He would bring his tools in the van, but perhaps Siân would leave the wheelbarrow out, somewhere near, for him to carry his stuff down the garden?

Siân trundled it to where the upper terrace joined the driveway, just inside the high-pillared gate. Parked there on the grass, it couldn't be missed. There was even room to put his van against the shrubbery and still leave space for Andreas when he drove in.

She hadn't long to wait for that. She had no sooner reached the boathouse than she heard the Peugeot drawing up outside. 'You've taken the afternoon off,' she greeted him. 'Lovely; what shall we do?'

He looked at her uneasily. 'I'm sorry, Siân. Just the reverse. I've come to pick up some clothes. I'm off abroad on a trip, leaving this afternoon.'

She stared at him in disbelief. 'Just like that? Abroad's a pretty loose term, isn't it? Somewhere plague-ridden, no doubt; and I'm *not to worry my pretty little head about it!*'

Confronted by her angry eyes, he gave a hopeless shrug. 'It's nothing of the sort, but I'm asked to be discreet. I'm not supposed to disclose where. In fact, for your ears only—' he eyed her quizzically—'it's Canada; Ottawa. How long for, I don't know. Certainly three or four days.'

'I see.' She waited to hear more but it didn't come. 'Do you need a meal first?' It sounded cool and distant.

'Love, don't be like that. You know I haven't chosen to disappear in this way. And no, I don't need to eat, thanks. But if you would drive me to the airport, I'd be happy. We should leave here about half past four, to miss the rush-hour traffic.'

Siân nodded miserably and left him to do his own packing. By the time she had made a pot of tea she felt chastened, but he gave her no chance to make up for her brusqueness. He wasn't apologizing any more either. She watched him covertly. He was certainly tense, but something more besides. Not positively suspicious, but on his guard. Unsure of her discretion, perhaps. He needn't fear she would blab about Canada.

'Since you'll be away in any case,' she said with studied calm, 'I might as well see if there's a vacancy on the botanists' outing, but as you said, it's probably too late now.'

He opened his mouth, made one grim line of his eyebrows and looked fiercely Greek for an instant, then consciously relaxed. 'You must do whatever you wish, of course. But Siân, please take good care of yourself.'

'You too, love.'

They clung together a moment, Siân pressing her eyelids tight to stop the tears, conscious that Andreas and she hadn't been a couple long enough to know how to part properly. Then it was time to be gone. They drove almost in silence to the Cointrin airport (where they'd arrived such a short time before) and on reaching it, Andreas said, 'Would you wait while I make a phone call? Just checking. It won't take long.'

She sat on for over ten minutes, with his luggage on the rear seat, expecting at any moment to be moved on by someone officious in uniform. When Andreas came back he opened the driver's door. His face was grim. 'There's been a change of plan. I have to drive to Berne again first, so I shall need the car. I'm sorry, but you'd better get one from the Hertz office here.'

'I can take a bus back into town.'

'No, we live too far out. You'd be cut off. Hire a car on your charge card. I'll get the office to settle it later.'

She climbed out and stood there while he took her place and fitted the seat-belt. His brown eyes were at their doggiest with concern, looking up at her. 'I'm sorry about all this— mess; I'll explain everything when I get back. Please look after yourself.'

She nodded, waggled her fingers feebly and stepped back, then he was away. 'Bloody job!' she told the Peugeot's back. 'Bloody, secretive, *deceiving* job!' This wasn't World Health business, she'd swear. It was something else he'd never admitted to her that he was involved in. Somebody's skul-duggery, and she didn't know whose. It angered her that she hadn't used to better purpose the little time they'd had together. She should have had it out with him about that cipher or whatever it was she'd found in his pocket.

With a sudden stab of fear she couldn't be sure she'd returned it. She'd meant to confront him with it. Hadn't she, temporarily, put it in her shoulder-bag?

She found a bench in the departure hall and emptied the bag over her lap. A folded receipt briefly raised her hopes, but her husband's list of letters and numbers wasn't there. She must have returned it to his pocket. Or could she have lost it? She seemed to remember at some point upsetting the bag over her feet. Yes, at the concert. The vital piece of paper could have ended on the Conservatoire floor, to be swept up later with toffee wrappings and cigarette packets, consigned to wherever refuse went.

Had Andreas missed it? And if so, what kind of trouble would result? Considering it now, she became convinced that this accounted for his manner when he left—anxious, almost guilty, unwilling to confide to her what had upset him.

He hadn't left her a phone number. She could hardly ring the Embassy in Berne and get him to contact her. That might advertise too widely that she'd seen the paper, and that by now it was irrecoverable. No, the damage was done, and she would explain when Andreas was back. But this left her terribly in the wrong, and vulnerable because she knew so little about what was at risk.

So, do what now? Hire a car, as Andreas said? Go home and wait—alone; not even Klara Zuelig for company, now that they'd said their goodbyes?

But she couldn't face the empty boathouse. As soon as she'd fixed up about the car she would drive over to the University and sign on for the botanical trip to the Canton de Valais.

CHAPTER 11

After such a diabolical day, and the maddening courtesies with which she had forced herself, almost masochistically, to treat the customers, Madame Kitty felt at explosion point. Yesterday that inflated fool Victor had crept off, like a spoilt child protesting the unfairness of it all, leaving her —the real man—to battle on. She had even pandered to his weakness, because of the uncertainty of his reactions under pressure. It was truly monstrous to be manacled to such a dead weight.

When she had first brought her expertise to the firm, he had had nothing to balance it but money. Some small skill in presentation perhaps, but no real taste or knowledge. He was an hotel person, all front and flattery, but it was the money, Zuelig money, which had made the arrangement viable.

At that time his father-in-law had been pouring in the uncounted wealth which he intended his daughter one day to receive from him. And the cunning old swine, Swiss to the fingertips, had quietly tied it all up in Klara's name. Victor—it was fatal that his parents should give him such a name, damning him forever to assume an easy win even while he was being taken for a ride—Victor had been so sure of himself that he had not properly considered all the provisions of property leases or the marriage contract. Such cautions as his legal adviser must surely have offered fell, obviously, on magnificently deaf ears. In the euphoria of his great good fortune, he had seen only what he wished to see, heard only the congratulations and the rustle of cheque-books.

He had been more cautious when he took Kitty on as a business partner. There had been carefully worded clauses restricting her progress towards a directorship and her involvement in decision-making; but she had found her own way round that, letting Victor make costly mistakes on his own, so that ultimately he became dependent on her advice (although always advertising the results as due to his own shrewd business sense).

And then gradually, as she learned more of his personal dealings, his parings of others' dues, his corner-cutting over tax declarations, she had become his confidante, then his sorrow-drowning drinking-companion, and finally she'd made him her creature in bed.

Was all that effort to come to nothing because the man was now proved so hollow? It couldn't! She must put some backbone into him so that he'd fight back. He must make Klara reinstate him, remarry her if necessary.

But Klara never would fall for that. Once the soft skin had been broken, she had revealed her father's tough frame and worldly cynicism underneath. And she was proud.

Yet there must be some way that Kitty could get at her, gain influence, make her see that the Maison Durochat would be worth her personal support, with Victor jettisoned. With Klara's money and Kitty's expertise unhampered by Victor's quirky direction, it could attain even greater artistic and commercial success. How then could she get this across to the wretched woman?

Any leverage exerted on Klara required some fulcrum, because she would never willingly entertain a business proposition from her ex-husband's onetime mistress. There had to be an avenue of approach unsuspected until now. Perhaps Victor could lead Kitty to it, using intimate knowledge he wasn't aware of possessing. What might prove to be Klara's Achilles heel: the Villa Montarnaud perhaps, or the simpleton son Freddy?

A little of Kitty's anger had been diverted into her scheming, but too much still burned inside her. She couldn't eat. Even brandy, after the first sips, set up fresh nausea. Perhaps if she could have got her strong, capable hands round that fool Victor's throat it would have stilled the trembling inside. What relief, to squeeze and squeeze!

But the real enemy, she must remember, was Klara Durochat-Zuelig. So she would tackle Victor first, patiently, hoping to find out the woman's vulnerable point, then ride to success on Klara's back. And to win Victor round she needed calm. Anger must wait, however much she felt that delay was like capping a volcano.

Kitty left her meal untasted on the table, shrugged on her jacket and closed the apartment door behind her. It was only five minutes' walk to where Victor lived, and the exercise should release some of her pent-up feelings.

A little short of his apartment block she recognized a car approaching with Victor at the wheel, his face pale and close to the windscreen as if he had difficulty in seeing in this combination of early dusk and the first wan artificial lighting.

She stepped to the edge of the pavement and held up her hand to stop him.

He had been drinking off and on all day. Then he'd been horribly sick and lay a while rigid on his bed, fearful of the way its four corners kept rising one after the other like waves on the lake in a storm. At times his mind drifted off and he was at the helm of *Cacahouette*, fighting a squall. Klara was somewhere about, wearing her yellow oilskins, and a miniature Freddy sprawled over a coil of rope like a drowned doll afloat on a lifebelt. But it was Kitty's malevolent face that kept swinging down towards his own, whispering and taunting him without any of the words coming through. When he slept, it was no peaceful sliding away but a series of chases and unresolved conflicts.

Towards evening, Victor awoke with a sense of outrage. His head buzzed with pain and he had an intolerable thirst. Bitterly he remembered yesterday's return to the *galeries*, exultant over the order from the hotel, expecting an equal delight from the others. Only to be met with harsh recrimination. As though all their roles were reversed and *he* were the employee. Or worse, the useless apprentice!

That damnable Kitty! She'd been his evil genius all along. But for her insinuating herself into every aspect of the business, he would never have started drinking with her after hours and ended up in her bed. Then Klara would have had no excuse for divorcing him.

Not that hers had been a normal reaction. What other wife in Geneva would have made such a drama out of discovering her husband had a mistress? And when the affair had gone undetected so long, was almost exhausted! Even poor Philippe's silly little wife had shown more sophistication over her changed situation. And Klara was supposed to be intelligent! She was a vindictive prig! Every move she had ever made was to one end only, to diminish him and make him a laughing-stock in the eyes of all his business rivals. It was quite unbelievable that such a small, colourless mouse of a woman should stand up alone and defy him. There had to be a reason, some sudden upsurge of bile that made her so venomous.

It had never seriously struck him until this moment, that there might be another man. His lawyer, when contesting the divorce, had employed a private investigator to look into such matters and he had come up with a blank. Which hadn't astonished Victor then, because Klara, past her best, had little to attract a man and had shown no desire for sex for some time now. Yet, to cause such a reversal in her behaviour, someone must secretly have sidled into his place, taken over first his home, then his money, now the security of the business. Everything. It was wicked persecution.

Well, he wasn't going to get away with it. *They* weren't, Klara and this unknown man. Victor would go back and claim his own before it was too late.

He stood leaning against the window, gazing at the street below awash with the tidal flow of traffic heading out of the city. It was the time of evening when men put off their cares and relaxed. Went home. For how many years had that been his habit too?

Even since the split with Klara, he had sometimes found himself, muzzy and forgetful, driving back towards the Villa Montarnaud. Once or twice he had even arrived, to find the place deserted. Then, deprived of any answer to his furious knockings, he had taken his revenge on the property itself. The dumb walls and the blind windows had raised such a fury in him that he had turned on them the hatred which he should have vented on the woman who rejected him. Bitch and cheat! He would go up there now, demand entry, insist on his rights, show that high and mighty Zuelig what a husband was for!

He started opening wardrobe and drawers, throwing clothing over the bed. He dragged a suitcase from the closet and tumbled everything in, added toilet things, razors, closed the lid, snapped the locks.

Then suddenly he was less sure. He sat on the edge of the bed, his head in his hands, and he wept with weariness. He heard the telephone ringing, and let it go unanswered. Then, when at last he stumbled across and snatched it up, the sound instantly ceased.

A new surge of anger possessed him. Before it could ebb, he went straight down to the car and threw his suitcase in. As he backed out on to the road, the first street-lights came on. He turned wide, just avoiding an oncoming taxi and headed towards the Rive Gauche.

103

It was as he pulled away from the traffic lights before the Courts de Rive that someone stepped out into the road ahead. It was a woman, waving him down. Immersed in resentment, he stared at her blankly, responding slowly to the too-familiar face with a further mounting tide of anger. He looked away, to the road clearing ahead, but he was not to escape. She had wrenched the passenger door open and was sliding in beside him, reaching back for the seat-belt.

She turned on him, oblivious of any plans he might have made, automatically overriding him with her own demands. 'Just the person I needed to see, Victor. Where are you off to?'

He pressed his lips together in a tight, straight line. 'Montarnaud. Where else?'

She swivelled to look at him assessingly. 'Ah! To confront Klara. Yes, it is time you did. I had something of the sort in mind myself. I shall come with you.'

Niall O'Diarmid divided the fruits of his afternoon's shopping between refrigerator, kitchen cupboard and drinks trolley, then rewarded himself with a *café filtre* and a *fine*. While he enjoyed these, with shoes off and stretched at full length on the settee under the open window, he pondered what lay behind Klara Zuelig's surrender of her old family home.

It was at this point that Régnier found him in and relayed the inquiry from Madame Zuelig regarding storage of stringed instruments. It flattered him to be appealed to as a professional. Or had she perhaps an ulterior purpose in consulting him? Could she still be seeing in her mind the windsurfer who had stripped off in her bathroom, momentarily disturbing her?

He wondered how adamant was her intention to dispose of the Bechstein: couldn't he perhaps persuade her to keep it and let him give her two or three lessons if, as Régnier said, she couldn't play it? Had she intended him to make such an offer? But apparently not, since she insisted on its being removed the very next morning, and she herself was going on holiday the same day.

Drifting about the affairs of his minimal housekeeping, it seemed he could be wasting an opportunity. Not only could there be a valuable item for sale, on which to make a personal profit, but there was also gratuitous information to be acquired. Using the piano as an excuse to call, he could sound the lady out about the sale of her town house. Being well-informed on such matters was never a disadvantage in Genevese society.

When he had walked in on her that other time he had come by way of the lake. Which he would do again, borrowing Jean-Sébastien's power boat from the Petit Port, and he'd wait until dusk, when from the windows she'd see his lights moving in on the boathouse jetty.

He dressed to a macho minimum, in *espadrilles*, white duck slacks, a check shirt unbuttoned half way; strapped a spare can of fuel for the boat on the Yamaha's bracket.

The shoreline was misty as he nosed in. La Zuelig's villa showed lights all along the front, in fine horizontals where she'd already dropped the shutters ready for leaving next day. So his romantically staged approach was all for nothing. He tied up by the dark shape of the boathouse, using a ring that already had a dinghy attached. This might have suggested other visitors, except that there were no sails or oars on board, and no motor. Niall stepped ashore to begin the zigzag ascent to the villa.

On the previous occasion he had gone to the kitchen door, but that end of the building was in darkness. Now he crossed the stone base of the villa and thought that from the lighted windows above he caught the sound of raised, angry voices. At the main door with its big brass lamps he paused, then rang. Immediate on it came a woman's terrified scream.

Niall was aware of the cool evening air raising gooseflesh on his bare arms. The scream was abruptly cut off. He reached out for the door-handle. It turned and the door swung inwards.

Down the dim hallway, light poured out of the drawing-room where Klara had once entertained him in her ex-husband's bathrobe. He had known what the score was then. Now he was totally unsure, as reluctant to act the hero

105

as to walk in on an embarrassment, telling himself that whatever silly situation the woman had got herself into was none of his affair.

It had gone utterly quiet now, and his native curiosity stirred. Whether he went away or entered the house he would surely regret it later. He stood uncertain, the edge of the door hard against his hand.

Part Two

CHAPTER 1

Siân awoke just before eight, vaguely discontented. Moving an arm across the bed, she reached for Andreas. The sheet over there was cool, as smooth as when she'd made the bed. Of course, he'd gone. She roused herself and went to make coffee.

Beyond the pale apricot gloss paint, the outer world was uniformly grey. Lowering sky and greasy lake met and merged without any sign of a farther shore. There were no boats, no birds, no movement of any kind.

Andreas could be in Ottawa by now. Or still held up in Berne. Whatever his movements, she must wait to find out. But she wouldn't make a full-time job of the waiting. It was essential to get to grips with her own life now.

Joining today's expedition into Valais hadn't been possible. Plans finalized the previous week wouldn't expand to take on individuals, especially as there was already a film crew going along, with all their extra equipment.

They had been very welcoming at the Bot. Soc. for all that, and she had signed on for the next trip, to Gruyère in six weeks' time. They had finished off the evening with a friendly students' supper at a bistro, and she had taken a longish walk in the night air afterwards between the wine and driving home. The hired car was a Fiat and she wasn't yet used to handling it.

She supposed that Klara was well into France by now. Perhaps she would visit her son at Annecy on the way.

Since the piano-removers could arrive as early as nine, Siân determined to be working on her projected Alpine garden by then. Last night she had been offered advice about suitable rocks.

She noticed that Monique's husband had made quite a production of treating the vandalized tree. It had a yellow bandage over the area where the cut had been made. A metre above this there was a soft leather cummerbund with bracing cord wound neatly round and attached to staples driven into the support wall of the upper terrace. So far the tree showed no sign of suffering.

She saw now why he had needed the wheelbarrow. As well as the first-aid items here, he must have required a pulley or windlass. Of the wheelbarrow itself there was no sign, so he must have put it back in the bunker.

Monique appeared on the top terrace, waved and planted the box with Siân's carton of milk and croissants conspicuously where she could claim it. She mimed extreme haste and left. Siân ran a tape round the pegs marking out her chosen plot and started to sketch the shape on her pad. She viewed the site from several angles before shading in where the main rocks should go.

The depository van had a little difficulty manœuvring the gateway. She went up to meet the three young men in long white aprons and the middle-aged Chinese who was in charge of the operation. It was all accomplished with calm and decorum.

With its legs removed, the instrument was shrouded and upended. The *cortège* passed out of the house with such an air of reverence that Siân thought a national flag and a floral wreath on top wouldn't have seemed out of place. As it slid gently into the van she was asked to sign the men's timesheet, and then received a contract card with the firm's name printed in chocolate copperplate on beige. Not quite the way it was done at home, but then the price would surely match the attention given.

When the van had left, Siân closed the front door and walked slowly back through the silent villa. The drawing-room looked even larger now, and although Monique would see to it later, she moved one or two chairs to give a better balance. There was a pile of dust sheets on a settee and some of the pieces had already been covered, giving the room a slightly sinister aspect. Indentations showed where the Bechstein had stood. There was also a rather darker patch on the carpet where yesterday someone had apparently spilled water in removing the flowers. She shivered, as though a cold wind blew through the house.

Immediately she was alert, listening. There had been a barely audible click, like a door latch lifted, and then the cold current of air had followed. No paranormal *frisson*, but a physical draught.

She edged back into the hall. Nothing moved in the rooms off it which were visible from where she stood. She pushed each door fully open as she passed, and surveyed the shuttered gloom. The stairway was empty. In the kitchen, which she reached last, she checked the outer door. It was deadlocked, and bolted top and bottom. There was only one other solid door besides the glass-fronted cupboards.

It must lead to the cellar. A key in the lock hadn't been turned. She pulled the door towards her and walked out on a small stone landing above steep steps leading down. And, below, there was a light on, a single naked bulb on a long flex which swayed slightly as if recently disturbed. The air made it feel like an icehouse.

'*Qui est là?*' she called. Nothing could have persuaded her to go down and find out.

The answering silence was frightening. She stepped back quickly, snapped off the light, slammed the door and turned the key. She didn't think the cellar had a window. If there was one, it would be shuttered like the rest of the house. Whoever was down there, lying low, was now a prisoner.

She could ring Monique's number. If her husband worked at home he might come over, and then together they . . . She had reached the third digit in dialling when a frenzied howling started up, and a beating on the cellar door. The voice was panic-stricken. For a moment it stopped and there followed the sound of metal crashing against wood, a straining of the lock. The voice rose in pitch through anger to triumph—a long-drawn '*a-a-a-aah!*' as the door gave way and a wild figure stumbled out clutching an iron stake.

He came straight at her, a thin boy-figure in jeans and a streaked T-shirt, his fair, curly hair in disorder, a darker growth of new beard outlining jaw and crimson mouth. 'Get away!' he screamed in French. 'Leave me alone!'

He came right up to where she stood paralysed with fear, and thrust his face into her own.

He had been eating pickles. The vinegar-and-onions breath was strangely normal and reassuring. This young vagrant had broken in because he was hungry. And he was as scared of her as she was of him!

'Who are you?' he demanded, holding the pointed end of the stake a few inches from her eyes.

'I'm Siân. I live in the boathouse,' she offered. 'Put that thing down. I shan't hurt you.'

'You . . . left me in the dark. You locked me in.'

'I—There was a light on down there, and there shouldn't have been. I did call, but no one answered.'

He seemed to think about this, still wild-eyed and clutching the iron stake. He put his free hand to his chest. 'I slept down there.'

'So who are *you*?' she risked asking.

He seemed puzzled. 'I'm Freddy. Freddy Durochat, but I don't know you.'

'You couldn't. I've only been here a few days.' She was eyeing him now with a new curiosity. He misunderstood, and insisted, 'I am Freddy, I *am*. Look, I'll show you. There are photographs in Mother's desk. Me, when I was little. I haven't changed all that much.'

He dropped the iron stake on the polished wooden floor and it rolled away unheeded. He turned towards the drawing-room and was half way across it when he gave a cry like a rabbit she'd once heard when a weasel got it by the neck.

Siân came in behind and gently touched his rigid arm. He seemed in some kind of fit, his body locked motionless, mouth agape and eyes screwed fiercely shut. 'Piano,' he moaned, and the sound of his voice seemed to free his limbs. He started rocking from one foot to the other.

'It's all right. It's gone to be stored, until your mother comes back.'

He started shaking. 'My—mother.'

110

'I'm afraid you've missed her. She left very early, going on holiday. She was driving into France first. Perhaps she's gone to visit you.'

'I'm Freddy,' he said again, hopelessly.

'Yes, she told me about you. You live at Annecy. And when you were little you learned to ski down the orchard. And you have a dinghy. It's tied up by the boathouse where I live. You see, I know quite a lot about you. I believe you. You are Freddy, Klara's son.'

'She's gone,' he said. He sounded desperate. 'I thought it was just a bad dream.'

'And the house is meant to be shut,' Siân explained. 'So I'd like to lock it up again now. Shall we go down to my place? Perhaps you're hungry? I know I am.'

How long could she keep this up, humouring him? Klara had said little enough about him, except that he'd been delicate. And he had painted that disturbing picture of the calf with two heads. Since then he had taken up abstracts, which Klara preferred. It seemed now that his paintings were disturbing because *he* was disturbed. Perhaps he had escaped from a mental institution, which could explain why he'd hidden away in the cellar. He could even have been there before Klara left, unknown to her.

Now Siân could see that he wasn't as young as she'd thought. Probably five or six years older than herself.

'How did you get here?' she asked gently. He let her lead him towards the path and they started down together. 'In a car,' he told her.

'Did you drive it yourself?'

He was looking around at bushes and trees which they passed. He stopped where the big bay of the support wall still showed traces of day-glow orange where the paint had not been entirely removed. As Andreas had done, he rubbed his fingers on it and then sniffed at them.

'Someone started to paint on it,' she said. He shook his head in wonderment and they continued down the path. She repeated her question. 'Did you drive yourself?'

He seemed very vague. 'I—no.' Had he hitch-hiked then? 'It's a holiday,' he volunteered irrelevantly.

111

'Then it's a pity you came when everyone is away.'

This seemed to distress him and he shook his head, trying to control the corners of his mouth. Then he stopped short at sight of the bandaged tree.

'It was damaged,' Siân explained quickly. 'A gardener's looking after it.'

Freddy continued staring and nodding. His face had gone smooth and childlike. They were deceptive features. Without the growth of beard he could have been taken for twelve or thirteen, but on his bare arms the muscles stood out harsh and knotted. When he had his haunted look a number of fine lines reappeared and he was obviously over twice that age.

'Are you hungry?' she asked again, to get him moving. 'What shall we have for lunch?'

He gave it thought for the rest of the way down, and then, peering into the box she had collected from the terrace, gave a sudden grin. 'Milk and croissants.'

'That's settled then. With butter and strawberry jam.'

While he slept—suddenly curling up after his nursery meal —she considered how to tackle this new development. With Klara leaving no forwarding address, must she approach the formidable Victor? It could be risky, since she couldn't predict Freddy's reaction to him. Where did the son stand in this divorce arrangement? He might well have a preference for one of his parents and a prejudice against the other.

Risking that he might wake while she was gone and wander off, she went up to the villa, looked up the Maison Durochat number and dialled.

It was the sexless person who answered—not so sexless, according to Klara's story—and Siân was informed that Monsieur Victor was not expected in that day. Furthermore, Monsieur Victor's home telephone number was ex-directory, and under no circumstances . . . No, she could not undertake to pass him a message. Any communication regarding Durochat-Zuelig affairs should be channelled through their respective solicitors, whose names she quoted.

It should be understood that Monsieur Victor was unwell and not to be disturbed for any reason.

It wasn't a simple brush-off. There was a touch of venom there, as though Victor himself could be receiving as harsh treatment from his woman partner as any inquirer might. She gave a definite impression of doghouse. Perhaps he had taken leave without giving notice, or was laid up after an alcoholic indiscretion. Either way, it left Siân with the problem of Freddy.

She rang the solicitors quoted, but the senior partner who dealt with the family was away. She wouldn't leave a message that made Freddy sound incompetent, when she'd no real proof of his condition. Best perhaps to set him on his way back to Annecy. If he'd made the journey here, he should manage to return.

When finally he awoke he appeared quite rational, if subdued, accepting her as someone he was accustomed to. He even apologized for his behaviour, admitting he'd been *nerveux*. She offered him a lift as far as the frontier. 'Have you got your passport safe?'

No passport. So he'd even entered Switzerland illegally. He would have to smuggle himself out. The prospect didn't worry him once he had accepted that he must return to Annecy. How it came about had little importance, except that he refused a direct route. Not Douvaine, because if he was caught everyone would know he'd been to Geneva. Suddenly it was essential to keep his visit home secret. He had plenty of money on him in French currency, so would she drive him to La Cure up in the Juras? That way he could return to Annecy from inside France. He would leave the car and go over the Col on foot. He'd done it many times in winter on skis. Once in France, he would hitch a ride with some truck-driver and so make his way south again.

She was doubtful. But it did offer one kind of solution.

They set off just after four, and in Nyon they shopped at a Migros market close to the station, getting provisions for an evening picnic. Freddy had lavish notions about food, and Siân added a spare pair of thick socks for all the walking he intended to do. Once his attention was drawn to this, he hunted for a good pair of mountain boots, a woollen ski-cap and a quilted anorak.

'*Voilà!*' he said proudly, modelling them for her approval. He looked like the anti-hero of some second-rate French Canadian film about trappers.

'It's getting dark,' she urged.

'By St Cergue we shall be above this cloud,' he promised. 'Then we shall have two hours of light.'

He was right, up to a point. They came through one layer of cloud into clear air, but above it was a thick greyish yellow fog.

'What's that white stuff?' Siân demanded, darting a glance at the open ground. It looked like fertilizer spread in generous handfuls. But no one would have thrown it up into the trees as well. 'It's been snowing!'

And then it wasn't 'has been' any more. It lay thick on the road. They drove straight into it, fine and barely visible at first, then falling in a heavy white cloud. It stuck to the car body and windscreen, freezing on. Before La Cure it drove at them obliquely and the wipers were juddering under the weight.

'How can it do this in May?' Siân complained. 'Look, I'll have to turn back.'

'You can't! We're so near the top,' Freddy howled. He was virtually wringing his hands. Beside the road edge Siân saw a stack of logs with enough flat ground alongside to turn, and she pulled up to reverse. Instantly Freddy threw the passenger-door open and was out. 'If you won't take me, I'll go on alone.'

'No! Not in all this. Freddy, come back!' But he had gone plunging on, heedless of her.

He headed off at an angle, up through a band of straggling conifers, and if she followed, it would have to be on foot. She switched off, pocketing the ignition key and praying the hired car wouldn't seize up in the cold. Then she ran after him through the soft snow, swearing aloud at the irresponsible oaf.

The soil underneath was spongy, and her shoes unsuited

114

to the terrain. Every few yards she slithered back, and there were sharp-edged rocks that grazed her ankles and shins when she stumbled. The way grew steeper, so that she had to reach up for splintery branches or rocks which sometimes came away with a liquid gasp. There were places where she could hardly make out his footmarks, because where the trees grew densely it was dark and the snow patchy. The silence was total except for her own soughing breath and occasional sounds of Freddy's progress ahead. She looked back downhill where the trees closed blackly together. No sign of the car. 'Freddy, please! We'll get lost.'

He called back to her, a crowing laugh which broke off, then a sharp cry of pain, and nothing after. Siân ploughed on, sinking into slush, clawing her way over ridges of greyish rock mouldering under lichens. 'Freddy, where are you?'

From nearby came a low groan. He was in a shallow sort of pit, lying half on his back, nursing one leg and rolling in pain. Speechless, he beat her off when she tried to examine him.

'Where is it?' she said impatiently. 'Don't be a fool, Freddy. I've got to see what you've done.'

'Ankle,' he managed to get out.

There was no blood, and she did what she could with a handkerchief packed with snow and the belt off his jeans. It was fairly dark by now and they would have a terrible time trying to find the car. As soon as she mentioned it he refused.

'There's a hut quite close,' he insisted. 'I know this part well. I'll lie up there for the night and go on tomorrow.'

She tried arguing, but it was wasting what daylight remained. She agreed to go and look. Just ahead and off to the left, she would meet a track. It wouldn't be more than fifty metres from there and on the level.

'Keep calling,' she ordered. Despite the pain he pulled an impish face. 'Maybe.'

The hut was even nearer than he'd promised. It had no padlock, only a heavy wooden bar across the outside of the door and a shutter on the single unglazed window. Inside there was a *paillasse*, a fire bucket under an open chimney and a shelf with empty jam-jars, a plastic-wrapped bundle of candles and a large box of safety matches.

'I don't believe it,' she said when she got back to him. 'It's Crusoe's island ready-made. What on earth is it for?'

'Occasions like this. The woodsmen sometimes stay up here overnight. Or anyone in a fix, like us.'

'Did you plan all along to use it?'

'No. I thought I'd get across tonight. There's another hut farther on if I got stuck. Will you help me up? I need to lean on you a bit.'

They made slow progress to the hut and he lowered himself with a groan on to the *paillasse*. 'Where are you going?'

'Back to the car to get our food, before all the light's gone.'

'Light a candle first and put it in a jam-jar outside the door. Then you'll see how to get back.'

She followed his instructions, darting him a swift sideways glance. He wasn't such a fool. It was hard to tell what his brain was capable of, but he could plan ahead when he needed to, when his emotions weren't involved. Perhaps that was because as an artist he had visual imagination.

Already the little Fiat had a quilt of snow over roof and bonnet. By morning, they might have trouble finding it, let alone getting the thing to start. It seemed better to leave it unlocked because she had no de-icer. Like whoever owned the hut, she had to trust any other survivors.

The candle helped a lot, now that she couldn't make out their earlier tracks. The hut was much farther left than she had thought. She shook the loose snow off her jacket before going in. The shoulders of her sweater were wet through.

Freddy had a fire going. He sat on the floor with his bad ankle stretched out to one side and fed sticks into the blaze. There was a foul smell of burning candle grease. Quite a boy scout. Boy, or man? 'Freddy,' she said on impulse, 'how old are you?'

His face, flushed crimson and with dramatic black caverns as the firelight flickered on its angles, looked sad and old now. 'Twenty-eight,' he said. 'It's a long time.' He spoke like someone at the end of his life, looking back.

116

Surprisingly, he didn't eat much. He had shown more enjoyment in shopping for the *pâtés* and cheeses. There was more than they could eat in two days.

Whether because of the pain of his ankle or some sadness that had overtaken him, Freddy seemed now to withdraw into his private world. It was only later, when Siân had put away the unused provisions and poured out the last of their wine into the carton cups that he started to talk, in a half-dreamy, almost bitter monotone, telling her a story while he stared into the blaze of holly branches and pine which they built up from the stack outside.

'There was this girl . . .' he said, 'and she was very young, still at school, and the boy used to try to make her come to him at night. For sex. But she wouldn't, because she'd been taught it was wrong—until one night when she'd hidden her head under the blankets because downstairs there was such a row going on, shouting and thumping and—' He shook his head wretchedly, affected by the story itself—'and *bad things*. So she was frightened and lonely, and she got up and looked at the moon. And the moon looked so sad. Such a very long way from anyone, and so lonely. And she climbed out of the window and went over the garden and they met.'

'The boy and the girl?'

'And made love. It was the first time. And she wasn't frightened any more, but warm and—' There was a longer pause now.

'She climbed back through the window. She got into bed in the dark and the sheets were cold. So she thought she'd get her sweater and pull it in with her. So she put on the light and—'

In the full blaze of the firelight, Siân shivered, watching his frozen face. 'Go on.'

'And there was a man sitting in the chair right opposite.'

Siân let out her breath slowly. 'How scary.'

'The little girl screamed. She screamed and screamed until she hadn't any voice left. She fainted. And next day she couldn't talk. She never did say anything again. She—wasn't any good any more.' His voice died away. The story had had a terrible effect on him, huddled with his head sunk on his chest.

Poor little girl, Siân thought. Scared out of her wits, but *never* talked again? Even with her newfound passion confused with old guilt, that wasn't a normal reaction. Children survived worse things than that.

'No good any more,' he repeated, and she caught the glint of tears on his cheeks. He spoke draggingly, as if he himself was in shock.

He nodded. 'There he was, just sitting. Right opposite. With half his face blown off by a shotgun.'

CHAPTER 2

Approaching the lake, Andreas's green Peugeot turned left on to the Quai des Bergues, and at once he saw the blocked road ahead, a concentration of lights, milling sightseers straining twoards the water at the Pont de la Machine. Traffic was solid in the roadway, but it was the tall bulk of an ambulance that made him head for the pavement, sounding his horn. He lurched on to the *pavé*, got out, brushing past a young gendarme. '*Je suis médecin.*' The policeman half shrugged and went back to crowd control.

'*Docteur. Médecin,*' Andreas repeated, ploughing steadily through the gathering of morbid voyeurs. He said it again to the back of a tall, immaculately clad civilian who was leaning over the parapet, gazing into the spotlit water below.

The man straightened, fine, straw-coloured hair blowing in the night wind. His face was long and lined, the nose high-bridged with grooves deeply carved from nostrils to wide, humorous mouth, but the eyes were sombre then, witness to so much violence, corruption and wastage in their forty-seven years. '*Médecin? Plus besoin,*' he said with laconic distaste. '*C'est un cadavre.*'

They were right above the sluice gates, where the water foamed and fought at the grids before dropping a metre or so into the Rhône. At this point, midway between the Old

118

Town of Geneva and the international city, lake calm once more became torrent, hurling its flotsam at the reinforced grille which splintered it with the force of the current. But occasional solid objects—tree-trunks, metal beer kegs, capsized boats—resisted the onslaught and had to be retrieved.

Animal bodies, only comparatively solid, would eventually become mangled offal. This had begun to happen now, and it was part of a human torso that was being salvaged with grapples, lifted on chains to a sort of mediæval gibbet.

'*Plus besoin,*' the tall man had said, dismissing the offer of help. Agreed; no longer any need for a doctor. Simply a skilled pathologist.

There was a general movement forward of men in oilskins. They had unrolled a groundsheet on the bridge and now steadied the body's descent until it lay in a grotesque lump, seeming half-boxed by splintered boards. Curious, that the water's mauling hadn't pulled the two fabrics apart, sorted animal from vegetable, before pulverizing each separately. Varnished wood gleamed darkly under the intense light. So, part of a wrecked boat? And then, as the Greek doctor identified the black cavern of the ribcage, he saw what had held the whole together. A shaft, riveted through flesh, bone and deckboards.

No way an accident. Something had been shot into the body from very close range to achieve such penetration. And judging from the end fins it looked like that very traditional Swiss weapon, a crossbow bolt.

'Oh my God,' he breathed in English.

The tall, well-groomed man took out a cigarette case and offered it. 'Perhaps,' he said, dropping into the same language, 'you would give your name to one of my men. We shall require an independent witness. To confirm,' he added drily, 'the body's deadness when received by my men.'

There was already an eager-eyed youngster in uniform with ballpoint poised. 'Vassilakis. Dr Andreas Vassilakis.' He spelled out the surname for them. 'I work at the World Health Organization, Avenue Appia, 1211 Geneva 27. I

119

have a card here with my extension number, and private address on the Rive Gauche.'

'Pierre Fourneval, Chef de Police Cantonale,' said the other formally. Andreas saw now that the dark suit was dinner dress. He must have been called out from some late reception. Like all the others here, apparently a Genevese who never went to bed. Soon it would be time for the rest of the city to get up.

The policeman watched while Andreas took the packet of freshly printed visiting cards from his jacket pocket, unsealed it and withdrew the top one. 'Such a way to start the set,' he said with some sympathy. 'You are new here?'

'A matter of days. I have replaced Professor Theodorakis.'

'Ah yes.' Fourneval was eyeing him with a new interest. 'The late Professor.'

'My appointment was already made. His sudden death merely brought it forward by a month.' Andreas knew there had been no call to explain so much, but he didn't want the man to take him for a stop-gap.

The policeman leaned back with his elbows on the parapet, and when he spoke again it was ironically. 'Welcome to Switzerland—once renowned for precision clockwork, and now, since Far Eastern cheap technology, only for Muesli.' He grunted. 'Geneva, you must know, was intended to demonstrate Swiss genius, in which equilibrium reaches perfection; the supreme engineering of complex triggers and balances creating harmonic movement. Now instead of balance we have Babel, an amalgam of unlikely international elements irreconcilably thrown together. We have all become foreign bodies here, even the natives.' His eyes brooded on the gleaming shape that had been lowered to the groundsheet. 'A macedoine of flotsam.'

He straightened. 'This part of my work, Doctor, I do not like.'

For a policeman addressing a stranger, he betrayed unexpected feeling. Or was it the wine speaking, because he'd surely come from some sort of celebration? Not so Andreas. He was exhausted and anxious. It made him edgy, more critical of the other's world-weary sophistication. This was

120

a body, no more; had been a person, and a person cruelly done to death. No call for fancy philosophizing. Yet, for the policeman, he admitted, it signalled the beginning of an unsavoury delving into animosities and malice. One could respect his distaste, even while disliking the hunter's motive.

The doctor moved restlessly, started to turn away, and the other's tone became more personal. 'Perhaps we shall meet again,' he said thoughtfully. 'Then you can tell me all about this admirable Professor you replaced.' His tone was bland enough, but the Greek sensed some menace behind it.

'Meanwhile—?' Andreas asked, glancing again at the drenched and mangled thing they had taken from the water. Male or female, there was no way at present of knowing.

Chief Fourneval nodded slowly, leaning again to stare into the black and swirling water. 'It is a recurring problem in this polyglot city: dark currents. Foreign bodies.'

That goes for my troubles too, Vassilakis echoed silently, marching back stolidly to his car: deep, fast waters; unwanted nonsequiturs and disconnected ends.

The remaining onlookers opened a path for the determined, stocky figure. He threw the opened packet of visiting cards on the dashboard shelf, and as the car started forward it was pitched to the floor, scattering the new printing over the passenger seat and carpet. A bad beginning, he thought, but it was the policeman who had put that idea in his mind. And his bad beginning dated from when Nikolaos Theodorakis had dropped dead with heart failure on the way to work, over a fortnight back. Which had brought him post-haste. Little since then had really gone right. This new life was so complex and diverse that he barely knew how many problems there were.

One, of course, was his neglect of Siân, neglect as unavoidable as it was hurtful to a bride of some three weeks. There was no doubt about either's affection. The strain arose from so much time spent apart, unkept promises, and information he wasn't permitted to share with her. She had a streak of impatience, which he admired, but he could well fall foul of it if he didn't make a better showing as a consort.

121

At least they had solved the problem of where to live. It was wonderful to have a whole house to themselves, something to work on together. He was coming now to the steep climb before their village and must look for the sudden turn at the stone pillars. His headlights found the driveway and he eased in. Despite the hour—dawn wasn't far off—the globes were still lit all down the zigzag path from the big villa. As the car wound quietly down towards the little house on the lake's edge the forecourt lights came automatically on and the panelled garage door began to rise. He ran the Peugeot in beside the blue Mercedes and heard the door close gently behind him.

Only darkness in the passage when he'd unlocked the inner house door. No lamps turned on in the other rooms either. Well, he hadn't been expected. Siân would have locked up for the night and gone to her lonely bed. If he crept in now he would surprise her as she woke.

Dark, but not totally. He realized that the curtains had never been drawn. The first, cold, silvery light of morning was stealing in even as the sky outside grew rosy streaks. Everything so tidy and incomplete. They were still short of furniture, but that pale shape over there was the bed.

Empty, never slept in.

He padded through the rooms. 'Siân, I'm home. Darling, where are you?'

He stood still and listened to the silence. No whisper of radio or plumbing. No leftover smells of cooking. No sense of being teased. She simply wasn't there. Gone on the botanists' expedition. Although she'd mentioned it when he left her, he hadn't expected it would come off.

He went into the bare kitchen and filled the coffee percolator, looked in the fridge and could see no difference from when he had last looked. So how long had she been gone, and why was there no note left?

It was disappointing, but at least he could now make himself a meal, supper-breakfast, and get some sleep before he had to give her an account of his doings. A carefully edited account for which he needed to be less weary than he felt at present.

The original plan to fly Subarsky out had been modified at the last minute. His new instructions, received when he phoned in from the Cointrin airport on Wednesday, were to pick the Russian up and deliver him immediately by road to a country house near Berne for preliminary debriefing. The man had been waiting under a neighbouring telephone hood with the contact, David.

Andreas had taken the business on as an unwanted legacy from old Theo, who had set it up with the Canadian Embassy, and he'd been much relieved that in the end his part had been such a minor one. He had no taste for international skulduggery, especially when it meant leaving Siân out on a limb, with no transport.

He buttered bread. Waiting for tinned mince to heat, he stared out over the lake. Lights strung out like a necklace along the opposite shoreline were fading into the general monochrome grey, and the palest tone now was the water, glassy and empty.

Something out there was vaguely disturbing him. He switched off the hotplate and went out by the kitchen door to stand on the wooden jetty. The lake made gentle clooping noises, nuzzling the piles the house stood on. He could hear the characteristic whipping *ping* of halyards against the aluminium mast of *Cacahouette* out at her mooring, but something was missing. It was the *clunk, clunk* of the wooden dinghy restless under the jetty. It must have slipped its mooring. A length of the painter still hung down into the water from its iron ring, but the boat was gone.

Not only Siân missing, but the dinghy as well. Yet if she had taken it out she would have untied the painter. To be quite certain he went back to the garage where they stored the sails. The waterproof bag was there, still bulging. So, unless she'd intended rowing . . .

He went back and knelt on the edge of the jetty, feeling about for the end of the rope. It came up stiff and slimy. Not rotted; cut short. He didn't like that. Maybe Siân hadn't gone on the expedition after all. If there'd been some kind of accident, it would account for her not leaving a note.

They might know something about it up at the villa. At

123

least he could use their telephone. Klara might have been told for certain where Siân had gone, and she'd know who should be notified about the drifting boat.

There was no reply to his ringing at the main door, although Madame Zuelig was an early riser. He walked round to the rear and thought there was a light faintly showing between the louvres of the heavy steel shutters. He pressed his face tight against the cold metal and made out a thin section of the kitchen.

As he watched, the light was extinguished. Nobody there though, and he remembered the villa had a time clock which lit sets of rooms in sequence, to fool would-be burglars. He tried knocking, then returned to the main door and continued ringing until it was obvious the house was empty.

He would wait for the cleaning girl. He needed sleep, but he wouldn't go back to that empty bed, had no stomach now for eating. He would stay here, squatting on the tiles under the deep-eaved porch until some better idea presented itself.

When he closed his eyes he seemed to be driving again through the night, with approaching headlights bearing down on him with yellow hypnotic eyes. His head fell heavily forward and he slept.

He only half-woke as the girl came stomping along the path jingling her keys. She stopped short at sight of him, then hurried forward dismayed, jabbering too fast in French for him easily to follow. Madame was away. It was just by chance that Monique had come in today, it being Saturday. She had been thinking to open some upstairs windows because it had suddenly turned warm. Yes, it was already past nine o'clock.

Madame Vassilakis? Ah, that she did not know. She had seen her two days back, putting marker pegs in the garden where she was going to dig. Of course Monsieur could use the telephone. She would show him where it was.

They went in together, by the kitchen, and through to the darkened hall where she operated the mechanism that raised the shutters and let daylight in. Andreas had been here before and admired the carved staircase with its wall of Swiss armour.

Now that he had access to a telephone, he didn't know who it was he should speak to, but there was always the memorized emergency number. He identified himself and waited for them to ring back. When he heard the right voice he explained what had happened, what had *not* happened. He was told they would find out if Siân had left any message for him. It would be passed to his office. They also explained who should be notified about the lost boat, and that the registered number, as on the sails, must be supplied for identification purposes.

'But I have the sails,' he said, 'so what use . . . ?

It was the correct procedure, he was informed. The Swiss were very particular about doing the right thing. On the form there would be a space for the number that had to be filled in so would he please find out what it was and send it to the appropriate official.

In the big rococo mirror he could see the girl Monique standing on the staircase as he put the receiver down. She was staring up, frowning.

'Something wrong?' He went to stand beside her.

She pointed. 'It was there yesterday, I'm almost sure. But it's been moved.'

'What has?'

'L'arbalète.'

The word went round in his mind, filling him with unease, although its meaning hadn't come through. He looked up where she pointed, at the empty space and the heavy bolt plugging the wall. Then he remembered seeing it there. *L'arbalète* . . . the crossbow.

He supposed later that all along he had gradually been moving towards just such a climax without admitting the terrible possibility. Now in an instant it all came together, and the life seemed to drain out of him. He saw the pattern, but couldn't believe it. Three things missing, which together echoed the horror down at the sluice gates. It had to be impossible; but Siân had disappeared, and the dinghy. Now the crossbow.

He said nothing, turned and went back to the phone. When he had the cantonal police he asked for Pierre Fourneval by name. '*Oui, le Chef. L'affaire du cadavre, Pont de la Machine . . .*' It was Saturday, so they regretted . . . He gave his information succinctly, his name and the number he was calling from. He was told to wait and someone would ring back.

The girl had heard enough to be alarmed. 'Shall I make you some coffee, monsieur?'

'For both of us, I think.' He went and sat on the stairs, waiting. Nobody phoned back. Instead, after some twenty minutes, the doorbell rang. A long, silver car stood in the driveway and a dark blue Citroën was pulling in through the gates. Chief Fourneval stepped forward. 'Excuse the funny clothes.' He was dressed for riding, in cream polo-necked sweater and matching breeches above brilliant boots the colour of new chestnuts. 'I see you didn't get to bed yourself.'

'Three things gone missing,' Andreas grimly reminded him, cutting through the social niceties. 'My wife, a dinghy, and a crossbow. I've been away since Wednesday evening. I last saw my wife then at the Cointrin airport. She was going to hire a car to get home.'

'Léonard,' Fourneval said over one shoulder, 'you heard all that? Check on it. And the dinghy?' He had turned back to Andreas.

'It was tied up to the boathouse jetty down there, where we live. The painter hasn't been untied. There's one end still on the ring, cut clean through.'

'We will look into that later. Any passing stranger might have seen the boat and taken it, but the crossbow was in the villa, as I understand. Someone had to come inside to get it.'

Andreas pointed to where it had hung over the staircase.

'Quite an armoury,' Fourneval commented wryly. 'Historical and decorative, no doubt, but fatally suggestive to certain twisted minds.' He lifted down a stout wooden handle with a chain and a spiked iron ball attached. 'This, for example. It could give one bad dreams.'

126

Andreas closed his eyes. The man was totally insensitive offering this obscene image. He opened them to find himself being shrewdly observed. 'Gilbert, a chair for Monsieur Vassilakis, but outside. We will talk again, in the garden, when I have taken a general look around. There will be all the usual specialist services, monsieur—photographs, fingerprinting, the lot. They are to concentrate on walls, doors, handrails, light switches, handles . . . *Dieu*, who's this?'

Monique had appeared from the kitchen, drying her hands.

'Have you been cleaning all the evidence away? When will people ever learn?'

'There was a mess in the sink,' she said, offended. 'I only . . .'

'Quite. Please go out into the garden and someone will come shortly to ask you some questions. Maurice, the kitchen.'

He walked thoughtfully from room to room, halting on the threshold of the drawing-room, his gaze on the carpet. 'A lot of action here at some time. I wonder why. But no dismemberment, of course. For such butchering one needs the bathroom or kitchen.' He skirted the centre of the room and went to the lacquered cabinet, unlatched its doors with the end of a ballpoint pen and nodded at the bottles and decanters, the precise rows of glasses sparkling in the recessed lighting. 'Not used,' he gave as his opinion, 'or else very carefully put to rights again. For myself I should certainly need something quite strong to steady me after the crime. Well, perhaps we shall strike lucky there: not with a glass, but possibly the shelves.'

He cast an eye over the experts who were already about their individual tasks, searching, dusting with powder, photographing. Two further cars had appeared in the drive and now the team numbered eight. 'Plumbing,' he commanded a small, bug-eyed man with a large canvas grip. 'Find me just a few drops of the red stuff and we are on our way.'

The little man smiled pleasantly. 'In the cause of duty I would bleed myself dry, sir.'

'Comedian,' muttered Fourneval under his breath, lit a cigar and went out into the sunshine. The day was really warming up. At last the weather seemed likely to catch up with the calendar.

Vassilakis had ignored the chair on the terrace. He was half way down the zigzag path, squatting on a rock and listening intently to the maid Monique beside him. They were both staring at a cherry tree in full blossom. 'What's this, then?' Fourneval demanded, reaching them and then seeing the tree's plastic cummerbunds.

'I think you should hear the whole story,' the Greek doctor said, 'beginning perhaps with the earlier damage to the property. Were you aware that Madame Zuelig had divorced her husband a few months ago?'

'A vindictive ex-husband? Bad blood between them, eh?' Fourneval said hopefully. Perhaps it was as simple as that. The majority of violent crimes turned out to be domestic. 'Tell me everything you know about it,' he demanded, resigning himself to hear a catalogue of scandals.

He heard Monique through and reserved judgement. He could get verification of the details from the Commune's police, Vassilakis told him. 'So when did Madame go away?' Fourneval asked Monique.

'Thursday morning early, by car, and Madame Vassilakis was to leave later the same day. When I brought the milk and croissants, she was working down here before going to join the expedition.'

'Expedition?'

'A botanical outing arranged by the University,' Andreas Vassilakis explained. 'She mentioned the possibility of taking part, but she didn't actually go. She was told there were no last-minute vacancies. I know because after contacting you I rang the University, to check when they would be back, and someone looked up their lists. My wife's name wasn't included.'

'We will ask them to look again,' Fourneval soothed. 'Perhaps an accidental omission.'

'God, I hope so,' vowed Andreas.

'But in case she has wandered off elsewhere, perhaps you have a photograph?'

Andreas picked up his jacket from the grass and took a folder from the inner pocket. Without comment he handed the policeman a wedding photograph of himself and Siân.

'This is recent?'

'Taken three weeks ago.'

'Ah.'

'My wife is British, twenty-three, speaks quite good French, some Greek. Her passport isn't with her things in the house. I've looked.'

'And you were away since Wednesday. When did she expect you to return, monsieur?'

'I—There was no way of knowing.'

'You intended to telephone . . .'

'It's not been reconnected at the boathouse. They're taking an unreasonable time getting round to it.'

Fourneval regarded him with an eyebrow raised. 'Ah! Perhaps I can be of some help in that matter. We need to be able to contact you. Perhaps your wife needs to as well. With her passport gone, she could be doing some travelling of her own. Sauce for the goose, I think the expression is.'

'I never chose not to make proper arrangements . . .'

'It is the job, yes. I am a policeman, Doctor, so I understand. Even now I am shortly supposed to be meeting my wife for lunch. As for the reconnection, the Telephone Bureau has emergency staff for Saturdays. I shall be ringing you myself as soon as your line is working. Meanwhile, please go and get some sleep.'

Fourneval gently brushed a sleepy bee off the sleeve of his sweater, then turned to the maid . . . 'Madame, I—'

'Monique, monsieur.'

'Monique, you will please take me on a tour of the villa and point out anything that strikes you as unusual.'

In the boathouse Andreas could not face the quiet room with the neatly made bed. He unbuttoned his shirt and sat back in an armchair facing the lakeside windows. The

129

telephone engineer woke him at a little after two, was let in and busied himself with the junction box. He padded through to announce that all was now in order. 'I have informed the department of police, monsieur. There could be a call for you at any time now.'

Andreas growled his thanks. But why couldn't such a minor adjustment have been made earlier? He sat forward in his chair, tense for the coming call, and aware of a background throbbing like a distant version of the aircraft in which they had arrived so few days before. It's the blood in my head, he thought dully. Pulsing because I am alive. Which I would not want to be if . . .

How could life have changed so utterly in so very few days? What in God's name had Siân become involved in while his head had been buried in the sand?

CHAPTER 3

Pierre Fourneval, Chef de Police Cantonale, liked to think himself hard-shelled. He accordingly expected to wipe the torso affair from his mind on leaving the Villa Montarnaud and, without qualms, to indulge his Saturday-morning custom of an hour's rough riding on the gelding Chicane, followed by massage and jacuzzi at a local private hotel. There he would down an iced concoction of his own devising which required half a lime, two *décis* of grenadine, vodka *ad lib*, and a touch of aloes. So braced, he would call in at the office to ensure that law enforcement in the canton was not falling apart over the weekend. Following which, under normal circumstances, he was his wife's for lunch and more or less his own man for the next thirty-six hours.

Today, he knew, would not be normal. The early hours had already brought the obscene discovery down at the sluice gates, and he had not been to bed since. He had just saddled up the gelding and was adjusting the stirrup leathers when the message came through, relayed from the Greek doctor, whose reappearance on his horizon shouldn't, by the law of averages, be scheduled for some time yet.

If his missing wife/dinghy/crossbow actually proved to be related to the torso case, then it was most unlikely that his presence at the recovery of the body was entirely fortuitous. Much more likely to be occasioned by a murderer's fascination for the after-effects of his crime.

But was Andreas Vassilakis a crude killer? The impression which Fourneval had gained of him at their first meeting was quite other. It was because of this, as well as the bizarre state of the corpse, that he hadn't been content to leave the case completely in the hands of Gilbert, who was competent enough (though it wouldn't do openly to admit as much). Also, the Villa Montarnaud had a reputation for elegance which he had never had the opportunity to judge, and there was a current interest in it among local estate agents since the Durochat-Zuelig divorce at Christmas.

As he pounded the turf and lifted Chicane over fences and hedges, what lingered in his mind was less the body's discovery than the later scene up at the villa; notably the blank space on the staircase wall, and the blanked-out face of the doctor staring up at it—masking apprehension because of his wife, or something more sinister?

He reined in to watch a flock of rooks rise from the coppice ahead and wheel cawing against the pearly sky. He tried to estimate their distance. If he had a crossbow, what range was it accurate over? How much practice did it take to handle the thing? It was a useful weapon, silent, transportable up to a point, but—bulky, and you had to get your target in one shot. If not, you were left vulnerable while you reloaded. An elitist weapon, one for an expert. Or else one to use on a defenceless target.

Then this question of penetration (and he could only guess here, having no practical experience): the corpse had been fired at from in front and near at hand. So what had he/she been doing while an enemy came so close, levelling a deadly weapon? Been asleep, unconscious, or dead already? A delectable puzzle, and one he'd need to call in expert opinion on.

Meanwhile there might already be developments at headquarters. Fourneval rang his wife with his regrets about lunch and went to check up on the Scene of Crime Team Gilbert had organized.

They were on the ball. Waiting on his desk was a scribbled note confirming the hire of a Hertz Fiat to Madame Vassilakis on the evening of last Wednesday at Cointrin airport; details appended.

So the doctor's wife had done as her husband wished. And now the car joined the growing list of missing objects. An Observe-and-Report Order on the Fiat had been broadcast throughout the canton. That should be extended to the Canton de Vaud, also to the French police in the Jura and Haute Savoie regions.

Next action would be to send scuba divers to the boathouse area and to notorious run-off points where large objects could be disposed of in the lake. It would be useful if the crossbow were to turn up inside the submerged Fiat, but perhaps that was too much to hope for.

There was already a report on action taken at the villa: scrapings from the drawing-room carpet had been sent for analysis. Ditto from carpet on the stairs. Fingerprint department had found the usual wealth of superimposed anonymous smudges and some significantly clean-wiped surfaces. Heavy quality beeswax had recently been used on furniture in the downstairs rooms, which might in itself be suspicious or merely evidence of conscientious cleaning. His men were now hard at work examining blown-up photographs and preparing computer entries.

Blood: visible traces had been detected in three places— the base of a velvet-covered footstool in the drawing-room; the side wall of the cellar steps; between tiles in the bathroom floor. All were deposited recently and were of two general groups. The first, a thick spurt, probably overlooked because under the fringed seam, was blood type AB Rhesus-positive. The other two—one a light, repetitive pattern recurring a metre above every second riser; the other partly washed away with a pumice solution—were identically Group O+.

So, two bodies? Or one body and a wounded killer?

How many persons had been present at the villa, and

when? Subtracting the legitimate marks left by Vassilakis and the maid, it looked as if several sets of shoes had marched over the floorboards since last vacuum-cleaning. The Chinese carpet was of superb quality, and therefore orientally inscrutable, except for one patch, shown on the diagram as being near the footstool, which appeared under magnification to have been rubbed at. Three indentations implied a piece of furniture had stood there a considerable time before removal: too central for a cupboard, too small for a billiard table, too heavy for a settee. Someone had written in 'piano' with a query. Be that as it might, no one performed rituals of heavy furniture-removing during the course of a murder, so it must be irrelevant.

Murder—or accident? Could they really be sure of that yet? A crossbow indoors? Fourneval asked himself. In a room with one long side all windows, even if shuttered, no one would be crazy enough to use such a weapon on purpose. But if someone inexpert were to be handling the thing loaded, with another person opposite . . . ? Could it have happened that way? He had thought it took a deliberate effort to release the bolt. Here again he needed an expert's opinion, and to recover the actual weapon, faulty or otherwise.

But what made this venue impossible, of course, was the timber attached to the torso by the bolt. He still placed his bet on it being part of a small boat, probably the missing dinghy. Dismembered bodies and sailing craft just weren't credible drawing-room adjuncts.

It was over-optimistic to expect a report on the torso yet, but he might resort to his link with Jourdain on the unofficial level. He shouted for Gilbert. 'Get the Path Lab on the phone.'

The pathologist answered with his accustomed calm. 'I'll have a word with the Chief myself, thanks. Hallo, Pierre? In your usual headlong rush, I observe. You'll end on my table twenty years too soon. No, nothing for you on paper yet. I'm taping my findings as I go. Let's see now. What we have is the headless, limbless torso of a recent cadaver, immersed within the past forty-eight to sixty hours and within an hour or two of death occurring. Yes, *blah, blah, blah, blah*—that won't mean anything to you, I'm afraid. Severe *post-mortem* mutilation. Fascinating, this, and strictly off the record as yet: I see the dismemberment as caused by sharp-cutting rotary blades at speed. How do you fancy the screws of a powerful launch?

'There are also random flesh wounds which tend to back up this idea. The splinters of varnished wood embedded in bone suggest to me two boats in collision. Our late friend came off badly, perhaps entangled by clothing in a position where the propellers would do most harm. Somewhere in the lake—it's my guess—the rest of the boat and missing limbs shouldn't be far from each other. I recommend you take an interest in beachcombing.'

Fourneval grunted. 'We have divers standing by. And our late friend; have we a him or a her?'

'We have a well-nourished, mature, male Caucasian; general blood type O+. Height, at an educated guess, between 1.70 metres and 1.80. Find me just half of one leg and I can let you have it accurate to 0.02 metres. That's all I can even hint at for the moment.'

Fourneval thanked him and replaced the receiver thoughtfully. Gilbert was balanced on one foot in the doorway. 'Do you want to see Dr Vassilakis?'

'Give me five minutes.' He looked through the papers again. The corpse's Blood Type O+ had turned up twice at the Villa Montarnaud: the washed-out stains between the ground-floor bathroom's floor-tiles, and the faint pattern of spots on the white wall by the cellar steps. So the torso wasn't connected with the thick splash on the drawing-room footstool or the rubbed patch of Chinese carpet. But how, *Seigneur Dieu,* could one manage to aim and fire a crossbow in a bathroom? It simply wasn't feasible. There just had to have been two separate attacks on the dead man, the wound in the bathroom (or cellar) coming first, the skewering later. Time and Jourdain's further finicky probings would reveal at what point in all this death actually occurred.

Since the corpse was found to be male, there would be some comfort to hand out to the Greek waiting—anxiously, no doubt—in the outer office. At least it wasn't his wife's, though the lady was still missing. Under the circumstances, one had to assume some connection between the body and her disappearance, and that might not be entirely good news for the waiting man. Killers had a tendency to disappear as well as concealed bodies. There was no scarcity of Missing Persons on file at present, including an unofficial whisper from Political Security that one of the Russian Permanent Mission had gone AWOL and everyone up there was at shit stations, suspecting a defection.

Ah well, Vassilakis had been kept waiting long enough. Fourneval pressed a button on his desk and spoke into the box. 'You can send him in now.'

'Can you hang on, sir?' the box answered urgently. 'Gilbert has an outside priority call and is making signs he wants you.'

'Put it through here on mike and send him in.'

There was a pause while someone slipped into the room behind him. Then a high, whinnying voice replaced the switchboard policewoman's. 'Guignard here, monsieur. Nyon, Vaud. Your Hertz Fiat on Observe-and-Report: we have it booked as stolen from the central car park here yesterday, Friday, between 14.00 hours and 22.30 hours. It later featured in a one-car fatal crash on the eastbound motorway near Chillon, timed at 23.57 hours. An illegal substance was found in the car; there was drug abuse by the dead passenger and driver, the latter injured and comatose. A Madame Vassilakis, who appears to have hired the car from Cointrin airport on Wednesday, is helping our inquiries regarding the drugs. She claims her husband is a doctor. I understand you have some prior interest in the lady, who has an implausible story. Would you care to sit in on the questioning?'

'With you in half an hour,' Fourneval assured him. 'Accompanied by the husband.'

He switched off the box and raised an eyebrow at Gilbert. 'God Almighty, now we have drugs! And I was beginning to smell international politics. Is my nose getting old, I ask myself? I want you to sit in the front with the driver, and watch the Greek in your spare mirror while I tell him the story so far.'

'Are you *betting* on a political killing?' Gilbert got in quickly before opening the door. 'Because I'll put a hundred francs on a domestic. We might get Guignard to back his third option.'

'Doesn't sound like a gambler.' Fourneval damped his enthusiasm, as he reached for his jacket. He recalled the whinnying voice and smiled. 'More of a runner, in fact.'

Siân was glad of the respite when the senior policeman pushed back his chair and got up to go. Wherever she'd encountered him she would have been put off by the peaked pink dome pushing through the carroty thin hair and the watery blue eyes fixed suspiciously on her. But here, under such circumstances, she found him odious.

You would have thought she was the criminal, not the complainant after a theft. She had tried to convince them all that she'd no connection with the juveniles who'd helped themselves to her car, but until the survivor recovered to tell his own story there was no back-up to her version. The police wanted someone to collar, and she was available. They hadn't cared for her story about seeing a friend off by train to Locarno, and then spending the rest of the day sight-seeing in Nyon, with a hotel dinner on her own before setting off back to Geneva. It was all perfectly true, right up to going to collect the car from the parking place and finding it gone. Nothing to feel guilty about in that. What she didn't want to tell them was all that nonsense about spending the previous night up at a woodsman's hut near La Cure.

By morning, yesterday, the snow had started to thaw and she was able to get Freddy back to the car. She'd driven him down to a doctor in Nyon, where no one seemed to have heard of the snowstorm. By the time they'd had a meal and she'd firmly refused to be led any more dances, Freddy had been remorseful enough to take on responsibility for his own departure. He'd opted for the train that connected at Brig with another bound for Domodossola and Locarno.

Somewhere on the journey, where the route crossed a corner of Italy, he expected to get off unobserved, hitch a ride down to Milan and get lost.

It was crazy, of course, but then so was Freddy, and seemed to thrive on being so. All he'd required her to do was to buy his ticket and to change half of his considerable French francs into lire while he rested his ankle.

After waving him goodbye, she had enjoyed the rest of her day in Nyon until she found the wretched car was missing. She'd gone back to the hotel where she'd had dinner, booked a room overnight, and reported the loss to the police by telephone.

Today the run of bad luck had continued, with the police discovering a small quantity of unspecified drugs in the wrecked car, tucked in an envelope addressed to herself at the Hôtel Stresa, Geneva. The unappetizing Guignard had produced it like a valuable item of evidence against her, although she explained it had held a letter from her step-mother in England, which she had picked up from her previous address on the way out of Geneva. She had kept the letter and discarded the envelope somewhere in the car. What happened to it later was nothing to do with her.

Now they had all gone off and left her alone. To worry, she supposed. But she'd nothing to worry about.

Then the door opened, and this time three men came in; Guignard, followed by a tall stranger. The third one to enter was Andreas.

He looked ten years older, exhausted and grim. He walked right past the other two and stood over her, just looking. She was scared. And then his arms were hard about her. He was rocking her gently, murmuring into her hair, *compelling* her to be comforted. She looked over his shoulder and caught the sardonic expression on the tall stranger's face.

'Siân, I shouldn't have left you.'

'You just turned your back and the world went mad.' She was almost laughing. 'They've got it all wrong.'

'Let's set it right then. I'm here to help now.'

More chairs were being brought in. The men settled down, two policemen on one side of the little table, Siân on the other, facing them, with Andreas just a foot back so that he wouldn't distract her from her story or prompt her answers. And she started telling it all over again. The same details, plus her explanation of the envelope. No mention of Freddy's part in anything at all.

This time when she had finished there were no questions, but the new policeman—so elegant in houndstooth jacket, tan silk shirt, cream leather tie—nodded and said, 'Now I have a story to tell you, also a curious one. Somewhere perhaps there is a link, but we cannot be sure, so listen carefully. We hope you can help us.'

Siân quickly looked round to Andreas who reached for her hand and squeezed it gently. Then Pierre Fourneval, glossing over the details, told of the dead body at the sluice gates, and of the crossbow bolt which had drawn attention to the villa, and finally of finding bloodstains in the house itself.

As he spoke, Siân lost her colour and sat tensed. 'Madame, are you feeling unwell?'

She shook her head. 'Go on, please. Who was it—the body?'

'We still cannot say, madame. A man, that is all we know as yet.'

'Thank God!' But she barely had the words out before a second awful possibility occurred to her.

'You think you may know who he could be, madame?

'No, *no!*'

'She assumes, as I do,' Andreas said in a low voice, 'that the vandal came back to damage the property, and someone caught him in the act . . .'

'That Victor Durochat returned by dark, and that his ex-wife, feeling threatened . . .' Fourneval suggested, revealing his familiarity with the situation.

'No!' they both said together. 'Not Klara,' Sian insisted. 'She couldn't have done it. She's been hurt badly, but she's learned to live with it. She's gone away to start a new life . . .'

'Go on, madame.'

Siân lowered her head, eyes tight shut to keep the tears

138

back. Andreas was conscious of her nails driving into his palm.

'If not Madame Durochat-Zuelig, who then, madame?

In the end I shall be forced to tell them, Siân told herself. If not Klara, who else could have caught the intruder and shown such fury, but Freddy? It explained so much about him; his state of unnatural excitement, almost paranoia; his hiding in the cellar; his insistence on no one knowing he had visited Geneva; his panicky need to return to Annecy by a roundabout route.

But Fourneval's last question had been purely rhetorical. Siân raised her eyes to find the policemen were in private consultation together. They seemed agreed, and then at last she was free to go, her report of a car theft signed into the log, and any suspicions of her own involvement with the junkies left for the moment in abeyance.

They went out into startling sunshine, to where the Geneva officer's car stood waiting, two plain-clothes men beside it. One of them joined Andreas and herself in the rear, while Fourneval sat by the driver. Andreas's grip on her arm felt like a jailer's. It had been bad enough before he appeared, but now there were even more half-truths between them, and a strange distance which her guilt made her believe was disapproval. And added to the loss of the car and the accident to the young men who stole it, there was now the awful reality of murder.

'When exactly did it happen?' she asked abruptly.

Fourneval answered over his shoulder. 'Either one or two days before we recovered the body from the water. Which offers us the nights of Wednesday/Thursday, or Thursday/Friday. We have to assume, I think, that the body's disposal could only be attempted after dark. Certainly the unknown man met his death just an hour or two before being immersed.'

'Killed at the Villa Montarnaud, carried down to the boathouse and placed in the dinghy,' Andreas considered. 'That took time. And all that without attracting attention, or waking Siân asleep in the boathouse? Surely no one would risk it if there were lights on there?'

139

'We don't sleep on the jetty side of the house,' Siân reminded him. 'And on Wednesday night I wasn't back until just after midnight. I had supper in Geneva with some of the botany department, and went for a walk afterwards to clear my head.'

'So it could have been then. Or while you were asleep the following night.' Fourneval nodded.

Thursday night. I was up at La Cure, Siân reflected, unsure how long she could keep that fact concealed.

'And we hadn't been there long,' Andreas was thinking aloud. 'Only since Monday. So, very few people knew the boathouse was in use again. They wouldn't have bothered to take precautions.'

'Who knew?'

'Madame Zuelig, Monique the maid.'

'And Monique's husband, who helped in the garden,' Siân added. 'Doesn't that put them all in the clear?'

'It may help. We need to trace the movements of interested parties.' Fourneval shrugged, looking ahead along the motorway. 'And prove who the dead man is.'

'You must already have some idea,' Andreas prompted, 'about who has gone missing lately.' He was still refusing to accept that it might be Klara's ex-husband.

The policeman settled his shoulders comfortably against the car door and turned back to look at them directly. He was a little too casual. 'There are missing persons, certainly. We have a choice of candidates for the body.'

'And Victor Durochat?' Siân dared to ask. 'Where is he?'

'He has not been sighted since he left work early on Tuesday afternoon. He is not at his apartment, and his cousin informs us that he is in Paris on business. But there are others who appear to have disappeared at about the same time. Notably a member of the Russian Permanent Delegation to UN. Which could be interesting, don't you think?'

Siân's throat was suddenly restricted. 'A *Russian*? Who?'

'We haven't a name yet.'

Did she imagine Andreas had tightened his grip on her for a moment and then relaxed? Or was it her own tension

140

as her mind leapt forward to the name *Subarsky*? The policeman was staring expressionlessly back at her, as though he
would read the flight of fears through her mind. Suspicious
of *her*, or of Andreas too? Because there *was* a link, Andreas
having inherited Theo's secret connection with the Russian.

She had to break the steely compulsion of the policeman's
eyes. 'And the others you spoke of?'

His lips thinned. 'There is always a list of untraced
persons. Elsewhere in the Confederation, among the worthy
burghers of Berne and Basel, Geneva is considered the sink
of iniquity. A sink certainly, because so much drains away
here—people, money, causes, principles. Being an international society, we attract what we do not need and have
no wish for. All the modern social evils flock here. When
the effluent chokes our drain, we are left to get rid of it. As
perhaps now.'

'Foreign bodies,' Andreas said sombrely, remembering
how Fourneval had first played the cynic philosopher down
at the sluice gates.

Their driver suddenly spoke into his mirror, momentarily
catching their eyes. 'Not that we are such a saintly lot
ourselves. We have been known to breed our own crimes.
But the Chief is a local patriot.'

Fourneval astonished them by smiling broadly. 'One has
to believe in something,' he excused himself. 'Perhaps I am
a trifle insular. Didn't you know that Switzerland is a
landlocked island?'

CHAPTER 4

In the car park at Geneva police headquarters they drew
up alongside the green Peugeot. Almost languidly, Chief
Fourneval bade them *au revoir*. Significantly not *adieu*, because there would be other meetings, questions, interrup-
tions of normal life. He stood there watching them depart,
tall, lean and not a little sinister, his fair hair finely blowing
in the wind above the spoilt-handsome face, and in his eyes

a quirky taunting that might have been suppressed black humour.

Siân was glad to see the back of him, but left alone with Andreas she was the more conscious of a grey zone of deceit stretched between them. And it was not all of her own making. Defiantly she left it to him to cross the no-man's land and make the first admissions. No way was she going to demand explanations, and even less was there any chance of him getting answers from her if he launched an interroation.

She almost relented when, stopped at a traffic light, she caught the worried glance he flicked across at her. Eyes like a wounded bear's, but—he hadn't the right to make her break silence over Freddy when there was so much he still hugged to himself in secret. What about the coded list of numbers and letters; his unlikely, sudden absences; the Subarsky connection and the Russian's possible disappearance?

Could it have been Subarsky's body that had been dredged out of the lake? If so, had that nervous little rabbit gone up to the villa on one of those two nights, looking for Andreas? And had Andreas anything to do with what subsequently happened to him? Where had Andreas actually been hiding up these last few days, when he'd started off for Ottawa by air and apparently been sidetracked elsewhere?

She knew that if she checked on the Peugeot's mileage she could work out whether he'd laid it up nearby or covered a considerable distance, but she was too proud to look. He could keep all his secrets and his distance, so long as she was accorded the same right to her privacy.

She had her own worries. Sooner or later someone would say there were no lights seen at the boathouse at all on Thursday night, and then the police would press her to say where she had been. How could she explain the night spent at La Cure without mentioning Freddy? Until she had that sorted in her mind, she felt safer with Andreas held at some distance. At the same time, and on a quite different, non-mental level, she ached for him.

'Where shall we eat?' he opened suddenly. (A man, so of

142

course, in a crisis he thought about food!) 'At home, or . . . ?'

'I don't feel like going out. I'm such a mess.'

He looked at her briefly. 'Not really.' His voice was unusually deep and gravelly. 'For myself, I'd like something light, then get to bed. But right now I have to make a phone call.' He ran the car down by the side of the Hôtel Stresa and got out. She noticed again how drained his face looked. 'I shan't be long.'

She remembered then that he'd told her the telephone was reconnected at the boathouse. The police chief had put pressure on to get it done. Was that why Andreas wouldn't use it now, suspecting it might be officially tapped? Surely he was no more seriously a suspect than herself? But police always thought the worst of everybody, and everyone had something they wanted to keep to themselves. No, it was more likely that he wanted privacy from her. He hadn't seemed all that concerned what Chief Fourneval might think of him. Perhaps he had watertight alibis for the two nights in question.

There were private phone calls she would like to make herself, to set her mind at rest about certain things, but she hadn't Niall's number to check on the Subarsky business, and had no idea where Freddy might be by now, nor Klara either. It was scary to feel so isolated when she hadn't even the security of being at one with Andreas.

Gilbert watched the green Peugeot pull out of the police yard. 'Another of life's grim little jokes,' he announced. 'Meeting the right girl just too late.' He sighed histrionically.

'Not your type,' Fourneval decided. 'They're a pair, but all the same something smells just a little off at the moment. Better check the girl's movements Wednesday night, when she was supposed to be with the botany students, and Thursday too. There's something she's not being open about. Probably not our main concern here, but *is* it drugs, or another man already? Or is the Greek simply getting paid back for masterful neglect of his bride?'

'A doctor, he *could* be involved with drugs. And he does keep turning up in things.'

'No, we leave that pair on the sidelines, I think, to play their own game. Unless, of course . . .'

'Unless?'

'Unless the torso does turn out to be Russian. In which case we take a second look at the Greek. There could be a connection there. International skulduggery. A pity our late friend had no teeth for Jourdain to inspect; there's no mistaking Soviet dentistry.'

There was a discreet police guard on the Villa Montarnaud. The iron gates, normally wide open, were now linked together with a chain. Andreas had to park on the bend, and when he got out a uniformed man stepped on to the drive from the shrubbery, spoke a few words with him and then opened up. As they drove down to the lakeside they could see that there were early lights on in the villa, although the steel shutters cut off full sight of the rooms.

'Andreas,' Siân said in a small voice, 'the police chief said you were up at the house this morning.'

'Yes. Monique let me in. She had come to clear up. I'd been ringing at the door, hoping you'd be with Madame Zuelig. I didn't know she'd gone away, and I needed to report the missing dinghy.'

'So you went in and—'

'While I was phoning, Monique noticed the crossbow had gone. *L'arbalète*. At first I couldn't remember what the word meant. But I'd already seen the—the body, down at the sluice gates, and suddenly it all came together.'

'And I was missing too, so you thought . . .'

'I never quite believed anything so—unspeakable.'

The car had come within control distance of the garage and the automatic door began to slide upwards. 'There's her car,' Andreas said, leaning forward to stare at the Mercedes. 'I never saw the significance of that before, because I didn't know of her plans to go away.'

'She said she was hiring a smaller one,' Siân assured him. 'Something less noticeable for a woman travelling on her own.'

'Did you see it?'

144

'No. She left on Thursday morning before I was up. Wednesday night I'd come back late after supper with the botanists, so I slept in late.'

'I see. And the hired car wasn't parked in the open?'

'No. I expect someone delivered it just before she was due to leave. I didn't get out to the garden until almost nine. Klara had left me a key. I was to let the removals men in when they came for the piano. I didn't notice anything wrong up there then.' She grimaced. 'I mean, no blood anywhere or things disarranged. So doesn't that mean that if there was some kind of violence, it happened later, on Thursday night, after we'd all gone?'

'*All?*'

'Klara, me, Monique, the men who came for the piano.' She sounded a little breathless in her haste to cover up.

Andreas was frowning, conjuring up a picture of the events. 'Possibly; it could have happened after that, but you weren't actively searching for blood as the police were. It could have been that you noticed nothing amiss because the place had been put straight afterwards. Did you go into the bathroom off the kitchen corridor, or down the cellar steps?'

She shook her head, uneasy again at mention of the cellar. That was where Freddy had been hiding. 'I—I didn't go right down into the cellar, but I pushed the door shut and locked it.'

She knew at once she had said too much. Her fingerprints were probably on the key and the panels, for the police to check on. But now she'd claimed to have locked the door, and it must have been found forced, as Freddy left it after going at it with the iron stake. The police hadn't mentioned that detail. Was that a trap? Perhaps they were waiting for her to let slip some reference to it.

'Siân, darling, it's been a terrible ordeal for you.' Andreas was holding her close again, stilling her trembling. 'Are you cold?'

She wanted to hammer at him with her fists and shout, 'No, I'm bloody terrified. It has to have happened Thursday night, or else I spent it alone with a killer up at La Cure!'

145

Instead she groped around in her head for a neutral gear and forced herself into it. 'Tired, I think. Hungry, perhaps.' It sounded ungracious. She tried again. 'Let's get some food inside us and turn in. Tomorrow's soon enough for working things out.'

He helped her from the car, switched off the garage lights and followed her up the stairs, remembering the last time, when the boathouse had been so eerily quiet and empty. 'Tomorrow,' he echoed. 'I've promised that tomorrow we'd lunch at David's.'

'David?' She couldn't place any David.

'You didn't actually meet. He gave me a lift into work once.'

That David. Well, no one important. 'You can call it off, can't you? Under the circumstances.'

'That's out of the question. His wife will have arranged everything. She has a baby to cope with as well.'

'Andreas, I don't think I could stand that sort of thing just now. Explain to them. They'll take a rain check.'

His jaw had gone very square. 'Too late. I just phoned to confirm it's on. We shall simply have to make an effort to seem normal, that's all.'

She stared at him and felt something like despair. *Make an effort* to seem normal! Because nothing was normal any more. Not she, nor Andreas, nor the chilling things that had been happening all round them.

He went off to shower while she warmed up soup from a tin and made a pile of buttered toast. She had changed into a housecoat and was beginning to feel more relaxed, when the doorbell buzzed. Through the glass panel, against the last streaks of a vivid sunset, she saw square shoulders and a jauntily tilted, neat head. She opened up to find it was Fourneval's assistant, the one he called Gilbert. He gave his cheeky smile. '*Madame, je regrette.*'

'Monsieur?'

He was sorry to disturb them again so soon.

Andreas had joined them at the door, looking like Greek thunder and kilted in a bath-towel, water gleaming among the dark hairs on his barrel chest. 'What now?' he growled.

146

Gilbert pointed outwards to a section of lake taped off between orange buoys. 'Can you keep clear of there? Our divers have brought up something interesting and there may be more. They'll start in again tomorrow when the bottom's had a chance to settle. There's not much detritus so early in the year, but what's there gets stirred up when they've been down for some time poking about.'

'What did they find?' Siân asked falteringly.

'I thought you might like to see it, might recognize it from somewhere.' He clicked his fingers and a man in a shiny wetsuit, with goggles pushed up into his hair, materialized and opened a package wrapped in plastic. It was heavy and about forty centimetres high: a bronze statuette of a rearing horse.

'Slightly damaged at the base,' Gilbert pointed out.

Siân shuddered. 'But what has this to do with—?'

'The blunt instrument,' he said cheerfully. 'Or so we think. Not so blunt at the edges, of course. And very solid. Have you ever seen it before?'

She realized she had, and nodded. 'In Klara Zuelig's drawing-room. It stood on a little table between the drinks cabinet and the window. There was another bronze on the opposite side of the room; of a horse grazing.'

'When did you last see it?'

She closed her eyes. Which of the several times she had been in that room? On the Thursday morning there had been one or two dust sheets already in use, and the rest in a pile, still folded. Had she actually looked in that direction?

The Chinese foreman had stood over there, out of the way while his men shrouded the legless piano. He'd been carrying something—a clipboard—and he'd put it down. On the embroidered mat covering the little table's centre. There had been nothing else on there with it!

She looked at Gilbert with horror and he saw at once what had been going through her mind. 'So it wasn't there on Thursday morning?'

'No, but—but the dead man was *shot*, with a crossbow, wasn't he? Nobody said anything about a blunt instrument.'

Andreas touched her arm. 'There were two blood types

found. So they think there may be another body. Or at least someone badly injured.'

'A dead body,' Gilbert said decisively. 'Otherwise why take the bronze out and drop it in the lake? It wasn't used to weight anything down. So a second body is what we now have to look for. I'm very sorry, madame, but tomorrow we shall have to start digging.'

He eyed her with challenge, a sad smile pulling at the mobile mouth. 'Where you planned your rock garden. It's the only place on the property where the ground has been recently disturbed.'

She stared back at him, hardly taking in his words, her mind still agape over the realization that it was *Wednesday* night that murder had been done. They wouldn't bother her about the following night up at La Cure, and she had an alibi up till midnight herself for the time in question. But Freddy—Freddy had admitted being up at the villa then, had hidden overnight in the cellar. He could have been there at the time of the murder. Had she all along been covering up for the killer?

CHAPTER 5

Pierre Fourneval could not settle to television or a book. Restlessness was part of the price he paid for an active mind, which when there was intriguing mystery in the air became hyperactive. This evening he was more of a prey than ever to frustration because Ginette was away, visiting her elderly parents, and the house felt empty without her.

When Gilbert telephoned to report the divers' discovery of the bronze horse, he felt the case pulling at him again. Down in Geneva they were all beavering away at it, and because of seniority he was expected to stay apart, wait for what they produced. A good team, and by tomorrow there would be reinforcements to poke and pry and turn up facts. What he needed now was to start moving about such facts as they already had, combining them, fantasizing a little on menus which these ingredients might produce.

'Gilbert,' he said on impulse, 'knock off and go home. Why not make a détour out this way? Come in for a drink.'

Better two heads than one. He needed counter-argument when the ideas started coming yeastily alive. Already he felt alerted, aware that discovery of the weapon and the girl's statement taken together fixed the crime almost certainly for the night of Wednesday/Thursday. (Unless the bronze had been removed in advance for a premeditated attack, which was most unlikely.) The primary fact to note from the incident's dating was that by then Klara Zuelig had not left on her holiday, and the inference was that she must have been, in some role, at the centre of the action.

He could barely wait to let Gilbert get seated and sniff appreciatively at the cognac he poured him before he started in on his theme. 'So now we have the time and the place. It remains to assemble the cast and recreate the drama. From an embarrassment of characters, we need only two victims and one killer.'

'One-plus,' Gilbert dared to contradict. 'Because of the disposal question. The O+ blood was mainly in the ground-floor bathroom. The body it came from was, we believe, transfixed by a crossbow bolt to the floor of the dinghy down at the boathouse jetty. That's quite a way to carry what was probably a healthy, mature, male body.'

'Unless he walked down with the murderer and was finished off there.'

They considered this, but neither of them liked it. 'The drive continues down to the boathouse,' Fourneval suggested. 'There were cars available.'

'You are supposing that the body was driven down. Yes, perhaps. We found faint tyre marks in loose sand on the macadam down there, but only of the Mercedes and the two Vassilakis cars.'

'There was a van called as well, to load the piano on Thursday morning.'

'It evidently reversed into the drive from the road. So it left no tyre marks, because it's only at the lower end that there's any sand deposit.'

'So either one of the cars you mentioned was used, or two people carried the body down by the shorter path. But couldn't one of the carriers have ended as the second victim?'

Gilbert grinned. 'No, because the body we haven't yet found—blood group AB+—was attacked in the drawing-room and the killer would then have had to dispose of *that* one single-handed.'

'The same problem again. You're right, of course, so I'll grant you your two victims and two killers.'

'I think it more likely there was a single killer and an assistant. There doesn't appear to have been a major rough-house at the villa. Nothing broken except a lock on the cellar door, which probably has a simple domestic explanation.'

'Has it?' Fourneval frowned. 'I can't imagine it being left unmended in a well-run household. How do you account for it?'

'It had been forced from the cellar side, which had no other outlet. Someone inadvertently locked in while choosing a wine perhaps.'

'Or deliberately restrained?' Fourneval half-closed his eyes, summoning the scene, but he couldn't put faces to the shadowy figures. 'So, supposing that visitors called to wish Klara Zuelig *bon voyage* before her holiday, we could have quite a crowd to choose from.'

'Including anyone with a real or imagined grievance against her. And she seems to have made plenty of enemies.'

'Petitioners,' Fourneval said thoughtfully. 'It was their last chance to get their views known before she went on holiday next morning. Protesters, even.'

'But they didn't have to be there *en masse*. They could have arrived one after the other, some possibly overlapping.'

'And some leaving before the main event, but possibly aware of which actors were still on the stage? How dangerous for them! Tell me who these people were.'

'Right.' Gilbert leaned forward, elbows on wide-spread knees, counting them off on his fingers. 'There would be Klara Zuelig herself; probably her ex-husband Victor, blustering and panicky over threatened disaster to the Maison Duro-chat; possibly the other two partners, his cousin Philippe and the formidable Kitty Wilson. Then Klara's brother Klaus, the banker, might well have dropped in to finalize arrangements. The concierge Régnier was also seen wandering in the general direction of the villa, ranting and raving, poor fellow, because he felt abandoned. I don't know if we ought to include the two remaining tenants of the town house which the Zueligs intended selling, but we'll throw them in for good measure: an Irishman called O'Diarmid and Philippe Durochat's ex-wife and present mistress, Céline. I'm sure you've heard of that amusing little scandal.'

'That makes a possible eight.'

'Plus any other unknowns who might have taken offence at La Zuelig's proposed new property-free life-style.'

'I wouldn't call that stage bare boards! We have far too many characters to fit into one scene. Can we group them into possible sets; two victims, one-plus killers? In view of the then prevalent mood,' Fourneval said, swirling the remaining brandy fiercely round in his globe, 'Klara Zuelig is undoubtedly the favoured candidate for victim, but who would qualify for the male torso with O+ blood?'

'How about brother Klaus, springing to her defence and being overpowered in his turn?' Gilbert offered with relish. 'Except—' and his face fell—'that that fat cat is still lapping at his cream bowl down among the bankers of the city. Who is your fancy?'

'Faithful retainer Régnier, suddenly remembering his loyalty to the family and regarded as expendable by the others.'

'But he's a survivor too.'

'So, who is missing?' Fourneval demanded.

'Of the likely group, no one officially. But I find Philippe's explanation of Victor's absence in Paris questionable, and Madame Kitty is distinctly vitriolic on the subject. I have instructed Bernard to keep her under pressure. She may eventually fire off with some useful revelation.'

'Klara-Victor-Philippe-Kitty,' the Chef de Police Cantonale considered. 'How is that for a quartet? The first two as victims, the second two in collusion. As surviving partners, they could only benefit from Victor's death in addition to Klara's, surely? Had Klara actually put a signature to her intentions? And what provisions about the business were made in Victor's will?'

'I have appointments with the lawyers on Monday,' Gilbert said gloomily. 'There is no violating their calvinistic sabbath.'

'Thank God it will be Sunday any moment now, since I never got to bed at all last night. However, I did snatch a nap in the jacuzzi this morning,' Pierre admitted.

'You could have drowned. Go to bed now, *patron*.' Gilbert swallowed the last of his drink and rose, presuming on their long association to give his chief advice. 'The case will still be around tomorrow, and you have eyes like pee-holes in the snow.'

Sabbath or not, next day was a working one for Fourneval. When he entered his outer office he found Gilbert already there, hands clasped behind his neck and smiling.

'I've cast our drama,' he claimed, 'and just written the synopsis. It happened this way: ex-husband Victor arrived, hoping to reason with Klara or bully her into some alternative decision. He'd been drinking and he went too far, actually struck her, making her nose bleed violently. (That's your AB+ group blood on the drawing-room footstool. There was also a splosh on the carpet which was later washed off.)

'They then adjourned to the ground-floor bathroom, Victor seeming abashed and helping Klara stem the flow. She managed unobtrusively to reach for, and secrete, a nail file from the toilet cabinet. Purely as a defensive measure, of course. But when the drunken Victor again got rough she plunged it into some available part of him which just happened to be a vital point. To her horror she realized she'd killed him. Plenty of O+ blood getting between the floor tiles, and Klara left surviving, to clear up afterwards.'

'Victim One, Killer One,' Pierre Fourneval scored. 'Go on.'

'While she is wringing her hands and all that business, her brother Klaus turns up. Victor had pushed his way in, leaving the front door ajar, so all Klaus has to do is wander in and shout for Klara. She falls on his neck weeping and shows him the corpse of her ex-husband. They decide that silence is golden, with more carats than a charge of unlawful killing in self-defence, so they start to clear up the mess.'

'Leaving the front door conveniently open for the arrival of victim number two.'

'No. Klaus Zuelig is a methodical fuddy-duddy with an eye to detail, the ideal accomplice for taking precautions and removing traces of any dark deed. Klara—who else?— goes to work with the beeswax polish and washes the carpet, bathroom floor etc. Klaus collects the refuse for dumping in the lake.'

Fourneval beat at his head theatrically. 'Marvellous! Let me finish it. They are loading the body and so on into the Mercedes, prior to taking it down to the dinghy, when— along comes A WITNESS. Now who have you cast for that?'

'Unfortunately all the best possible victims have survived. But don't jeer, because now we *don't need* a second corpse. We have the requisite two types of blood in the right places, and two worthies to carry the heavy body off. So how do you like that?'

'Quite your best reconstruction yet. So then Klaus returns home unseen and Klara leaves early next morning, as planned, for her lone French holiday—a pair of convincing innocents.' Fourneval's voice was at its most ironic.

'Why not?'

'Because Klaus Zuelig has a gold-mounted alibi. Nothing less than a Consular Reception with three hundred witnesses to swear he dined and danced and dallied from dusk until the early hours. I checked, after you left last night. A number of my most reliable acquaintances can back him up.'

'Highly suspicious,' Gilbert declared grandly. 'I like an alibi that's a challenge.'

'This one's unassailable. But there's another drawback too. The bronze horse. It didn't get a part written in.' Fourneval continued into his private office, leaving the door ajar. 'Try again, Gilbert. Something more Hitchcock this time.'

*

The news of Subarsky's defection to the West—country as yet unspecified—was broadcast on the ten a.m. news. Warned of it by a call from the Mess, Pierre Fourneval heard the last of the bulletin, then with relief scored out the Russian's name from the list of claimants for the sluice-gates torso. His elimination removed the dreaded possibility of an international crime. Now there would be no need for any cover-up, and it was totally acceptable to proceed with solving the crime and using reasonable publicity.

There was still no one to vouch for Victor Durochat's activities since Tuesday afternoon when, according to Philippe, he had been shattered by the realization of Klara's power to embarrass the Maison Durochat. Madame Kitty claimed to have spoken to Victor twice since then by telephone, but there was good reason to regard this as partner's bluff. She struck Fourneval as a woman who would lie through her teeth with ice-cold calm if it were of benefit to the business.

It had been confirmed from medical records that Durochat's general blood group was the same as that of the corpse, but the Chef de Police did not regard this as conclusive. Perhaps it was too convenient, therefore one could easily deceive oneself.

The man was definitely not at home. A search of his apartment had given no clue to his sudden disappearance. Yet for some indefinable reason Fourneval hesitated to make the obvious assumption.

Why so reluctant? he demanded of himself. Gilbert's overall thesis had been so reasonable: Durochat, after the histrionics at work, reinforcing himself with liquor and perhaps legal advice, encircled by further frustrations, rushing up to the villa to threaten his ex-wife, or worse. And she, alone and packing for her departure, finding attack the best method of defence.

Fourneval picked up the pathologist's report and re-read the relevant sentences: death almost instantaneous . . . not as the result of the crossbow bolt, but of a previous wound caused by the direct penetration of the left ventricle of the heart by a long, flat-tipped instrument driven in upwards

154

with considerable force. Possibly, he suggested, a screwdriver or chisel. Either the blow had been made with precise anatomical knowledge, or else it was an extremely lucky one.

Gilbert had guessed a nail file, because such an object might have been to hand in the bathroom. They would need to check with the lab people on its suitability.

The crossbow bolt had been fired into the body, almost obliterating the earlier injury, anything up to an hour later. The implication was that the killer had wished to disguise the manner of the killing, but it had a further quite separate and horrific purpose: namely, to pin the corpse to some wooden framework, like a butterfly specimen for display. There being a need to hold the body rigid while some other operation was undertaken? Some essential phase in the disposal business?

And further tests had confirmed that the wood was indeed part of the outer curve of a small boat's bow.

So why a boat? Well, the lake was good and deep at its centre. One could simply take the body out, weight it, and roll it over the side. For all the police department knew, the lake was already the depository for countless bodies over the past few centuries. Certainly Calvin's political embarrassments had tended to end as corpses in sacks committed to water. So, this recent nameless killer had made use of a dinghy conveniently to hand, had sailed it out to unload the corpse, when—

No; hadn't *sailed*. Vassilakis had said the sails were still bagged in the boathouse. Had the dinghy an outboard motor, then? They must verify that, but it seemed unlikely, when the family already had a powered craft. It would be quieter to row, but in a dinghy there wouldn't have been enough room, with a corpse spreadeagled at one's feet. No, there had to be a second boat, towing the dinghy with the body in it! Yes, he liked that; and the corpse fixed to the pierced bottom boards, which guaranteed that the holed boat would ultimately fill with water as it was pulled along. Just before it went down, the painter would be cast off and the leading craft go free.

Yes, that was a vastly improved scenario. So what of the extra boat written in? Dared he assume the killer had arrived in it, intending to leave by water too? Or had it begun as the victim's transport, and the killer had no need to come back?

But in that case, what happened to the vehicle the killer arrived in, if any? Had the killer come on foot, by bus, or taxi? If a car, he would have had to come back to fetch it later.

While on the subject of transport, they hadn't yet traced the 'smaller car' Klara Zuelig had ordered for her holiday. There was no booking for her wtih any hire car firm locally, so perhaps she had borrowed it—the spare car in some multiple-car family of her acquaintance. In which case, a public announcement must go out, or it could take weeks to catch up with her, the woman having been so reticent about her private arrangements. Inquiries made for her through the French police had so far brought a blank equal to that following attempts to locate her ex-husband.

Fourneval pushed a button on his desk and invited Gilbert in to act again as sounding-board for his further thoughts. The younger man sat forward in his chair, hands clasped loosely between parted knees while he listened, staring at the floor. When Fourneval stopped talking he hummed for a second or two like a computer between phases of action. Then: 'Can we go back to the blood groups? We have two kinds, with the corpse (possibly Victor) having bled in the bathroom and very slightly marking the wall beside the cellar steps.

'Now, why should Victor go down into the cellar? Was he carrying something down? Or did he go to fetch something? It doesn't seem to fit in with a flaming row with his ex-wife. And then the forced lock on the cellar door. Ever since you drew attention to it last night I've been trying to see what it means.'

'We know there is no body in the cellar,' Fourneval said firmly. 'Not so much as a beetle's. Bernard doesn't overlook things like that. And the door was forced from the inside, don't forget. Which may account for a small spot or two of

156

blood. Someone at sometime was shut in and broke out. Someone with Victor's blood type.'

'And according to the maid the marks weren't there Tuesday. But how, in the middle of the mother and father of a family row, could La Zuelig have persuaded her ex to trot off to the cellar for something? All very conveniently so that she could lock him in.'

'The newly divorced have been known to approach insanity over the disposition of property,' Fourneval said drily. 'Perhaps he had a sudden urge to push for custody of the lawnmower or a crate of claret.'

'So what was down there that might fit the bill? There was wine, of course, but apart from that, mainly junk. Winter sports stuff, tennis net, an empty rabbit hutch, various dismantled gadgets that the family had lost interest in but not totally discarded.'

Fourneval sat up abruptly, looked sharply across at the younger officer. 'You know, I like that word "dismantled". Let's go out there now and take another, more informed look at what's still in the cellar, keeping in mind the screwdriver (or chisel) quoted in the pathologist's report.'

They found skis, in adult and junior sizes; a *luge* painted bright red with a buckled left runner; various garden furniture and canopies; three bicycles; a child's swing and its tubular frame; a great number of bottles of wine on several long racks against the outer wall. One rack was pulled slightly forward and an irregular shrouded object leaned behind it on the stonework. The swept floor gave no clue to recent activity, but this time Fourneval was taking no chances. He reached a long arm across and twitched the damask cover aside. 'What the—! A *harp*?'

On closer examination it proved to be the strung frame of a piano. Gilbert passed his fingers lightly across the strings and they gave off a ghostly *glissando*. Fourneval stiffened, reached forward and deliberately plucked the start of a major scale. '*In tune*, would you believe?'

'Which means it hasn't been here any great time.'

'Take the cover right off.'

Gilbert gave it a tug and this was followed by a metallic clatter. Something relatively small fell to the floor and rolled out from behind the wine rack.

'Luck!' Fourneval breathed in a voice of awe. 'That's all it takes a little of, when you have genius already.'

Gilbert was opening out a clean handkerchief to lift the heavy screwdriver gingerly by its centre. He looked up. 'So the piano was disembowelled before it went. But the removals men would have noticed the weight was wrong.'

'Unless,' Fourneval put his thoughts into words, 'there was a compensatory load: another foreign body, in fact.'

Old Antoine Régnier had made the removals arrangements. As the town house was on their way back they called there in person instead of phoning. They found the concierge in a fever, barely able to creep to the door to let them in, but there was nothing feeble about his outpourings. Their wanton souls were verbally buffeted and exhorted to penitence before the doctor they summoned could arrive to sedate the old man. Burning with zeal, he had overridden their requests for information and provided instead texts of admonition.

The affair of the missing piano would have to wait. 'Patience,' Fourneval had advised Gilbert, quite untypically. 'Tomorrow will do.'

CHAPTER 6

Out at the Villa Montarnaud there were two groups hard at it soon after dawn, the diggers and the divers. Siân was secretly relieved to be getting away from the domain for lunch, however much the idea of making small talk with strangers daunted her while she hadn't full command of her mind.

At unexpected moments she found herself reliving scenes of the past few days. Every time Andreas caught her staring into space he would come across and gather her into his

158

grizzly embrace, and then she was afraid of softening too far and letting slip things best left concealed.

Not that she was protecting a guilty person. It was more that any stranger who hadn't seen the vulnerable side of Freddy, as she had done, was bound to be critical. She believed she understood his painting now, the one Professor Theodorakis had said made a 'valid statement'. It meant that there were things in life which could injure an innocent, and the horror lived on in dark corners to haunt you. Freddy had said it again, as self-excuse, in the macabre story he had told her. It was an allegory, and at the same time a disguised bit of autobiography. There was some happening in his own childhood which had permanently scarred him, a parallel to what the little girl had seen in the chair when she turned on the light.

Siân didn't feel ready yet to share all this with her husband. Although she didn't think of Freddy as a real man, mature and demanding as Andreas was, he was male and she had shared a hard, narrow bed with him overnight. It wasn't a recommended risk for a bride of three weeks, much less one married to a possessive Greek, however enlightened.

Andreas was aware of the gap between them and tried to bridge it with a threadbare brand of humour. 'Actually,' he said, standing foursquare, fists on hips, and glaring uphill at the excavations in progress, 'this could save you a lot of hard work. Why not ask them to drop in a load of humus while they're at it?'

Siân didn't comment, wondering whether she would ever have the heart to continue her project. There might be no body discovered in the ground she had chosen, but the idea was upsetting enough.

'When must we leave for this lunch with your friends?' she demanded abruptly.

'I think twelve-forty will do. It isn't more than twenty minutes by car. Have you something in mind for before then?'

'I'd like to look in on Madame Durochat in Geneva. If I find she's out, I can always go to church instead.'

She thought at first he would suggest coming with her,

but he was more keen on seeing what the police might turn up. 'There's petrol in the tank,' he said, handing her the Peugeot's keys from his pocket.

It was a cloudless sky and, even as early as ten, the warmest day yet since they had come to Switzerland. The cream and gold façades of the Old Town basked under a clangour of bells that chimed or pealed or puritanically tolled from a dozen directions, and cars buzzed on warm tarmac like homing honey bees.

A day designed for delights, but at the Zuelig town house the blue-grey uniforms were in charge. At sight of them Siân almost turned back, but she was called in and asked her business by a blond officer like a young Siegfried from some wartime German film. She thought better of admitting that she'd come to seek out Niall O'Diarmid, and gave the same reason for her visit as she'd offered Andreas.

Céline Durochat was at home, they told her, and allowed her to go up to the first floor. Their own presence, it appeared, concerned the little office of the concierge near the entrance. Siân came out of the lift to find Céline's door ajar. When she pressed the bell there was no response, except after a few seconds the sound of shoes on the stairs behind her.

Madame Dorochat, slightly breathless, came down the last few steps and peered at Siân in the shadows. '*Ah, c'est vous, madame!*' She smiled her relief. Perhaps the police had been harassing her. 'Come in, come in,' she pressed. '*Quelle horreur que cette affaire à la Villa Montarnaud!* Excuse me, but I forget all my English, I am so *étourdie*.'

She was more flustered than dazed, and Siân wondered how many flights she had come down. From Niall's attic, or one of the two empty apartments in between? She seemed somehow deflated. Siân had expected her to be almost relishing this new disaster as a super-scandal.

Suddenly Céline managed to catch up with her image. She pulled a face and threw out her hands. 'Poor child, 'ow terrifying for you. I 'ear you were *there*, living in the boat'ouse. Did you see anything, 'ear anything *extraordinaire?*'

'Nothing,' Siân said firmly. 'No one seems certain when it happened, or even exactly what, but I must have been away. It was my husband who walked in on it afterwards and informed the police. I'd gone off the same day as Madame Zuelig, which was lucky as it turned out.'

'Yes. Yes, I see. One moment, madame, and I will fetch some fresh ice for our drinks.' She put together the makings of a dry Martini and turned her back on the girl to fill their glasses. 'I am not clear what it was your 'usband found at the villa. The *Tribune* gave only 'eadlines and 'ints.'

Siân grimaced. 'The crossbow had disappeared. You heard about part of a man's body being found in the lake by the Pont de la Machine? Andreas was there when they fished it out, so he saw the crossbow bolt and the bits of smashed boat. Another connection was that the dinghy was missing from the jetty by our boathouse. So the police looked over the villa and found signs of violence. But they don't know who, or why, or exactly when, even now. It's horrible. I don't know how they will break the news to Madame Zuelig when they find her.'

'She 'as not telephoned, then?'

'There's no one there to take a call. And we hadn't had our line restored when she left.'

'Nobody tells me anything,' Céline complained unfairly. 'I 'adn't 'eard until the late night news that you were living at the boat'ouse. A Greek doctor and 'is wife, it said. So I guessed. But 'ow alarming for you, all this. And police everywhere, one supposes. 'Ere they crucify old Antoine. The concierge, you know? 'E is a little unmarbled, as you say. With this terrible news about the 'ouse being sold, 'e loses 'is memory. 'E was gone for days. They find 'im up at Vandœuvres, out your way, with 'is feet all bleeding because 'e 'as walked for days, it seems. And 'e is preaching to an orchard; yes, to *fruit trees*! 'E thinks 'e is Calvin again, and we are all to be sent to 'ellfire, the Zueligs especially.'

'I thought he was devoted to the family. What happened?'

'Before she goes on 'oliday, Klara 'ands over 'er 'alf of the 'ouse to 'er brother Klaus. And Klaus, 'e as no sentiment. 'E will get us out and sell it for a great amount. Now that the Professor is dead, also their mother, there are only Monsieur O'Diarmid and myself 'ere any more. And old Antoine, 'oo is mad as a goat and will be thrown away like last week's rubbish. Well, it is in'uman, that is what it is.' She was rocking herself with emotion.

'And Antoine has nothing but his rooms here? I'm sure Madame has made some provision for him.'

''Ow can 'e tell that? She 'as said nothing. Nothing to any of us. What am *I* to do, I ask you? I 'ave no 'ome now, no 'usband. She does not think of me, because she 'as everything she wants. She 'as always been like that. *C'est dégoûtant, ça!*'

She thrust herself from her chair, screwing up her face myopically. 'You 'ave not finished your drink, madame. I drink too fast, myself. So 'e says, *mon cher mari divorcé.*' Her voice was climbing to a petulant squeak. Not the smooth mask of the doting little ex-wife any more, but unleashing all the rancour which the words had previously concealed.

Céline seized the bottle by its neck and refilled her own glass, not bothering with such refinements as ice, olives or lemon. It struck Siân that her hostess, at whatever speed, had been well liquored before her own arrival. 'Is Monsieur O'Diarmid at home?' she asked, to change the subject.

Céline's hand hung suspended in the air. She frowned. ''Im upstairs? Always 'is *sacrée musique*! Yes, I 'ave just been to complain. So 'e stop.'

'Maybe I should go up and thank him for the concert ticket.'

Madame Durochat waved her glass, slopping Martini on her knee. Her eyes narrowed. 'Per'aps 'e 'as a woman there. 'E would not come to the door, rude man. Most weekends, *pfui!*' She shrugged and pouted. 'But you can try. Maybe you find 'im in bed.'

Warned off, Siân didn't fancy hanging around to add to anyone's reputation, but she had to know if he'd deliberately tried to place her as a contact for Subarsky. Surely just a couple of forthright questions could settle that.

She stood up and returned her glass to the tray, thanked Céline, who was watching her with glazed intentness. She didn't attempt to rise as Siân started to leave, turned,

162

thanked her again. The girl went out, pulling the door shut behind.

It was quite silent on the landing; no whirr of lift, no music escaping down the stairwell from O'Diarmid's attic. When a door on the ground floor opened and shut it released a low rumble of male voices as suddenly cut off.

Down there the police were still grilling the concierge. Did they seriously believe that old Régnier was involved in the Montarnaud violence? Could the shock of the Zuelig's destroying his security (as it must seem to him) have tipped the precarious balance of his sin-obsessed mind? Had he really gone berserk about 'the Lord's work of retribution'? More likely that the police, balked of a serious prey, were merely enjoying an easy revenge on the world outside their closed order.

She felt outraged for the inadequate old man, who should surely be receiving comfort and medical aid, not an inquisition. This must be the way false confessions were obtained, by force of numbers and persistent repetition of what authority wanted accepted as truth. It made her so angry that her discretion fled. She determined to beard O'Diarmid, whatever his present state, and demand to know what he thought he was setting up in passing on Theo's ticket.

She ran upstairs before the anger could cool and, still breathless, rapped on the panels of Niall's door. There was no sound from inside, but she felt sure he was listening for her departing footsteps. She knelt and opened the letter-box flap. It pushed inwards against some felty fabric which obscured the view and stopped draughts. 'Niall!' she called through. 'It's Siân Vassilakis. I need to talk to you.'

Then she heard the clatter of some small metal object disturbed—brass ashtray on table?—knife on kitchen counter? She couldn't define it, but she knew he was there, listening to her listening to the ensuing silence.

She waited, called again, but—for whatever reason—he wouldn't declare himself. 'Damn you then, Niall O'Diarmid,' she said under her breath, picked up her shoulder-bag from the floor and went away furious.

As she reached the ground floor the concierge's office

door opened. Siân looked right through into the tidy little bachelor-flat beyond. Two men in white jackets were manoeuvring a stretcher round an angled doorway, followed by a middle-aged woman carrying a doctor's bag. So at last the poor creature was to get caring treatment.

As he was carried past, she glimpsed grey, drawn features above the wispy beard. '*Bon courage, monsieur,*' she said firmly, and his eyes seemed to register the message with bewilderment.

'He has enough for Genghis Khan,' said a droll voice in English from the interior. Leaning against the door jamb was the stylishly dressed Chef de Police.

Siân regarded him coldly. 'I doubt,' she said, 'if Genghis Khan had to suffer such an inquisition.' She would admit it was cheap satisfaction to catch Fourneval open-mouthed, but at least it discharged a little of her anger.

He walked beside her to the street door. 'He has told us plenty,' Fourneval said seriously. 'The difficulty is to get him to stop. We all know now the folly of our ways and the ultimate price we shall pay for them. I wish he could work on some of the hard sinners I come across.'

'Poor old man. I suppose you heard about the house being put up for sale? It must have been a terrible shock to him.'

'I hear most things eventually, yes.' Was there some underlying threat in those words? She listened carefully for what was to come, but he went off at a tangent that had no immediate relevance to her. 'I heard about the business property too, from a young employee who had fallen out with Durochat-boss. I think that by the time the taxman has unravelled certain claims, and they are obliged to pay a genuine rent for the galleries, the Maison Durochat will be in some embarrassment. Which gives for to think, as we are supposed to say in French.'

'To think what, monsieur?'

He waved his hands elegantly. 'Just to think. Knowing is another thing. I should like to believe that in an hour or so we shall know for certain the identity of the second body. Thanks to that poor deluded old man.'

164

She looked hard at him. The policeman's face had lost all trace of sardonic humour.

'For a brief moment Régnier remembered who he was,' Fourneval said simply. 'Next time we talk I hope he will tell us where the second body is.'

Back in the car she made a wide sweep of the Rive Gauche to give herself time before re-encountering Andreas. Sun and the sabbath had brought out the well-dressed family crowds, strolling in little groups, waiting at piers for boats, lining the lakeside to feed ducks or swans. Among all these anonymous, sunlit faces there sprang out at her a little dispirited trio seated on a *brasserie* terrace as she pulled up for the lights. It was the *cher mari divorcé* himself, seated morosely between a fleshy blonde half his age and a small child with a pony-tail. All three were frozen into dejected silence. Not so much washed-up survivors as the recently condemned, was her impression.

They reflected so accurately the despair already settled on Céline and the old concierge that she thought for a moment her mind had projected them, but the man stirred and plucked nervously at his moustache, just as she'd seen him do among the shop's crystal display. It was indeed Durochat the lesser.

So where was Victor? Was his the body to which the police expected Régnier to lead them? But why should Régnier kill Victor, if it was Klara and her brother who had overthrown his world? Did he blame the husband for the marriage breakdown which had led to all this? Or had he merely killed the nearest to hand when his brain went?

And if he had been the maniac at the villa, wasn't it most reasonable to suppose that the two victims he had chanced upon up there were Victor and Klara fighting over the Maison Durochat's fate? Which would mean that the male torso in the lake was Victor's, and Klara's the one Fourneval was now out to discover. It was too horrible!

Klara had certainly not deserved that, even if unwittingly she'd pushed the old man too far. If she had considered him at all—and surely she must have—there would be some

165

provision made which he had yet to learn of. Unfortunately, gossip on what she intended had run ahead of her lawyer's provisions.

All that Klara was guilty of was finally to say to her husband, 'Enough!' and attempt to throw off the habitual submission of years. She'd had a right to make a stand against Victor's outsize ego. But it didn't end there. It rebounded on others who were already hard pressed.

Pushed too far. The words drummed in Siân's mind as the Peugeot took the hill towards the villa. She still wasn't sure who was pushing and who pushed. Damn Fourneval! Why hadn't he followed up the clue of the blood types? Klara had once borne a child. There must be a record somewhere of which group she belonged to.

She had the question ready on her lips as soon as she saw Andreas. He left his balcony seat in the sunshine and came down when he saw the car reappear. 'I'm sure there will be a record,' he agreed. 'Perhaps they have already checked and found her blood is different from the samples they collected. They would hardly mention a negative detail like that to us.'

'But, Andreas, if the bronze horse had disappeared by Thursday morning, and if it was really used as they think, it must be that the violence occurred while Klara was still there. And either she herself let someone in, or they had a key—which implies Monique or me. Perhaps her brother Klaus as well.' (*And Freddy*, part of her mind insisted.) She stopped, confused.

'What you are afraid of is that Madame Zuelig may never have left the house; that she was killed as well as the unidentified man. Well, if it helps, the police have given up digging. They found nothing there at all.'

She moved restlessly away, staring out over the water to where the white plastic tape twisted and retwisted between the orange marker buoys. She very nearly burst out with a demand to know *Subarsky's* blood group. That would certainly have put the cat among the pigeons. No one had used the name to date. Even the police had referred only to 'a member of the Russian Permanent Delegation'. It was obscene to have to be so careful what you said to your own husband. A lifetime of this would be unthinkable.

'Are you changing for lunch?' Andreas reminded her. 'I'm going like this, casual.'

Siân looked down at her own white cotton slacks and T-shirt striped with turquoise. 'Will this do? I'll just get my jacket.'

She used the few minutes to give her face a cold splash and put on fresh mascara. Any armour at all would help, when she felt so nakedly alone.

She strapped her watch back on her wrist and looked at the time. By now, according to Fourneval, the police might know the identity of the second body.

CHAPTER 7

Andreas drove out in the general direction of the Salèves. 'David rents a cottage on a poultry farm,' Andreas announced. It sounded unpromising.

After a hotch-potch area of mushrooming factories and market gardens, they turned on to a track through more open country. The promised hens eventually revealed themselves to view, then to the ears and finally, faintly, to the nose. Beyond a screen of willows a long, single-storey house stood on a knoll, broad windows turned to the sun, golf umbrellas and lido furniture scattered across a flagged patio pillared with roses already in small bud. The scene was human, comfortable and welcoming, as were the couple who waved and came down to meet them.

David, about thirty, was a little heavy for his less than medium height. He had a chubby face with round, dark-rimmed glasses and a short, unexpectedly sharp nose. His eyebrows and hair were sparse, almost colourless, and he walked with a disguised limp as though it was just one of those things, from birth onwards. He had a way of looking at you, Siân found, as if meeting you made all the difference to him. And Penny was a beauty; lean, long-limbed, her face a sudden presentation of laughing eyes, slanting cheekbones, generous smile. But she didn't use her looks on you; instead she was taking you in, eager to be friendly.

There was also a minute barking monster exhibiting a single bright eye among the wild disarray of its tangled hair. 'Florian,' David introduced it. 'A sort of Yorkshire terrier, we think, which came out extra miniature. No bite, though he sounds fierce enough to scare a bulldog.'

Florian promptly proved the point, provoking a crescendo of wailing from inside the house. 'Come and meet Poppy,' Penny invited. 'Our bilingual baby. She goes *wah* in French and English.'

'Have you called her Poppæa?' Siân inquired, overawed.

Caroline exchanged a guilty glance with David and laughed. 'No, she's Petra really, but David's father has a rather attractive stutter and we liked the sound of it.'

Poppy-Petra proved to be a quite ordinary sort of baby, redfaced and roaring, or else milky-calm when asleep; domineering and defenceless by turns, terrifyingly fragile when you were expected to stand and hold her. 'I don't know anything about this sort of thing,' Siân warned Penny.

'I shouldn't worry. Andreas is more than competent.' Penny was happily mistaking her meaning.

So Andreas had already been here, had handled the tiny creature. He might have been called in for advice, as a doctor; but more likely he'd homed in with the instincts of a prepackaged father. Siân hoped she hadn't been brought here to be sold the rôle of motherhood.

Whatever the motives, she had to admit that the overall experience was enjoyable. David and Penny were easy and natural. There was plenty to discuss since both missed England (David a Winnipeg-born Anglophile), and both were curious about Greece. David knew Athens a little, having been there once for ILO, but it was Crete and how they'd met there that fascinated Penny. About Switzerland they were open-minded, admitting their good fortune in having so safe a place to raise a baby, and had no clever, waspish stories to tell about the medley of nationals David worked among.

168

'I like change,' he modestly claimed. 'I like a challenge.' Siân would have taken him for a good-natured, easygoing, mid-Atlantic nobody, if it hadn't been for what happened after Penny cleared the luncheon table.

She had declined Siân's offer to help with the dishes, because there was a village girl who came in specially, and Penny excused herself to go and feed the ravening Poppy. The last object she removed on going out was Siân's coffee cup and saucer. On the little side table left bare there remained a piece of paper with writing on it.

Siân leaned forward to examine it and froze. On either side of her, David and Andreas sat waiting for her reaction. Taken unawares, she had difficulty in controlling her voice. 'How did this get here?'

David said mildly, 'I put it there. We thought you might like to talk about it.'

We. Andreas and his friend David, in an alliance against her. She looked up and met her husband's eyes. They weren't accusing, nor even puzzled, just patient. 'Why me? I imagine you both know more about it than I ever will,' she said defensively.

'We have ventured some guesses.' Again David was the spokesman. 'Just the same, it would be helpful if you told us the whole story.'

'But I don't know the beginning.' Siân smoothed creases from the paper with an index finger. The writing looked dimmer now, as if it had been well handled since Andreas first set down the list of letters and numbers.

'It would spoil the dénouement if we started the story for you,' David said, smiling. He was still friendly, but there was a vein of authority there that she hadn't recognized before. 'What did you think when you first found it?'

She tried to remember the exact sequence. 'It embarrassed me, because I hadn't been searching my husband's pockets. It simply fell out when I removed a handkerchief for the wash.'

'And when you saw what it was?'

She shook her head. 'I was mystified. It looked like a list, but coded. I meant to ask him about it, but things started happening so fast just then—I think I must have put it in my shoulder-bag to give to Andreas next time I saw him, but when I looked for it later it had gone. I thought I must have lost it when my bag was upset at the concert.'

She suddenly cut off and faced David squarely. '*Subarsky*. He could have taken it. You know all about him, don't you? He's the Russian who's disappeared. What have you done with Subarsky?'

'He's in Ottawa, Siân. He flew out of Zürich with a bodyguard yesterday.' Andreas had taken up the story now. 'When you left me at the Cointrin airport, I met him with David. The original plans had been changed. I was to drive Subarsky to Berne for initial debriefing. He claimed political asylum there.'

'He was Theo's man, then?'

'In a way, and I inherited him. But that was only because inadvertently you had stepped in, Siân. It had been a personal arrangement with Theo: nothing to do with Greece. He was afraid that ill-health might prevent the completion of his plans for Subarsky, so he tried to warn David, and wrote asking him to take over if necessary. Then, within half an hour of sending that note, he had a fatal heart attack. He was driving to work, began to feel unwell, abandoned the car near David's office and tried to get to him. His heart simply gave out on the way.

'It was a natural death all right, and purely coincidental that David worked in the building between the Soviet Mission and WHO. Everyone assumed Theo was hurrying to WHO, but it was really to see David and finalize the departure arrangements for Subarsky. It was his abandoning the car in the road, presumably to avoid a dangerous accident, that made the police think there might be a Russian connection. And Subarsky himself feared the whole plan was blown.'

'All I knew for sure,' David explained, 'was the Russian's identity, that his desired destination was Canada, and that he had supplied—was still supplying—suppressed material dealing with conditions following Chernobyl and earlier disasters on which the West hadn't any data. Despite the comparatively more open policy of the present Soviet government, there is still a great deal of information held back which the whole world is in need of. Nikos Theodorakis, the internationally acclaimed ecologist, was the ideal recipient, especially since the Greek government is not unsympathetic to the Russians. But Papandreou's Socialists would never have agreed to Subarsky's price of secret transfer to the West. Which is why Subarsky approached Theo on a one-to-one basis, and the old chap took it on.'

'He was brave.'

'And so was Subarsky. Lucky he had no family left to suffer any backwash, except an older brother who was involved in early attempts to cool the number four reactor at Chernobyl. The worst has already happened to him. But once he had passed on the collated information, Ivan too acted treasonably in receiving it. If discovered, he would have been sent back immediately to the USSR, tried and probably executed. Just before Theo was ready to move him, Subarsky was notified of his next posting—to Czechoslovakia, back behind the Curtain.

'Once a move from a Western capital is on the cards, a minder is put on the Soviet subject until he's actually on his way. This happened to Subarsky and he was petrified, half convinced that they'd found out about his plans, and too scared to initiate a fresh move towards any influential Westerner.' David grimaced.

'I discovered from his dossier that he was a quite accomplished musician and had obtained tickets for the Conservatoire concerts from one of the staff . . .'

'Who just happened to live in the same house as Professor Theodorakis?'

David nodded. 'Exactly. I don't suppose the Professor confided in Niall, but that young man has a taste for imaginative romance, and when Theodorakis asked to be given the consecutive number to the Russian's seat, he saw himself as breaking into the Big Time of international skulduggery. A volunteer James Bond. Geneva gets some people that way.'

'So when Theo died, Niall O'Diarmid assumed that his

replacement would carry on with the same arrangement?'

'It seems so.' David sounded rueful. Theo must have passed Niall my name and phone number in case of his own inability to complete, but he hadn't got round to saying as much to me. I was acting in the dark, hadn't a notion what the score was when O'Diarmid phoned to say that you, Siân, had made contact.'

She shrugged. 'At the concert Subarsky caught sight of my Greek paperback and greeted me in that language. So, reasonably enough, he'd taken me for Theo's replacement. We started chatting and later went for a drink at a little Czech-owned restaurant.'

'And when my "coded list" got into his hands, he was sure he'd received his departure instructions,' Andreas offered wryly. 'We learned all this from the man himself once David had picked him up. He traced your surname Vassilakis to my office, via the UN lists of new appointments, and managed to evade his minder and ring through direct, frantic because he couldn't decode the cipher.'

'And from then on, Andreas and I fixed it up between us to get him away,' David summarized blandly, making it sound simple.

Siân considered him. David, it seemed, represented what Andreas had referred to as 'Security', and still she didn't see who exactly he worked for, probably never would know.

'I realized there was something peculiar about Theo buying a concert ticket,' Andreas said. 'I remembered he was tone-deaf. He had no interest in music at all.'

'And your "coded list"?' Siân reminded him.

David and Andreas grinned at each other like a pair of fourth-form schoolboys. 'Show her,' urged Andreas.

David reached for a drawstring bag from a shelf behind him and poured its contents over the side table. 'I have a friend along the main road who has a small plastics factory. You passed it coming here. Among other items he designs embossed tiles. But nothing as small as these. These are a one-off, strictly non-commercial order executed for a personal friend of mine.'

Siân picked up the little cream-coloured squares, one at a time: Z_{10}, K_5, V_4, P_3, Z_{10} again . . . As near as dammit, (from the back and except for the figures' colour)—Scrabble tiles!

'Our English Scrabble set hadn't enough of certain letters to make it work with Greek words,' Andreas explained. 'So I worked out how many more of each we would need in Roman capitals to play in either language. Then David had them made up for me. Now I find that a Greek version of the game already exists.

'Siân! Siân, love, what on earth are you crying for?'

On their way home Siân laid a hand on her husband's wrist as he drove. 'Stop somewhere quiet, Andreas. I need to talk to you.'

He had been open with her, at last, about Subarsky, waiting only for news of the defection to break officially. Now she must be as frank herself, and the fact of murder overshadowing the background made complete honesty essential.

Confession wasn't easy for her, but as the details about Freddy came out, hesitantly at first and then in a flood of relief once she found Andreas holding her tight, black-browed with apprehension but fiercely supportive, there was no need to keep anything back.

'Fourneval has to hear this,' Andreas said in a low voice. 'We haven't enough facts to judge the case ourselves. At best this Freddy was there when something happened. He's a material witness. At least he must know who else was present, even if the actions remain in doubt.'

If he hadn't assumed straight off that Freddy was a homicidal maniac, yet he must be considering the possibility that he'd taken an active part in whatever family battle took place. Siân watched the grim face for some clue to how he was thinking. 'You should have seen him, Andreas. I can't believe he's a killer. More a born victim.'

'Why was he hiding in the cellar, then?'

'Because he was scared. He was badly in shock. He's not as tough as most, and he'd either seen, or guessed at,

173

something really horrific. I'd have hidden too. In his place I'd have appeared every bit as witless and unstable to anyone meeting me for the first time. Just think what he could have seen.'

'Murder. Of his own father.'

'Or even both parents, because I'm not sure any more about Klara having gone away. Fourneval said two bodies . . .'

'If Klara and Victor are both dead—' There was a deep, warning note in Andreas's voice—'isn't the son the most likely one to have been the killer? A domestic crime. Time and time again you get this claustrophobic pattern, the intolerable strain of a close love-hate relationship, and the murderous response of a sick young mind.'

She wouldn't accept that Freddy was a psychopath. 'He's just oversensitive,' she insisted. 'Sensitive and rather cut off, like Klara herself.'

Andreas was frowning at her. 'There's something you should know, Siân. While you were getting ready to go out for lunch, I rang Chief Fourneval and asked about Klara Zuelig's blood type. I thought that as a doctor I could remind him of maternity records.'

'And what did he tell you?'

'That Klara Zuelig had never had a child. Remember, she had been married less than twenty-six years, and Freddy told you he was twenty-eight.'

'So he was adopted? Who were his true parents?'

'I asked, but all Fourneval would say was that that was a long, unhappy story.'

Siân sat silent. 'So you believe it's a case of bad blood. Can one inherit a criminal tendency? Doesn't the love and care of foster-parents have any power to cancel out?'

'We can't judge. We have to see Fourneval, Siân, as quickly as possible. If you sent Freddy off to Northern Italy on Friday, he could have made his way back to Annecy by now.'

Back at the boathouse he rang through to the number Fourneval had given him, but there was only a clerical aide

174

who took the message and asked them to wait at home until the Chief could make contact.

Since his visit to the Zuelig town house that morning the Chef de Police Cantonale had made startling progress. As the ambulance men negotiated the passage with old Régnier's stretcher, the Greek doctor's wife had appeared from the stairway and bent to wish the old fellow well. Fourneval draped himself across the doorway and made some remark to let her know she'd been observed.

Gilbert, still in the little office, missed what was said but noticed his chief's look of suppressed amusement. Even more he noticed how the nautical white slacks and T-shirt showed up the girl's neatly rounded figure. He followed his chief out and looked down the road after her.

'We don't have to wait for Régnier to answer our questions tomorrow,' he said happily. 'That delectable girl. I've just remembered something she said: about the removals team. A Chinese foreman. That shouldn't be hard to trace.'

The pieces were starting to slot together, but at the depository Monsieur Denglos was evasive. 'Yes,' Fourneval agreed, with more calm than was to be expected of a senior police officer long deprived of the first essential in a homicide inquiry—the victim's identity. 'I understand. I am a professional man myself, monsieur, and appreciate how standards must be upheld.'

Material standards here were beyond reproach, as witnessed by the effectively controlled temperature and humidity levels. Discretion over viewing of clients' property was as strictly maintained. Monsieur Denglos and his Chinese foreman, each plucked from the enjoyment of an after-lunch Sunday nap, stood as firm as honour and commercial obligation required, fully aware that retreat was the only direction ultimately open to them.

Fourneval presented his case. 'You received telephoned instructions from Madame Zuelig, who is unfortunately on holiday abroad and therefore beyond our reach. The specific arrangements were made through Antoine Régnier, concierge at her town house—who is temporarily indisposed in the Hôpital Cantonal. So it is to your discretion that I must address my request. A warrant to search would take valuable time, and possibly arouse unwanted comment.'

Labyrinthine, but eventually effective, Gilbert appreciated, watching the two men's eyes meet in a shared signal of defeat. 'The key?' he suggested.

The piano had no key. It had been locked before collection. It was preferred if owners adopted this precaution. Not that Monsieur Denglos's employees would ever take liberties with the instruments, but it facilitated insurance arrangements. Perhaps Monsieur le Chef de Police Cantonale should return when he had obtained the key from Madame's agents?

'No matter; I am sure we have something that will fit,' Fourneval assured him. His patience abruptly deserted him. 'Gilbert, open the thing.'

Monsieur Denglos, already shocked at the police presence, observed the inappropriate air of distrust with which the senior officer regarded the superb Bechstein grand. He waited at attention, breathing out disapproval as the younger one tried a set of skeletons in the lock.

There was a soft click. 'Ah!'

Gilbert raised the lid to reveal an immaculate keyboard. Then he walked round the side to join his chief in the curved angle of the sounding box. He took the main lid's weight on the heel of one latex-gloved hand and began to raise it. At shoulder level he paused. Both men peered inside. Then slowly the movement was completed, the lid set on its stay.

'*Seigneur Dieu!*' moaned Monsieur Denglos, and trod back on his foreman's toes. '*Un cadavre!*'

'I think you will agree,' Fourneval told him, 'that Madame Zuelig would have wished us to open this.'

Without touching any part of the interior, Gilbert was closely examining the contents of the slightly clouded plastic. The body lay on its front with the head turned in profile. The smashed skull had crusted over and there was considerable *post-mortem* staining, but no doubt at all about the cause of death.

176

CHAPTER 8

It was not until seven in the evening, when Siân was preparing a salad, that the doorbell buzzed and Fourneval stood there, leaning against a verandah post and gazing out across the lake. 'Police,' Gilbert unnecessarily announced. 'You wanted to see us.'

They came in wearily and accepted the offer of coffee. 'The story begins to take shape,' Fourneval said, sinking into an armchair. 'We have received a report of damage to the bow of a large, powered launch suspected of making smuggling runs to the French shoreline without navigational lights on moonless nights. It would appear that it ran down some small, equally unlit boat adrift on Wednesday night. Those on board, except for our informant, are lying low for fear of a manslaughter charge. I'm having them rounded up. Our man swears the boat was already half submerged. What they actually saw may be of some help in our case, because it could account for the state of our dismembered corpse, particularly since in circling for possible survivors our informant mentions something fouling the screws.'

Siân turned her face away in disgust.

'And still we have no name for the dead man,' the policeman admitted, 'but it could be Durochat, since he is missing. So I ask myself whether this story Madame Vassilakis has to tell us concerns him.'

'No,' Siân said in a low voice. 'It concerns his son Freddy. He was at the villa, hiding in the cellar, Thursday morning. I found him after the piano-removers left and I gave him a meal here. On Friday I drove him to Nyon in the Fiat and saw him on to a train going east. He took a ticket for Locarno, but I think he was going to make a detour back to Annecy where he lives. I haven't seen him or heard from him since.'

'*Ah!*' Fourneval considered this a moment, steepling his fingers and watching her under his eyelids. He leaned forward, his voice steely. 'You have deliberately suppressed any mention of him in your earlier statement to my colleagues at Nyon. I am afraid we shall need a great deal more detail than you have offered. For example, at what point you discovered him and how; also how much you already knew at that time of recent events at the Villa Montarnaud.'

'I knew nothing about any murder,' she said quickly. 'And I've no reason to think that Freddy did either. I was only at the villa to let the removals men in. After they'd gone I went into the kitchen, and I noticed the cellar door wasn't quite closed—'

The policemen listened in silence while she told the story again, including the farcical snow incident up at La Cure. 'I can believe you knew nothing of the murder,' Fourneval said drily at its end. 'Otherwise you would never have taken such risks in a stranger's company. Unless, of course, you already knew that the killer was someone else.'

'How could I know?'

Gilbert sighed, then tilted his head pertly and took up his part of the two-man act. 'If you'd been an eye-witness. Or were the killer yourself.'

They played a mild version of cat and mouse with her until the whole story was laid open.

'Is that absolutely everything?' Fourneval asked, when she felt she had talked herself empty.

'There is that story he told you,' Andreas reminded her quietly.

'Oh, that—'

'You thought it went some way to explain the sort of person he is.'

'I could be wrong.' Siân felt she was being pushed into total betrayal. Any interpretation she put on the story now was tainted by the knowledge of the murder, which Freddy might indeed have known something of. She had thought the tale was allegorical, referring to some trauma of childhood; but it could have been a twisted version of something much more recent which weighed on him. He might have felt compelled to get it talked out of his mind before he could sleep in peace.

The two policemen were waiting, watching her face. 'Let us judge for ourselves,' Fourneval said, almost with sympathy.

So, reluctantly, she repeated the story of the little girl in bed who heard arguing and fighting going on downstairs, who left by the window to meet with the boy, discovered sex and came back to the grisly discovery of the dead man in her bedroom.

'Oh, oh, oh,' Gilbert confided quietly to the toecaps of his shoes, but the Chief just nodded. 'Not a reassuring bedtime story. And under the circumstances we have to question just what prompted it. Tell me, did you think at the time that it was a fiction?'

She found it almost impossible to answer, but all the time she hesitated she was conscious of increasing the impact of whatever finally she had to admit. 'No,' she mumbled, head down. 'I thought maybe something like it had frightened him as a child.'

She was barely aware of them leaving. Andreas came back and sat on the arm of her chair. She felt drained of energy and self-respect. 'It sounds so *stupid*,' she said miserably, her face crushed against his chest.

'You took a terrible risk,' he grunted, 'with someone so unstable—all that time together up at La Cure, miles from anyone. You weren't to know the danger, but weren't you instinctively afraid?'

She tried to remember. Despite her repeated telling, the events were becoming unreal—except for isolated details: the cellar door bursting open; a moment on Friday morning as she stood carefully rewrapping the candles in waxed paper; cradling the thin, almost fleshless body as she comforted Freddy in the night. She believed now that she had once half-woken to feel him racked with sobbing. Strange, that until this moment she hadn't been fully aware of it. Why had he been crying? Was it a killer's remorse, or the early-hours aloneness all humanity was a prey to in despair?

No, after the first few moments when he burst out of the cellar, she hadn't been afraid of Freddy. Only fearful for him.

Before leaving, Fourneval had spoken to Andreas on the verandah. Now he had the task of breaking to Siân that the piano had been traced, and the fearful discovery inside it. So now it was certain that Klara was dead. And unwittingly Siân had played a part in hiding the body away.

All evening her mind kept returning to that Thursday morning, projecting a silent, slow-motion replay of the scene, with the removals men like some macabre Daliesque ballet. Whenever Andreas spoke his voice broke through momentarily, dissolving their moon-gravity movements, the distorted close-up of their faces, the foreshortened hands.

Klara killed; so unbelievably, and yet the fact hadn't really astonished her. At a deep level she had known for some time that Klara Zuelig must be dead.

Now, following Fourneval's laconic observations, what did she feel about Freddy? What difference did it make to know that the considerable sum of French currency she'd changed for him against her passport at Nyon could be what Klara withdrew for her holiday, money missing at the villa along with her travel papers and luggage?

'Will they make some announcement on the radio?' she roused herself to ask Andreas. 'He'll panic if he knows he's being hunted. If he has reached Annecy, the French police . . .'

'Will take care to bring him over unhurt. Don't go imagining a thousand horrors. Pick on a quiet outcome and believe in that.'

'Anodyne Andreas,' she said, almost impatiently, and stirred in his arms.

'So, we all have our functions. Make use of mine. You comforted this Freddy once. Perhaps he will remember it and manage to hang on. I'm putting out the light now, so we can get some sleep. After I've loved you well again.'

Monday arrived abruptly. It was like a shutter instantly opened: one moment, dark nothing; and then brightness, a cup of tea being handed to her. Behind, a little out of focus as yet, Andreas looking speculative and saying he would be off in ten minutes and could be make her some toast? After all that had gone wrong, how could it be an ordinary week beginning?

Siân struggled to catch up. 'Thanks, no. Will you be late tonight?'

'As early as possible. I don't want to go in at all, but with being away a few days I'll have a cluttered desk.'

Yes, Andreas as an international civil servant, when really he was a healer. This change, made to accommodate their marriage, to make them equally foreign, and save her being stranded among his fellow Greeks, left her in his debt. She must make some positive effort to use his generosity and repay it.

'I love you, Andreas Vassilakis,' she said earnestly, sitting up to receive his morning kiss.

He gave her the old, comfortable, ursine grin. 'We have a lot of love between us. How do you intend to spend the day?'

'I have to go and sign my statement at twelve. The High Noon confrontation. Shall I phone you straight afterwards?'

'Yes. If, for some reason, I'm not in my office, then I'll phone you here at two.'

'Right. And this morning I may go into Geneva shopping, perhaps call in on Céline Durochat, see how she has taken this new horror. I hope she's feeling more charitable towards Klara now.'

Andreas considered this. 'Surely Klara had yet to sign all those papers about the property? So both the business and the tenants of the town house have a reprieve. Madame Durochat won't be the only one who should feel relieved.'

They could even be glad Klara was gone! It was an unpleasant thought to leave her with, but at least Siân now had an alternative topic to divert her from brooding on Freddy's fate and her own responsibility for his disappearance.

She found herself wondering who else would benefit from Victor's and Klara's deaths. It must depend on the order of their deaths and the contents of Klara's will. Would she have thought to make a new one since the divorce? And if not, did divorce automatically nullify a husband's inheritance? Would his business partners be likely to benefit from more than the postponement of the rent scandal? She thought about the mannish partner Kitty, the cousin Philippe and his second wife and child, Klara's banker brother Klaus. All of these, as well as the tenants of the town house, stood to gain from what had happened to that unhappy woman. How many of them would truly grieve?

While she showered and dressed, Siân was vaguely conscious that she had left someone off the list; not Monique, who would be distraught over Madame's death, nor Monique's husband, who was barely involved. Who then, other than family, tenants, and the Durochat connection, stood to gain from Klara's removal?

Of course: Régnier, that pathetic old man with religious mania, toppled over the edge of sanity by the threat to his familiar way of life. Klara too seemed to have overlooked him, forgetting to reassure him that his future was taken care of. Régnier was another reason why Siân wanted to see Céline and hear the latest news from the town house. The police had been on his back only yesterday. But above all she wanted to know more about Freddy's past, anything that might prove he couldn't have hated his adoptive parents enough to kill them.

Céline Durochat didn't answer her ring, but again the door was ajar. Siân could see through to the drawing-room with its champagne velour carpet slatted with light from the half-closed venetians. She called and there was no reply. Yet the mousey young replacement down in Régnier's office had assured her Madame hadn't gone out. So, doubtless, she was upstairs again in one of the other flats.

Siân went back to the stairwell and listened. Distantly she caught the sound of music, Niall's clarinet, unaccompanied. The melody came clearer as she climbed the first two flights: *Pavane pour une Infante Défunte*, hauntingly beautiful and sad.

Then, abruptly—in mid-bar—it stopped, and there was silence. Or silence punctuated by an alarming human sound, not quite sobbing, not just breathing, but something between.

Half way up the last flight, Céline Durochat was crouched, one hand clawing at her chest, the other desperately clinging to the curved iron rail. Her face was grey, the features pinched, and her stiffly lacquered hair was shredded in disarray. She seemed not to see Siân until she touched her, and then the woman swung round, wild-eyed. 'Niall! How could he, how could he—?' she moaned.

Insensitive fool! Siân agreed. What a time to inflict sad music on others, when the shock of Klara's death was so fresh. All right, so it took him that way, but he'd no right to be so totally inconsiderate. Céline seemed on the point of collapse, rubbing the heel of one hand against her forehead in a tormented way and twisting her head from side to side.

She shouldn't be left here in that state. Easier to take her up the few steps into Niall's rooms than two and a half floors down to her own. After that first burst of reproach she didn't seem capable of speech, but her wide-staring eyes followed the girl as she ran up and knocked at the Irishman's door.

It gave under her knuckles, swinging open a few inches with a feeble squeak. From inside the flat came no sound at all. 'Mr O'Diarmid,' she called. 'Niall! Madame Durochat is unwell. Will you help me?' It was like shouting in a void.

The silence began to affect her. She turned back to Céline who had a hand to her mouth in horror. It wasn't any kind of seizure, Siân realized, but sheer fright. Not even shock at the news of Klara's being murdered would have put her into this state. Céline was terrified by something here and now. Had she actually been *coming from* the upper flat?

Siân again put a hand on the door, hesitated, then resolved to go in. 'Niall!' she called more loudly. *'Please!'*

He had to be there. She'd heard him, only a minute or two before, playing the *Pavane*. So why didn't he come out, or call?

'Are you all right? Look, I'm coming in.' She moved cautiously, not knowing what to expect, pushed the door back against the inner wall and took three steps forward into the little square hall. Straight ahead was a closed door.

To the left she could look into the empty, sunlit kitchen. Next would be the bathroom. On her right, in the still darkened bedroom, duvet and pillows were heaped untidily where he had slept. Nobody spoke or moved anywhere. She went forward towards the closed door, although every instinct in her warned her to stay away.

As she turned the solid, faceted glass knob, she knew she must run, but it was too late. The door was torn from her grasp and she fell forward into a lunging figure with upraised arm. She tried to fend him off but something came whistling down on her and burst in a white pain.

With the identification of Klara's body by her brother, and the removal of Subarsky from the list of possibles for the sluice-gates torso, Gilbert felt he was more than half way to winning his bet against the *patron*. He knew well enough why Fourneval had put money on a political crime: he detested such tentacled and labyrinthine cases above all others. So if this still proved one, at least he'd have the slim consolation of a hundred-franc win.

But Ivan Subarsky had surfaced in Ottawa and was even now facing the Press out there, having passed to the appropriate international committee at WHO detailed information on the medical outcome of successive radiation-leakage accidents within the USSR.

Although political ramifications might still burgeon before the Montarnaud murder case was solved, Gilbert's diagnosis of a domestic crime was now the most likely. His win appeared doubly certain when, on entering the office on Monday morning, he was handed the memo from police headquarters at Nyon, Vaud, where money had been laid on the Geneva murder having a narcotics background. He presented the memo smirkingly when Fourneval made his own entrance at mid-morning.

'As we supposed.' The Chef de Police Cantonale shrugged it off. 'The car thieves merely made use of the girl's discarded envelope when sharing out their drugs. Small-time stuff. So, if the driver admits this, it appears he is recovering from his injuries, although at this moment I cannot believe he will

184

be feeling so grateful for that chance. What else has come in?'

'Nothing from Dublin yet on O'Diarmid. Perhaps they don't have Mondays there.'

'It is their Sundays that drain away. I went there once to buy a horse for a friend. Headstrong women and horses, and heady old whiskey. One might give the Irish ample time to recover from their weekend. Nothing else?'

'Confirmation from La Cure that the girl's hired Fiat was parked overnight off the road near the Col. Evidence that someone entered a woodsman's hut, lit a fire and had a meal. The girl appears to have told the truth about that. Also a train conductor, on the Domodossola-Brig leg, remembers a young man with a first-class single ticket who answers to the description of Freddy Durochat.'

'And from Annecy?'

'A negative. They haven't seen young Durochat since Wednesday. If he does turn up there they'll hold him and get in touch immediately.'

'And his father, Victor? Any sightings?'

'Still nothing.'

Fourneval rolled his eyes elaborately. 'Right, then. Let's go through everything again. See if we can pull out a roast chestnut.'

They were deep in computer printouts when two calls came simultaneously, one from Annecy, which Fourneval switched to a policewoman for a transcript while he dealt with the urgent local one.

'The Vassilakis girl,' he snapped at Gilbert, slamming down the receiver. 'She was to be here at noon to sign her statement.'

'I was giving her leeway. Women—'

'—can be vulnerable as well as unpunctual. Get the car while I contact the husband.'

They met at the exit, Gilbert stiff-faced at the rebuke and apprehensive, Fourneval tight-lipped but ready to share his anxiety. 'There's a replacement concierge at the Zuelig town house. He found the girl at the bottom of a staircase, unconscious and bleeding from a partly congealed head wound. She'd gone up some time before to call on Madame Philippe Durochat, who just happens to have taken a large dose of sleeping tablets and is being removed to the cantonal hospital. *Two* unconscious, Gilbert, and on the high risk list. I don't like the apparent coincidence at all.'

Gilbert pulled up behind an emergency ambulance parked with the rear doors open. On the first-floor landing Siân lay covered by a blanket, with another insinuated between her and the ceramic tiles. Two uniformed attendants stood back against the wall with breathing apparatus while a young doctor knelt beside the girl, frowning over his stethoscope. 'How bad?' Fourneval demanded as he sat back on his heels.

The doctor took no notice, pulled up each eyelid in turn to shine a pencil torch in, then leaned forward and deliberately sniffed at the unconscious girl's lips. 'M'm. Something a little odd here.' He eased the dress loose from her neck and shoulder, sniffed again along the skin and across the cushion on which her head lay. He looked up, puzzled and annoyed. 'Who gave the young lady brandy?'

No one spoke. 'Somebody did,' the doctor insisted. 'Stupid thing to do. Never, with concussion . . .'

'Spare us the medical instruction,' Fourneval said tightly. 'How bad? Can she be moved?'

'She should be all right, I think, but we must admit her for observation and X-ray. I'm giving her an injection, then in a few minutes she can go down in the lift.'

'Chalk her outline,' Fourneval growled to Gilbert. 'Go on. She can't see you.' Gilbert dug in his pocket and unearthed the requisite stub of chalk, conscious of the unspoken hostility of the medical team.

'Did you move her at all?' Fourneval asked.

'No,' said the doctor shortly. 'The carotid artery was exposed and I used that for her pulse.'

The Chef de Police Cantonale pursed his lips. 'She didn't get that gash by falling,' Gilbert told him unnecessarily.

'We simply lifted her to slide the blanket under,' one of the ambulance men volunteered. 'She was already in recovery position.' He looked uneasy. 'The cushion was under her head when we arrived.'

Fourneval looked around for the concierge who dumbly shook his head. 'It wasn't me, I never saw it before. And I don't have any brandy either.'

'Right. You can go ahead and move her,' the doctor allowed. Fourneval and Gilbert stepped back while the dispositions were made. The chief eyed the visiting card set in a brass holder by the door he stood alongside. 'And Madame Durochat?'

'Barbiturate overdose,' sighed the doctor, 'if one can believe the label on the bottle. And an alcohol intake as well. Fortunately she vomited, but I can't say one way or the other until we clean her out and do tests. I sent her in the first ambulance. Stand aside, please. We're going down now.'

At the outer door they almost collided with Andreas Vassilakis who had parked on the pavement. He pounced on the medic and there was a swift interchange of question and answer. Both climbed into the ambulance after the stretcher. 'See you later,' Fourneval called in as he turned away.

Vassilakis seemed to notice him for the first time. 'Oh, Monsieur le Chef, thank you. Yes. But for the present—' He shrugged his heavy shoulders and turned back to the stretcher.

Married a month, Gilbert reflected; to a lovely girl like that. Too much happening too fast. What a life! Almost as bad as being a policeman.

CHAPTER 9

'If necessary,' Fourneval instructed his team before dismissing them, 'take the house to pieces, but for God's sake find something significant.' And fat cat Klaus Zuelig, seemingly transformed into a distinctly bedraggled feline, had sat in the Chief's office nodding assent. 'Anything, anything,' he agreed. 'We have to get to the bottom of these appalling happenings. Is it Niall O'Diarmid, do you think? I met him only once. He seemed so—innocuous.'

'*Negligible*', Fourneval corrected inside his own head. Klaus Zuelig would have flicked the man one glance and written him off: assets nil, authority nil, usefulness nil. Yet the financier wasn't totally a cash calculator; there had been evidence of real distress over his sister's death. And shock, because the unspeakable had cruelly invaded his circle, breached his couldn't-happen-to-me security.

'If I can help in any way,' he offered, the gesture of his muscled and manicured hand as ineffectual as a flipper's, 'please let me know. I am not without resources.'

Fourneval's mouth lifted at one end. He nodded gravely as the man took his departure. The financier had no resources of the kind this case now required. Let Zuelig go back to his balance sheets. There was paperwork of a different kind to tackle at police headquarters, while the technical experts beavered away on the new scene of crime.

He had only one more instruction to give Gilbert. 'No more casualties,' he ordered, one cynical eyebrow raised. 'We do not need a complaint of overloading from the Hôpital Cantonal.'

Gilbert bit back the repartee. Damn the man, he was actually rattled. And he'd been as much in the picture as Gilbert himself, and hadn't seen fit to put a guard on the girl. 'I'm putting Baptiste in charge at the house, sir,' he said briefly. 'I'll take a quick look myself and be back in an hour. By then I should be able to speculate on what happened.'

Speculate, Fourneval thought, and smiled grimly. That had been their main occupation since the case began, because investigation had never got past point one: knowing who the first victim was. The first-*found* victim, he corrected himself; because the skewering, he was sure now, was done as cover-up after the impetuous attack on Klara Zuelig with the bronze horse. The scene at the villa was slowly coming alive for him. What remained unclear were the features of the principal actor's face.

*

Gilbert returned within fifty minutes and Fourneval's greeting consisted of tossing him the day's menu card from the Mess. 'I'm having it sent up. There's no point in missing meals. Suit you?'

'Fine.' Gilbert squinted at the list, took a ballpoint from his pocket and ticked *Crème aux Asperges, Poussin Provençal, Haricots verts, Tarte aux Fraises*. Fourneval, he noticed, had settled for *Pâté Normand, Sôle Dugléré, Petits pois, Fromages*. If this was hardship, then it was a form he could take in his stride. Luckily there was a separate table to eat at, so their papers wouldn't bear witness. Incident Room staff had to make do with a staggered thirty-minute dash to the canteen and eternal damnation if they later stamped their output with coffee-mug rings of brown.

Then he observed that Fourneval had stacked his files on the floor. All that his working desk now held was an unlined scribbling block. So they were going to build the story up themselves from scratch, relying on memory. But first there was an apéritif from the cabinet, and two young cadets bearing in discreetly covered trays.

When they had paid due respect to the lunch and Gilbert had deposited the trays in the corridor, Fourneval tore off one half of the block and handed it to him. 'We first list all the *personæ*, dead or alive.'

They compared their separate sheets and found them identical, apart from order. 'So?' Fourneval prompted, 'taking account first of the incidents at the Villa Montarnaud—'

'We eliminate those without opportunity.'

Out went Klara Zuelig and Victor Durochat, as being deceased; Klaus Zuelig, impeccably alibied; Dr Vassilakis, vouched for by diplomatic unquestionables in Berne; Monique the maid and her husband, seen by half the commune at a church supper on Wednesday night and various neighbours on Thursday morning; Philippe Durochat (with a query) who was supposedly with his wife Caroline until she delivered him by car to work next day.

'Leaving,' Gilbert claimed, 'the Vassilakis girl from midnight Wednesday onwards; Madame Kitty from Wednesday evening until nine a.m. on Thursday; Madame Céline Durochat; old Antoine Régnier wandering uncharted; Niall O'Diarmid (included because a tenant of the house) and the totally unpredictable Freddy Durochat. Not,' he stipulated, 'in order of preference.'

'And X,' Fourneval reminded him. 'There is always the unknown. So our killer could be any one of those, or any combination of them.'

'Ah,' said Gilbert, requiring further light shed.

'The strung frame of the piano,' Fourneval obliged, 'was carried to the cellar by two persons. No marks have been found anywhere of it having been dragged or dropped. One person his own must have left scratches on the steps and the frame itself. And one of those involved has scraped knuckles or elbow from the wall going down.'

'Blood of Victor Durochat's general group, O+. So did he take part in his ex-wife's murder and the hiding of her body before receiving his own quietus?'

'Or was X the piano-frame porter; being, in fact, any other O+ blood type in the canton?'

'In whichever case, we are looking for a second person, who was either the killer of Klara, or at least an implicated witness.'

Fourneval showed his teeth in a vulpine grin. 'So who is your fancy to be in harness with Victor?'

'If the first piano-handler was indeed Victor.'

'Assuming for the moment it was so, then we'll not consider the Vassilakis girl, who probably had never met him; nor his cousin's ex-wife who, despite equal financial motive, appeared to detest him. Niall O'Diarmid?—No, they'd be poles apart mentally. Old Régnier?—Just possible, I think, if he'd been ordered up to the villa for some job. He was involved in making arrangements for the piano's storage, after all, so he would know that the body could be carted away next day without bother. And then Madame Kitty's a favourite for the stakes. She was Victor's corespondent in the divorce, unlikely though that seems, and she was in financial harness with him as well. A very forceful lady, that one.'

While Gilbert turned over these speculations and evaluated them, Fourneval began tearing up sheets of blank paper with the aid of a stiletto from his top desk drawer. Now he began to print names on the postcard-sized pieces. He laid them out in a row. 'Let's set up partnerships,' he suggested. 'And we don't have to insist on one of the pair being Victor. He could have been skewered by then.'

The first set of duos Gilbert produced consisted of Victor-Régnier, Victor-Kitty, Victor-Freddy. 'We know young Durochat was in the locality at the time, perhaps already in the villa, and some family row could have erupted during which he and his father took sides against the mother.'

Fourneval was busy printing fresh sets of names. 'Right, so we take each of the second elements and make new partnerships. Who goes with old Régnier?'

Gilbert's hand hovered, then settled on O'Diarmid's name. 'Because they lived under one roof, knew all the parties involved, were both stranded by Klara's invention to sell the town house,' he said without much conviction.

'O'Diarmid had the reputation of a womanizer. That wouldn't have gone down well with Calvin II. I can't see them in harness together to commit any crime.'

'Unless O'Diarmid had something on Mr Purity and threatened to use it against him. Enforced cooperation. The old man is certainly in an abnormal state. Something drove him into crisis: perhaps being compelled by the sinner O'Diarmid to witness, and be accessory to, the act of murder?'

'I'll accept that for the present,' Fourneval allowed. 'And the same might be true for Régnier-Céline Durochat, if we can imagine her issuing blackmail threats. She's more one for telling all than offering discretion, whatever the price.'

Gilbert considered it. 'I like that pair, especially if it was Régnier who killed Klara Zuelig in a mad surge of anger because of the house. Then Madame Durochat might have been scared enough to agree to helping him cover up. Remember, there were no fingerprints at all on the screwdriver and the piano frame. A half-mad old man might not have thought of cleaning them off, but an experienced housewife would. And as we know, they don't come of easily.'

'Then we have another possibility: Régnier-Freddy. The old servant had known him from quite a small boy, was close to the family and has a strong sense of loyalty to past Zueligs. If the young man had killed his adoptive mother in a rage, because she denied him something—money or the right to live at the villa, his sometime home—then Régnier might have helped conceal the crime out of misguided affection. Young Freddy has appealing ways, acording to Siân Vassilakis. He may be twenty-eight, but he's mastered the rôle of little boy lost.'

'That gives us six possible pairs already,' Gilbert counted glumly. 'And more to come. Who's next? Ah, Madame Kitty Wilson. A toughie, if ever there was one, and she had a lot to lose. We've considered her in harness with Victor. How about with Philippe?'

Fourneval made a balancing movement with one hand. 'She would act alone, never pick such a feeble back-up. Of course, if Philippe Durochat had inadvertently been a witness, she might well have used her considerable powers of persuasion to make him her accomplice after the deed. We have no evidence to support a link between her and any of the others.'

'O'Diarmid.' Gilbert took up the tally. 'We don't know that he had any connection with the Maison Durochat partners, but he certainly knew the ex-wife of Philippe, Céline. They shared the same roof and the same risk of losing it through Klara's new intentions. So we can team up those two. They might have gone up to the villa together to appeal for Klara's sympathy. He was already on visiting terms with Madame Zuelig, according to the maid Monique, who even suspected a bit of attempted dalliance when he turned up once from the lake in wetsuit and swimming trunks. So was there some more personal reason too for him to wish his landlady dead?'

His chief nodded. 'And having met the Vassilakis couple by chance, he contrived an introduction for the girl to Klara

Zuelig, which resulted in the Greek couple getting the boathouse. Then, in the husband's absence, he gave the girl a ticket to one of his concerts. We know she visited the house on several occasions, ostensibly to see Madame Durochat, but she could just as well have gone up to the top floor. As did many another flighty young female, as it happens. Monsieur O'Diarmid should have an interesting tale to tell us when he gets back from his half-term vacation and honours us with a call.'

'So are you pairing O'Diarmid with Madame Vassilakis as well as with Madame Durochat for the villa business?' Gilbert queried.

'Why not? It's no more tenuous than some of the other partnerships we've considered. And while on the subject of those two ladies, bracket them together too. There's some connection there. This business today: did Madame Durochat attack the girl, think she'd killed her—in the same manner as Klara Zuelig—then attempt suicide? It makes a sort of sense, and yet . . .'

'Someone certainly had given the girl brandy after the attack. There was spilt brandy, but no vomit, on the cushion. I took a look round Madame Durochat's apartment, and all she had was table wine and vermouth. No empty bottles either. We don't know yet what she was drinking along with the barbiturates, but they could have been forced on her. In which case someone was out to remove both women, or at least put one of them out of action for a time. They were her own tablets. I found her doctor's number on a phone pad and checked with him. She'd been prescribed them for some months now.'

'Did you look in on the other apartments?'

'No. They were locked. The Irishman was out, still away over half-term, and the two floors between him and Madame Durochat are unoccupied at present. The new concierge was sending to the Zuelig Bank for duplicate keys when I left. Baptiste will let us know the results of the search in due course.'

'So we'll leave that for the immediate present and go back to the partnership theme: Céline Durochat's links with the partners in her husband's firm. If we discount the present wife's word, Philippe might have been up at the villa Wednesday night together with Céline. Both were thought to be very upset by Klara's recent decisions. But I don't see Monsieur Philippe using anything more lethal than a balloon on a stick. I think too that to save his own skin he would have come to us before this and poured out all he knew, however much under his ex-wife's influence. He doesn't continue his relationship with her from any sense of loyalty, it's said, but from inadequacy. He was manœuvred into a regretted exchange of wife with mistress, and still needs the older lady's shoulder to weep on. But his own safety would, as ever, be uppermost in his mind. If we do accept them as possible partners in crime, they should, as with the Kitty-Philippe link, be entered strictly in parenthesis. Who else remains?'

'Siân Vassilakis,' Gilbert said regretfully, 'with Freddy Durochat. Unless the fact that she was attacked today means that we can view her throughout as an innocent?'

Fourneval's lip curled. 'What a romantic we have in you, Gilbert. Just because she is pretty and has all that glorious red hair! We have accepted that she might have acted in concert with either Céline Durochat or Niall O'Diarmid. You don't like the Freddy connection now because it seems a little too likely. We might well have our finger on the killers there. They stayed so closely in touch after the event that one cannot avoid assumptions. And if she was herself attacked today, on the home ground of at least three of the other suspects, doesn't that seem too neat a way of diverting suspicion?'

'She couldn't have given herself that injury.'

'No, but *he* could. He still hasn't turned up at the nursing home at Annecy. There's been no *brouhaha* simply because he's a voluntary patient and he has more or less finished the course, but he hasn't surfaced anywhere else, so—'

'You think he could have circled back to Geneva? That would be crazy, if he's the killer.'

'It would be *unexpected*, and so quite a clever move. He doesn't lack brains, that one, just stability. Even before he started experimenting with acid he had bad dreams. You have read the *résumé* of his early life, the traumas?'

Gilbert nodded. 'Durochat's illegitimate son by a hotel chambermaid bought off by his father; brought up by her and the dumb ox she married. At the age of eleven he found his mother's body after the drunken sot had blown out her brains with his shotgun.'

'Rows and fighting were nothing new in that household, but on that occasion she had run to the child's room for safety. The man followed and killed her there, for the boy to find when he crept back after a night on the tiles. That, barely disguised, is the story which Freddy told to Siân Vassilakis. Aged eleven. And scarred for life as a result. Can you imagine the connection in his sick mind: his mother and murder?

'What state would he be in when he found that in anger he'd done the same to the woman who'd taken her place, given him a new home alongside his natural father? His mind could have blown completely. He could have killed Victor then as cover-up, might even have come back to wipe out the girl who'd helped him get away.'

'That implies he was in the town house today and attacked her. Where would he be hiding? In Céline's apartment? And did he provide the girl's brandy, and force the barbiturates on the older woman because she'd seen and recognized him?'

'We'll know more when she wakes up, which I hope won't be too long in happening. You could go along and relieve the officer sitting with her, see if she's said anything yet. Take a look at Régnier too, on the way. It's superfluous, of course, to tell you to show some interest also in the red-head.'

As Gilbert closed the door behind him, Fourneval rose and took the pairs of names across to his pegboard where he pinned them on display. Then he went back to his chair and sat regarding them. Now and again in the next half-hour he went across to change their order on the board, but he wasn't satisfied. On an impulse he strode across and counted the times each name recurred.

Rearranging them in order of high score brought Céline Durochat to the top, tying with Siân Vassilakis and Régnier. Freddy came later, although he was almost certainly at the villa when the first crime took place, or very soon after. Fourneval sighed. Leaving aside the cast for the moment, what about the play itself? Three acts: Murder One, Murder Two, and *L'après-meurtre*.

In Act One, X killed Y; in Act Two, X killed (or was killed by) Z. In Act Three, either X or Z disposed of the bodies of Y and Z (or X), aided by a possible anybody-on-God's-earth.

No, algebra had never been his strong subject, and anyway there were two many unknowns. So, back to speculation informed now by fact.

Klara Zuelig was killed by a single blow from the bronze statuette, her body enveloped in a plastic blanket-store and crushed into the piano case after removal of the strung instrument. The removal of this, and its transfer to the cellar, had required a second pair of hands. One of those four hands had bled in scraping against the cellar wall during the operation. At that time the cellar door was supposedly whole, because Siân Vassilakis didn't lock Freddy in there until the following morning. The cellar blood might have come from Victor, killed later; or from Freddy, who could have inherited his father's blood group.

Next, somebody of that same group—Victor?—bled in the bathroom, having been run through fatally with the screwdriver used in the piano operation, was transported to the dinghy and ineffectually disposed of via the lake. At some point between or after the murders, the house was thoroughly sanitized and wax polish used on surfaces which might otherwise have held significant prints. Since the screwdriver was not well hidden, it had probably been dropped behind the cellar wine rack *after* it was pushed back across the shrouded piano frame. Was the killer getting rattled by then, working alone and against time? There had been a terrible lot to be done to cover up an original crime of sudden anger.

Did it mean there were two killers after all—one impul-

ve, the other to some extent a planner? Suppose Victor, in
ncontrollable rage, had killed Klara; and Freddy, turning
p just then, had been somehow forced to help him dispose
f her body. Couldn't he have contrived to turn the tables,
eize the screwdriver and use it on his father, either in
elf-defence or a revenge killing?

One needed to know more about the complicated Freddy's
elations with the other two. And was he strong enough to
omplete the disposal arrangements for Victor's body? What
neans had he used for moving such a weight? And why did
t have to be Freddy at all?

Back to facts then, he told himself. Reconsider oppor-
unity. How did the *personæ* get to the Villa Montarnaud?
He took a blank sheet and headed it Transport. Then he
started through the whole list again.

CHAPTER 10

Because of his advanced age, Antoine Régnier had been
placed in the geriatric unit. There the patients fell into two
categories: the mentally inadequate and those present for
purely bodily reasons. These latter, affronted by being cate-
gorized as senile, spent disproportionate energy on protest at
the indignity and on defiantly organizing mental Olympics.
Marooned between both groups in an open ward, the ema-
ciated old Puritan was attempting to regain his own world
by means of more or less silent communion with his stern
Maker.

Sedation, adequate food and bed rest had already helped
to restore him, but some confusion persisted. Régnier appeared to take the dark-suited Gilbert for something between
a pastor and an apocalyptic visitation. The old man's
revelations were therefore highly personal and mainly of
spiritual content. Undaunted, Gilbert accepted the rôle as
unavoidable and filled it as best he knew how. Eventually
he arrived at the information he required.

Régnier remembered some events of the previous Wednesday with quite acute perception. It was after that that he had started on his physical and mental wanderings.

He had certainly made the telephoned arrangements for Madame Zuelig's piano to be stored. Monsieur O'Diarmid had advised on the depository offering the best care for the instrument.

No, he did not drive a car; had never been in a boat apart from the big lake steamers; when he went anywhere locally he always walked or took a bus. Yes, he believed he had walked a considerable way recently; the bloodied and blistered state of his feet gave him to think this, but he could not say where. Enough that he had been about his Lord's business. Whether he had actually gone to the Villa Montarnaud in the past few days was uncertain. He did recall Monsieur O'Diarmid mentioning on Wednesday his intention to call there concerning piano lessons.

Speaking of his own recent state of mind, Régnier confessed to a sense of impending doom due to the corrupted nature of society. He had felt the need to point out to others the folly of their ways. No, he had never raised that subject with Miss Klara because it was not appropriate. She was under no obligation to compensate her tenants for loss of a protecting roof, since they were already so indebted to her for past kindnesses. They should instead rise and gird themselves, for the time had come to go forth with nothing but a staff in the hand and the Word of the Lord on the lips. All else was Vanity. Now was the Time of Reckoning when the grain should be separated from the chaff.

Gilbert was of like mind about the desirability of this, but there was still much chaff to be blown off the information he was after. When at last he felt the garnering, as such, was complete, he bade the old man trust in the abiding good in all men and went pontifically on his way.

As yet there was no chance of interviewing either of the women. Although both were now conscious, a medical embargo had been put on all access to them until the next morning. In any case Madame Durochat was claiming to have lost her memory.

*

ourneval, made restless at Gilbert's departure, went through to the Incident Room where there was a sudden rush of information. All the telephones were currently in use. The blonde policewoman with the heart-shaped birthmark on one cheek made a beeline for him. He read the note she passed over. *Wheelbarrow?*

The divers had found it twenty metres farther out than the bronze horse. Of course, used for the body's transport from villa to boat, it could have been run down the zigzag path, and any marks made then would be indistinguishable from those made previously during gardening and tree-doctoring. So disposal of the male body could have been a single-handed job. And apparently the killer wasn't trained to put his tools tidily away after use. Dumping in the lake was easier. There was still a chance there for Forensic. It was amazing how many people thought that fingerprints couldn't survive immersion in water.

'Sir,' the girl prompted, 'that report from Annecy this morning.'

'A negative on Freddy Durochat. What of it?'

'It was a "No, *but* . . ." Did you want a follow-up?'

He made an effort to get on the same wavelength. 'No. But *what* . . . ?' He patted his pockets and retrieved the crumpled note he'd barely scanned on his way out to the emergency at the Zuelig house. 'Just a second.' He smoothed out the creases and checked. *God Almighty!* True, nothing on Freddy, but the name Durochat had automatically been passed on to regions. A Victor Durochat, aged 45–50, 1 metre 85, dark brown eyes, near-black hair with white wings, had been reported in, victim of a mugging at Grenoble, Thursday at 01.45 hours. Nationality unknown due to absence of identity papers, charge cards, currency etc. The same, but no address, was stitched inside his suit jacket. No apparent means of transport. He had gone into coma. Skull injuries with brain hæmorrhage.

'Full details required,' he snapped. 'Get Philippe Durochat pulled in to go and identify.' Down the drain goes top candidate for the torso, he reflected.

He wiped off the scowl he'd been fixing the girl with.

Referred anger, he reminded himself: you commit a cras
stupidity, so you go and kick the dog. But the PCW wa
resilient; she looked satisfied at getting a positive reaction

There was a message coming in now from the Petit Po
of slow sinking of a power boat with damage to the starboar
bow. Corresponding markings on the quayside suggested
careless return after a stolen joyride. The owner, a Jear
Sébastien Claudel, studio engineer, was looking the cra
over now, reported no break-in or fiddled ignition. The onl
other keyholder had been a friend, Niall O'Diarmid, wh
occasionally borrowed the boat on condition he replace
the fuel used.

'O'Diarmid!' Fourneval muttered between his teeth
'Control, get me through to Baptiste, at the Zuelig tow
house.'

'Sir, he's back. Just seen his car come into the yard.'

The detective came in humming; he had taken on a glov
that must mean they were on to something good. 'Bee
through O'Diarmid's attic,' he reported succinctly. 'Con
tents of the fridge slightly putrescent, and the thermosta
hadn't been altered to allow for the rise in temperatur
these last few days. A half-empty milk carton dated from
Wednesday; the latest edition of the *Tribune de Genève* th
same. Some items of unopened mail—mostly circular
with two local letters addressed by hand and one from
Ireland—stacked tidily on a side table in the sitting-room
On the kitchen table half a wrapped loaf, quite fresh; crock
ery for one; a knife and a jar of peanut butter; a bag of apple
a half-bottle of brandy, with two-thirds gone. (There's n
space for said bottle on the crowded drinks trolley in th
sitting-room.) The electric kettle, when examined, was sti
quite warm.

'According to old Régnier, Niall O'Diarmid was the onl
tenant with a key to the rear door giving on to the courtyar
He used to come and go that way when he used his Yamah
bike, wheeling it through the cobbled archway. The rea
doorkey is missing from its hook in his kitchen, and th
bike's not in the stable.

'O'Diarmid's double bed is unmade since being slep

in. Two short, curly fair hairs were found on a pillow. O'Diarmid's own hair is rather long, very dark and straight.

'There is an expensive sound-reproduction system and an assortment of music tapes, including some home-recorded practice cassettes of the man himself. Significantly, several of these were "looped". That means that they could be left running and would repeat themselves until a time switch turned the power off.'

'Thank you, I am aware of what "looped" tapes are: commonly used as background music, or alternatively to give a false impression of someone's presence. What else? I know how you save the best for the end.'

'A second cushion,' Baptiste said, smirking, 'identical to the one under the unconscious girl's head, was on the sitting-room settee.'

'That I really like. Cushion and brandy by favour of the top floor. The two unconscious women down on the first floor. Did O'Diarmid descend to attack the girl, or did he risk carrying her down by lift all that way afterwards? And was she knocked out by error, hence the later efforts to revive her?'

Baptiste treated all the questions as rhetorical. 'Finger-prints,' he reminded his chief. 'The flat's general housekeeping standard was good, but several people had been there lately, some possibly women. There was a fine coat of dust overall. Outside, on the banister and handrail of the top stairs, a considerable overprinting a few steps down. Something happened there—a protracted conversation at least. I tend to link this to the women; small palm prints of two kinds. No evidence of anyone having actually fallen.'

'So what do you propose to do, Baptiste?'

'Fix an electronic button to the back door downstairs, bleeping an officer posted up in the flat. Pick up O'Diarmid next time he comes in.'

'Why not?' Fourneval's aquiline features broke into lines of something like merriment. 'See to it, then.'

'What about the two women?'

'Gilbert radioed in: both conscious now, but no access until tomorrow. So if you need me I'm at home.' Fourneval turned back at the door, one corner of his mouth turned up. 'I hope your trap comes off. For some reason I am reminded of the first one I set as a boy. For a fox that had taken my uncle's chicken.'

'Was it successful?'

'Of course. I killed my grandmother's Siamese cat.'

Tuesday. It was just after ten and the warm sunshine of a perfect May morning carried the scent from acacia and lilac blossom in the park. The two policemen turned their backs on springtime and headed for the aseptic precinct of the Hôpital Cantonal.

When Fourneval and Gilbert went in, Siân Vassilakis was sitting out in a chair by the open window, with her husband already installed on the arm looking grimly possessive.

The doctor opened by demanding what likelihood there was of a further attack being made on his wife. Fourneval could give no guarantee, especially—he made the point emphatic—since he'd been denied an opportunity to discover exactly what happened. 'Would you tell us now, madame,' he invited, 'what precisely you heard and saw before you were struck down? For example, where did this take place, and why were you there?'

Siân played with the rug's fringe on her knees. 'I went to call on Madame Durochat.'

'To offer your condolences?'

'Perhaps, but more to get information about Freddy. She must have known him quite well as a child. You see, I'm absolutely sure he couldn't have been involved in anything so awful as Klara's death.' There was an edge of fear to her voice.

'So what did you learn?'

'Nothing. Madame Durochat was out, although the door was ajar. I felt she must be somewhere close. Then I heard Niall's clarinet. He was playing the Fauré *Pavane*, but it broke off. I assumed he'd given up practising, so I decided to go up and talk to him.' She stopped, frowning.

'Go on, madame. I believe you paused for some moments on the top flight.'

202

'Yes, I did. That's where I found Madame Durochat. She looked ill, crouched down on the stairs and gripping the railing. She muttered something about Niall playing that music, and I was angry too because it had upset her so. Then—'

'What happened next?'

'I wanted to get her to a chair or something, so I went up and tapped on the door, thinking Niall would help me with her. There was no answer, and the door fell open. I could see right through the hall. It looked as though no one was there. I think I called out, and then I went in. It was when I opened the door at the far end that it happened. Something hit me.'

'Something fell on you, or some*one* struck at you?'

She stared at her clenched hands and shook her head. 'Siân,' her husband appealed.

'All right, then. There was somebody there, just a dark shape. Little more than an impression.'

'Man or woman?'

'I think—a man.'

'And he came from that closed room? Not from behind?'

'He was in the room, yes. He must have heard me calling, but he never moved until I started to go in. I'm sorry, I really can't help you any further. I couldn't even say for sure that it was Niall.'

'It's good that you remember so much. That means, I hope, that the damage is not too serious.'

'Just a headache now, no sickness.'

'You knew perhaps that you were found outside Madame Durochat's apartment? Have you any recollection of getting there?'

'Andreas told me. I'm not sure. I think maybe there was a sensation of being carried, someone bending over me, but I could be muddling it with when I arrived here. Really, I've no clear picture. It's all horribly confused.'

'Thank you, madame. I am sorry to disturb your rest, and I hope you will continue to make good progress. Is there anything we can do to make you more comfortable?'

'I'd like to know about Madame Durochat. Is she all right? What happened to her?'

'That is what we hope to discover ourselves, madame. She too seems to have suffered some temporary mishap and is now recovering.'

'She was petrified,' Siân declared. 'I thought at first she was ill, but actually she was frightened almost out of her mind. By something or someone inside the top flat.'

They found upon inquiry that Madame Durochat had discharged herself from hospital against professional advice and gone home in a taxi summoned by telephone. The bed she had occupied was already neatly made up for its next occupant and the little room cleared of personal possessions. The officer left on duty in the corridor had gone off duty at midnight, and not been relieved due to an administrative oversight.

Fourneval was livid, Gilbert gnawed by apprehension. They went down to join the others waiting in the police car and Gilbert drove them all to the Zuelig town house.

To Fourneval's surprise, Céline's door was opened to their ring by Madame Kitty wearing her mannish business suit. 'I am on the point of leaving,' she informed them distantly. 'I dropped by to make sure Céline had all she needed. It is a time when we should all pull together.' She nodded unsmilingly and swept past.

Céline called out to them and they went through to the pale green and gold drawing-room. She lay on a chaise-longue, voluptuous in a cream satin négligée frothing with fine lace and silk-covered buttons. ''Oo is it?' she demanded in English, then switched to French as she recognized the two policemen.

'Ah, I suppose you've come to worry me with your questions. It will be of no use. I cannot remember what occurred. Yesterday is a complete jumble of faces, like a nightmare.' She lay back, exquisitely delicate, too fragile to be brutally pursued.

'We thought we might help you to remember, madame,' said Fourneval gently. 'In fact we have brought along a visitor for that purpose, who is waiting just outside.'

204

CHAPTER 11

'A visitor?' Unease showed through the *Dame-aux-Camélias* languor. Céline put a delicate hand to her head. 'No, I don't think I want to see anyone yet. I'm not at all well.'

'This is someone you went half way to see just yesterday. And on that occasion too your courage failed you. You crouched a few steps down on the stairs and let Siân Vassilakis go past and make contact instead. To her considerable inconvenience.'

Céline drew back against her cushions. Her voice came breathlessly. 'I—I was afraid. Of the killer. Yes, he had killed before, killed Klara, and—and Victor!' Her voice rose desperately. 'How could I go in there?'

Fourneval outstared her. 'The killer, madame? You have been more adept at identifying him than ourselves, then? However, we will leave that for the moment. You let the girl go in, without warning her.' He leaned forward, holding her gaze with his own. 'And what happened next?'

'I don't know. I can't remember. I must have fainted. Or else I struggled back here. Something, but my mind is a blank.'

'Shall I suggest a scenario? You heard perhaps a cry or gasp, and the girl fall, and then you turned tail and ran. And back in your own apartment you quickly downed two or three drinks to stop the trembling.'

'Perhaps. I do not know. I tell you, it is a blank.' She hid her face like a shamed child, but Fourneval pressed on with his attack. 'And what are we to suppose next? That you decided to take a long, convenient sleep, and so swallowed all that remained of your barbiturates? Or that someone followed you down and forced them on you, to make sure it was your final sleep?'

She moaned and covered her face, the gesture only half theatrical. There was real distress there too.

'And one puzzle exercises my mind above all,' Fourneval

said softly. 'Why were you there at all on the top stairs? Was it because of something you heard? Music perhaps, when there should be none? Siân Vassilakis claimed she heard O'Diarmid's clarinet. Doubtless you had done so too. But you lost your nerve on the way up. You were petrified, suspended between a need to know and fear of what you might find. I want you to meet now the man you failed to face then.'

He nodded to Gilbert who opened the hallway door. Someone outside came quietly in and stood looking down on Céline.

She had tensed herself for some horrendous encounter, and the change was almost laughable. Her mouth sagged open behind the hand clawing at her cheeks. The taut-ness went out of her and she was suddenly no more than a flaccid, ageing woman wearing a model's make-up. 'You?' She sounded incredulous. '*Freddy?* What are you doing here?'

Freddy said nothing, staring balefully.

'What was he doing in Niall's room?' Fourneval repeated for her. 'Were you expecting Niall because of the music? Surely not, because Niall is dead. As well you know. Niall, never Victor. Killed at the Villa Montarnaud, with a screw-driver into the heart. A skilful thrust, with a knowledge of anatomy behind it. But then you were a qualified physio-therapist when you met and married Philippe Durochat in Lyons, weren't you, madame?'

'This is madness!' Céline sat bolt upright and waved her arms to dispel the scene. 'It was Victor killed at the villa. You said so yourself. What would Niall O'Diarmid have been doing there?'

'Perhaps the Irishman went to see Klara, and came upon her dead. And then confronted her killer. He was a quick-witted young man with strangely quixotic notions. Maybe he thought he could swear to keep silence, leave no trace behind and fade from the scene. For some misguided reason he even decided to help you do the same, or was he buying time? Was he temporarily promising you help to save his own skin?'

'*Me?* I was never there!'

Fourneval continued unabashed. 'O'Diarmid knew about the plans for the piano's removal, because Klara had consulted him about a suitable depository. So it could have been his wild idea to remove the frame and put the body in instead. Did you help with closing the lid down, adding your own weight to crush the body flat? It could not have been easy. The sounding box is very shallow. Then you locked the instrument and carried the frame between you down into the cellar, and set about clearing away all traces of the killing and your own presence there.

'But you couldn't trust such a volatile, quirky young man to hold deadly knowledge about you, so he had to be silenced. Cold-bloodedly, with the same tool which he had used for you on the piano, you killed him. What was one more death when you were already so committed? You had shot your bolt when in fury you picked up the bronze horse and struck down Klara Zuelig.

'By now you were beyond all feeling or reason and, with the added strength of panic, dragged his body across the polished tiles and loaded it into the wheelbarrow left ostentatiously for the tree surgeon. There again your earlier skills stood you in good stead. For all that, it was a nightmare journey down to the boat, madame.

'Niall had told you he came in his friend's powered launch, which he frequently borrowed from the Petit Port. Old Régnier remembered that Niall once took you out in it as a sort of joke, thinking to make you sick, but you weren't. In a show-off mood perhaps, the Irishman demonstrated the controls to you, allowed you the run of the cockpit. Even such a poor driver on land as yourself can handle such a craft on a large, calm lake empty of traffic—until coming in to tie up, when the bow received a bad gash. I think we shall find O'Diarmid's Yamaha somewhere beneath the boat's mooring. You were not quite up to riding the thing back here.

'You made some unfortunate mistakes. When the body was loaded and the dinghy hitched to the power boat, you still needed to be sure the body would sink. That was when you remembered the crossbow. It could ensure that the stoved-in shell took the body down with it. You weren't to know of the grisly dismemberment that followed when the half-submerged boat was run down by a powerful launch. Boards from the dinghy are still being recovered as flotsam. A considerable part had buoyancy enough to reach the sluice gates, with the torso attached.

'You cast off the towed dinghy too soon, madame. The unlit smuggling vessel hit it broadside on before it could sink. In the ensuing panic, and the circling for supposed survivors, the body became caught up in the screws. The limbs were severed and most of the head . . . Madame, am I distressing you? I merely *speak* of what happened. Surely it took a stronger stomach to—Gilbert! Look to her.'

Freddy Durochat turned away, sickened. '*She* did all that? And that *little woman* killed my mother? From the hall gallery I only saw her dead between them on the floor, and the man holding the bronze horse. One of them had just come in from the open front door; I didn't know which. I thought the murder was his doing. And then later, when she followed him into the bathroom, where he was being sick, and killed *him*, I wasn't sorry. It seemed like justice. She never saw me because I was out in the corridor then. I went away and hid in the cellar, and I must have blacked out. I think I was out of my mind for a while. I am a terrible coward, I know.

'Later on, everything went quiet and I slept. Then there were fresh sounds in the house. It must have been when the removals men came. It was daytime, and I opened the cellar door to listen. But someone entered the kitchen and locked me in, so I got angry and broke out, using an iron bar I found. And it was Siân Vassilakis out there, and she was scared too. Scared of me, which was ridiculous. But we— made friends, and she helped me to get away. They'd taken the piano by then, and Mother's body had gone. I couldn't tell Siân what had happened. She was too nice. But she seemed to understand I was very upset. I think she helped me stay sane.'

'Was it you who removed Madame Zuelig's passport and travel money?'

'No. I never saw any. I had money of my own. I get a regular allowance from the family bank. They send it to me in Annecy.'

'So perhaps we must go on looking for those things in the lake, somewhere near where the divers found the wheelbarrow, her suitcase and the crossbow.'

Gilbert had been watching the prostrate woman closely and caught the facial tic that registered she listened. 'But perhaps Madame Durochat couldn't bear to waste good money,' he suggested. 'Do you think we may find it somewhere here if we look? In her purse, or tucked away in a drawer? Quite a lot of French currency, I understand. Some of it undoubtedly traceable.'

She began grizzling then like a child, drawing her knees up and locking her arms about them under her chin. Her lacquered hair, sticking out in stiff wisps where she had dragged her fingers through it, hung over her face obscuring the features.

'She-devil,' Freddy hissed, but Fourneval restrained him as he moved in. 'Leave her. She's broken.'

The woman raised her head. 'I never meant to kill her,' she moaned. 'But it was *so unfair*! She had everything. She was secure; never any need to *ask* for anything, to wait for a handout. She controlled everyone, and all the time so *nice* about it, so refined. I hated her, yes; but I went up there to *reason* with her. And she said it was out of her hands: it was all settled. *Settled!*

'Do you know that that wretched Philippe was being squeezed out of the Maison Durochat? This would be the end for him, the end for me. He was going to continue supporting that—that other woman and her child as best he could, but he would leave me with nothing, nothing! All my lovely things, that took me so long to collect—' she gazed around at the furniture and china figures—'they would have to go, and the apartment besides. I should have to find rooms somewhere, perhaps over a shop or in a village, while she—No, it was unthinkable!'

Fourneval went back to the outer door, opened it and

called in a woman *agent*. 'See to packing a bag for her. Gilbert, the formalities.'

He waited while her night clothes and toiletries were put together, more pretty things which to her might well matter more than human lives. Already she had begun to draw away inside herself, presenting an outer shell from which only the hard blue eyes continued communicating, with a withering hostility as she moved past the policemen.

'How did you get to the villa on Wednesday night?' Fourneval asked conversationally, holding out a coat for her to slip on.

She halted her movement, facing him with scorn. 'Victor gave me a lift. By chance I saw his car when I was looking for a taxi. I stepped out in front of him at the lights or he would have driven past. He was at the end of his tether between Kitty and Klara, so he was going up to the Villa Montarnaud to make himself its master again!

'While he drove I talked to him, quietly and reasonably, to bring him back to reality. He began to see it was impossible. He had some luggage with him, and on a sudden urge he decided to run out on everyone and everything, take an unscheduled vacation, try to lose himself. He dropped me by Klara's gates and intended heading into France.

'Poor fool, I almost pitied him, but he's only himself to blame. He'd had Klara eating out of his hand for years, and he threw it all away, seduced by an ambitious dike! Ha!— he didn't know what she was! Kitty fooled him for nearly as long as he fooled Klara, but he was no use to her in the end. She finds her pleasure elsewhere. She even came to me for a while.'

There was a silence while they absorbed this. Céline smiled sourly. 'I had to break it off, because whispers might have got about. I couldn't risk putting off my *dear* divorced husband, my only regular source of income, apart from the divorce settlement.'

She was watching their eyes. 'No, Kitty didn't come this morning to renew our relationship. She has an eye to business. She wanted money for her silence—and I might well have had the money to pay her if we had handled Victor the right way on his return. Kitty had worked it all out, you see. She had guessed what happened up at the Villa Montarnaud.

'That evening she had been on her way to see Victor herself when we went by in his car. She and I recognized each other, but Victor never noticed her waving to stop him. Later that night he phoned her from over the border. He was drunkenly abusive and bitter. He said he had taken me to Klara's but not gone in himself. Kitty thought that if we both swore it was the other way about, everyone would believe it was Victor who'd done the killing. Sooner or later he would turn up and then you would know that the body in the lake wasn't his.'

She was almost enjoying herself now, in the release of malice long held in. 'Now you tell me something,' she challenged Fourneval, slit-eyed. 'How did you identify the body in the lake as Niall's and not Victor's? The blood type was right, and you admitted that the head—was not there.'

Fourneval shrugged. 'Because at some early point in his sudden vacation Victor Durochat had the misfortune to be mugged and robbed. He has been in a state of coma in a hospital at Grenoble since Thursday.

'So we knew the body was someone else's. It was you who pointed us in the direction of O'Diarmid, because Siân Vassilakis told us you were "petrified" outside his door.

'It is one thing to play a dead man's tapes to make it seem he's there. It is quite another when they start to play themselves. Are you afraid of ghosts, madame?'

She seemed to shrivel, and then her gaze lit on Freddy who had watched and listened in horrified silence. 'And really it was you up there, wretched boy, fooling about with his things. What brought you here?'

'I—it doesn't matter now.' He turned away, revolted by her.

'Monsieur Freddy Durochat was eye-witness to the killing of O'Diarmid, as he will testify later in court,' Fourneval said with quiet authority. 'He left the villa in a state of

211

shock, but later came back because he intended to see justice done. He came to this house, knowing that the top rooms would be empty. You may be glad that you didn't go in yesterday but stayed on the stairs. Otherwise it would have been you concussed. He mistook Siân Vassilakis for you pursuing him, and he struck out wildly, to prevent himself becoming your next victim.

'You have known him for many years, it seems; ever since he came to live with his father and Klara at the Villa Montarnaud. Can you doubt that with his history of suffering he will prove a very determined witness against the one who murdered his second mother?'

She almost spat her defiance. 'No one will believe him, with such a record of instability and drugging. It will be his word against mine!' She turned on him with contempt. 'You will make a mess of it, Freddy, like everything else you attempt.'

'We shall see,' Fourneval warned her as she swung past on her way out. 'Would you care to know why he turned up unannounced at the Villa Montarnaud that night? He had come to tell Klara two things: that he had a clean bill of health, was quite free of the after-effects of the drug abuse; and that he had just become engaged to be married. The young lady is an experienced nurse at the Annecy Institution and has known him for a long time. You would be mistaken if you thought of him as anything less than a formidable opponent.'

CHAPTER 12

'It astonishes you,' Freddy remarked, watching Siân's expression. They were all four together on the stone promontory of the boathouse. He had been joined by his fiancée, Louise Pierrel, who had driven across from France to spend her three days' leave with him.

'Despite all that has happened, there are only good ghosts for me up at the villa. That foolish little woman's flash of malice can't wipe out all the good years, or her greed make me believe that things matter more than people. My childhood—the better, second half of it—is built into those walls. Everywhere I look, everything I touch, reminds me of Klara's steady love. I need it. I can't let it be wasted. And Louise feels too that it's the right place to start our life together.'

'So please don't consider moving away yourselves,' the nurse pleaded. 'When I leave Annecy I shall miss all my old friends. We need some good ones here. Besides, there is the alpine garden for you to work on, Siân. There are a dozen reasons for you to stay.'

'What do you think?' Andreas asked Siân, after their guests had left. 'Do we stay on here? Could you bear it?'

'If Freddy can, I suppose I could. How about you? Does it give you bad vibes?'

'I'll know that next time I go down to the Pont de la Machine,' he said sombrely. 'I never want to relive those moments when I thought that *that* might have happened to you.' He stared over the lake and they linked arms to walk back down the drive.

Siân looked up at him. 'I keep remembering something Klara said the last time we really talked together: about anger. She'd learned to value anger; it was company for her. Anger could be a good thing and should be used constructively.' She stood still.

'So—?'

'It was anger that destroyed her. A sudden burst of jealous rage in a self-absorbed, greedy little woman who felt her life-style threatened. Death must have come too suddenly for Klara to know what happened but, in a way, I think she would have understood the anger. It's the deliberate wasting of Niall O'Diarmid that I find so chilling. And all that careful clearing up afterwards.'

Andreas looked serious. 'I'm afraid that O'Diarmid is going to be a talking point for some time to come. The Press are building him up into a picaresque hero. Someone seems to have leaked to them that he was the one who master-

213

minded Subarsky's defection to the West. So he's to be the shadowy spymaster everyone expects to be lurking in Geneva's diplomatic byways. Already he's become a myth with an ironic ending.'

Siân faced him, frowning. '*Somebody* leaked it—that's David, of course. Andreas, he's a—'

'He's doing his job, Siân; and someone has to. He tries to cause as little distress all round as he can manage.'

She still looked ruffled, then suddenly she softened. 'And he's taken the pressure off you. If everyone accepts that Niall arranged the whole business, they won't look farther —to you and Theo.'

They walked in silence along the jetty and Andreas produced a bag of crusts from his pocket for the ducks. All four of the regulars were there again today, the trio and the hanger-on. He looked up to find Siân considering him. 'That was a political decision you made, Andreas.'

'Yes. I seem to be getting reconciled to my environment. Expediency.'

'Perhaps,' Siân said slowly, 'it's time to go down to the Pont de la Machine and see where we stand. Get it over with.'

There were white-overalled workmen down by the sluices, paint-spraying the metal struts. Lake water poured through clear as from a filter, sparkling under the spring sunshine. 'Yes,' Andreas decided, 'it's different already. Time has moved on.'

One of the taller workmen, goggled and masked against inhaling the spray paint, reminded him of the lean, loose-limbed Chief of Police.

What was it that Fourneval in philosophic mood had said about this paradoxical city? No longer the clockwork precision of the past, but *muesli*. And the fair face of Geneva masked a sink of iniquity, the place where the dregs were cast up as flotsam. His work concerned what would not integrate: the foreign bodies.

Well, Andreas considered, gazing about him, Siân and

e had been foreign when they arrived, but by now they ad their place here.

'Let's take the steamer to the far end of the lake,' he said, losing one hand over hers. 'I'll point out for you all the elebrities' houses: Palais des Nations, Boathouse Vassi- akis, the infamous Villa Montarnaud . . .'